THREE DOGMA NIGHT

THREE DOGMA NIGHT

THE ELVEN PROPHECY™ BOOK THREE

THEOPHILUS MONROE

MICHAEL ANDERLE

DISRUPTIVE IMAGINATION

LMBPN Publishing
PMB 196, 2540 South Maryland Pkwy
Las Vegas, NV 89109

Version 1.00, June 2021
ebook ISBN: 978-1-64971-835-8
Print ISBN: 978-1-64971-836-5

THE THREE DOGMA NIGHT TEAM

Thanks to our Beta Team

John Ashmore, Rachel Beckford, Kelly O'Donnell, John Scafidi

Thanks to our JIT Readers

Veronica Stephan-Miller
Dave Hicks
Debi Sateren
Jackey Hankard-Brodie
Dorothy Lloyd
Jeff Goode
Zacc Pelter
Diane L. Smith
Peter Manis
Angel LaVey

If We've missed anyone, please let us know!

Editor
The Skyhunter Editing Team

PROLOGUE

I pivoted on my back foot, narrowly evading the assassin's dagger.

Focusing my mind, I blasted him in the back with a magically enhanced shove. He flew into the first row of pews. Thankfully, they were made of oak. If we'd broken one, well, I don't know how I'd explain it. I was already on thin ice with the congregation.

Not bad, I thought. Not that I had a lot of time to bask in well-earned glory for pulling off an evasive maneuver against an assassin who probably had a lifetime's worth of training and a lot of experience murdering people.

Not a résumé I'd consider career-boosting, but he'd come from New Albion. He wasn't looking for a job at a Fortune 500 company.

The assassin quickly leaped to his feet. The dumbass looked like a ninja. You know, the kind who appeared as the villains' lackeys in any number of action flicks from the eighties. I wasn't sure why he bothered covering his face anyway. I mean, if he killed me, it wouldn't matter if I saw who he was, and if he failed, which I was holding out hope would be the case, it wasn't like I knew anyone I could reveal his identity to.

I hadn't met many elves from New Albion outside of Layla, her father, and a handful of legionnaires. I probably wouldn't recognize this guy, even if I could see his face.

He leaped up like he hadn't just about snapped his spine across the back of an oak pew. I mean, I'd hit him with one heck of a magically enhanced wallop, and he'd jumped back up like an acrobat hopped up on Twinkies.

I shook my head.

Why hadn't Layla taken the shot?

That was the plan. I glanced up at the balcony. She should have been up there somewhere, hiding in the organ pipes.

We'd rehearsed this. Where the hell was she? She'd said she just needed a little space, enough to give her a clean shot. A foot or more of separation between the assailant and me, and she'd take him out with an arrow.

All I needed to do was stay alive.

Easier said than done when throwing down with a professional elven assassin.

That Layla didn't take him out meant one of two things: either she was tangled up with a second assassin and she never got into position, or this one had gotten to her first, and he took her out before he turned on me.

I shook my head. It couldn't be that. I mean, would King Brightborn have his daughter killed?

Maybe she just didn't have the right angle. I had to hope that was the case. I had no way of knowing for sure that she was up there. Could I risk it? It wasn't likely the assassin would fall for the back-foot pivot maneuver a second time.

And I only had a few moves I could use.

I inhaled again. I might not be able to beat the assassin outright, but I could send him elsewhere thanks to Ensley, the fairy who'd left a little of his portal magic inside me.

I focused on a space about six inches in front of me as the assassin charged again, his dagger glistening green. He came at me quickly, leading the way with his blade. I formed a portal between us, sending the energies required for it from my eyes.

The assassin's momentum carried him through the gold and green magic gateway.

"Take that, asshole," I said.

Then I smirked. I'd just called someone an asshole *in the church*.

Not that I hadn't wanted to use that word more than once here. When I was in pastor mode, though, I had to watch my language.

I quickly closed the portal. I'd put him on top of the St. Louis Arch. No, not inside the arch. *On top* of it.

It had been the first thing I thought of.

I'm not a killer. I'd killed once, and even though the elf had it coming, I wasn't in any hurry to add another body to my conscience.

Of course, if the assassin fell off the arch, I supposed I'd be partly responsible for that. And there's no way he'd survive the fall. Not unless he had level-five magic like me or knew how to fly.

Not likely. Layla said that before me, there hadn't been anyone capable of level-five badassery in centuries.

Why not just portal the elf to Antarctica? Or better, back to New Albion?

So far, I hadn't managed to cast portals that took people more than a few miles away. I knew I could; the ability was there. Ensley was able to use the same kind of magic to create portals that took him all over the world. I had to have a clear mental picture of where I wanted to open a portal—somewhere there wouldn't be an object, or heaven forbid, a person in the space where it opened on the other side.

But I was still an amateur when it came to magic in general, and even more so with fairy magic.

"Layla!" I called toward the darkened church balcony.

No response.

My stomach churned. Where the hell was she? I hadn't heard so much as a scream, much less a struggle.

I mean, this was an old building, and the place was well-insulated and sound-proofed. It didn't mean she wasn't somewhere on the church grounds.

I took a deep breath as I ran out the front door. What was I worried about? Layla could hold her own even against some of New Albion's nastiest elf assassins.

Focus, Caspar.

Then it dawned on me. I didn't need to use magic. I could just turn on the stupid lights. Sometimes the easiest solution is the best one. When you can do magic, there's a temptation to use it to do everything, even things that are more easily done the conventional way.

I sprinted to the back of the sanctuary, where the light switch panel was located. I've been a pastor there for the better part of a decade and still couldn't remember which switch did what.

The first few I knew, but after that? One of these days, I'd get a label maker and fix the problem.

Flicking them on and off, I eventually turned on the lights over the balcony. I took off up the stairs, skipping every other step on my way up.

"Layla?" I called.

Nothing.

No evidence she'd been there at all. I grabbed my phone from my pocket and called her. It rang. No answer. I sent a text and waited.

No response, not even the three tiny dots that indicated that she was typing.

What the hell had happened? Then it dawned on me. We had

our phones hooked up on one of those find your friends and family GPS apps. I opened it, and it showed her icon-sized head-shot just outside the door.

I ran back downstairs, nearly twisting my ankle as I jumped down the last five. I blasted through the church doors, almost knocking them off their hinges. My heart raced.

I expected the worst as I looked around.

"Layla!" I shouted.

Then I glanced down. Something caught the sun, and the reflection almost blinded me. On the small patch of grass along the sidewalk leading up to the church was Layla's phone in its hot-pink case.

Shit.

CHAPTER ONE

Four days earlier

I'd never been to a cult meeting before. It's generally ill-advised for ministers.

I take that back. There are a lot of folks who think AA is a cult.

My former bishop had believed it was. Too bad he hadn't tried it. It might have saved his career.

I get it, I suppose. A lot of random "God talk" goes on there, and some of the folks live and breathe the program. Their whole world revolves around meetings. What the folks who call it "cult-like" fail to understand, though, is that for a lot of AA members, the alternative to that is drinking again. Joining something people think might be a cult is far preferable to any of the other destinations that untreated alcoholics are destined to reach: jails, institutions for the criminally insane, and the grave.

And if I was honest about it, the Order of the Elven Gate, what non-members colloquially refer to as the "Elf Gate Cult," wasn't all that different.

They had learned a grim truth: that the elven legions intended to conquer the world. They'd admitted they were powerless in the situation, so they'd decided to do what they thought they could to prepare themselves to be on the elves' good side.

Of course, kissing elf ass isn't exactly my style. I mean, I'm dating one, and I won't even kiss hers, literally or metaphorically. Just not a butt man.

I expected they'd all swoon when Layla, an elf princess, an elf of elves, walked into their meeting, but they had been distracted. Another kind of elf, a more exotic breed, had shown up.

The drow. They'd come to find me because the magic I was wielding got their attention. They had felt a great disturbance in the force.

That's my best Obi-Wan impression. Of course, anyone who knows anything realizes that Obi-Wan continues, "...as if millions of voices cried out in terror and were suddenly silenced."

Hopefully, the drow's visit wouldn't be quite that ominous. I mean, with a lot of luck and a ton of help, I'd thwarted the elven legion a couple of times. I wouldn't stand much of a chance against a world-destroying death star, though.

Yes, I have most of those movies memorized. The original films anyway, the ones that matter—and *Monty Python and the Quest for the Holy Grail.* "Your mother was a hamster and your father smelt of elderberries!" Sorry, I know that quote was random, but I couldn't control myself.

The Elf Gate Cult had grown, even though I'd prevented the elven invasion at least temporarily. I'd never seen so many people wearing silicone elf ears in one place, not even at the renaissance festival where we'd first met Fred, the larper who played both the King and the Blacksmith (depending on the day of the week). He'd helped us craft a faux Blade of Echoes and was, coincidentally, one of the leaders of the Elf Gate Cult.

"This way," Jag said.

Jag was my personal trainer. At least, he was while Layla had been off-world. I figured we'd probably stick with the arrangement. People who were romantically involved shouldn't enter a trainer-client relationship. One of two things was bound to happen. Every session would either end in a fight or with lots and lots of screwing. Not that I'd know that from experience.

I'm a minister, after all. We don't do that sort of thing. We don't believe in fighting outside of marriage.

Jag led us through the crowd. I mean, I figured we'd be a big deal. An elf princess and the "chosen one" of the elven prophecy has to be worth some celebrity in a cult that worships elfkind.

"Well, this is underwhelming," I blurted.

"They don't all realize who you are," Jag said. "We don't have portraits of you in our homes or anything. I mean, if Jesus walked into your church, would anyone recognize him?"

I snorted. "I'm not Jesus. Not even close."

Jag laughed. "I agree. Jesus wasn't a pussy."

I chuckled under my breath. It was an inside joke, or I told myself it was. It helped me not take it personally. In the gym, he was a firm believer in self-deprecation like calling yourself a pussy, a wimp because you're always speaking to your present. If you don't want your present self to become a past self, you need to become a badass future you and kick your past self's ass into nonexistence.

The power of positive thinking and the culture of affirmation was all bullshit from Jag's perspective. Self-loathing and deprecations unleashed the power to change.

The past you is soft and flabby. The future you is huge and ripped.

The past you eats donuts for breakfast. The future you drinks protein shakes. Even if they taste like lawn, you choke them down. Let the past you complain about the flavor. The future you will thank you for it.

I'm not sure I agree with his philosophy, but strangely, it worked. I mean, I didn't have six-pack abs, but I'd gotten rid of most of the keg I used to carry around my waist. The love handles were almost gone. I couldn't flick the band of fat that hung over my waistband and watch the waves ripple across my abdomen anymore. It made standing naked in front of the bathroom mirror a bit less entertaining but much more satisfying.

I couldn't believe how many people were here, and they were all crowded around the three drow who had come looking for me.

Jag started pushing people to the right or the left. He was a big boy. I'm pretty sure his momma had to shop in the "husky boys" department at Sears when he was growing up. He wasn't fat, just one of those large-framed men who, with a ton of muscle, wasn't the kind of person you wanted to make angry. Jag was to this crowd of cultists as Moses had been to the Red Sea. He moved forward, and, whether it happened willingly or not, the crowd parted.

I didn't need to ask who the visitors were. They stood out in the crowd.

Fred was there, talking to them. When he saw us, he pointed at us, and all three of them peered our way.

They had ears like Layla's, but their skin was a dark purple-gray. Their hair was white, and they wore long robes that were more ornate and colorful than anything I'd ever worn preaching. A brocade pattern embossed in gold covered their robes.

Their clothing resembled traditional Indian dress. I suppose, with darker skin, the drow probably blended better there than in, say, northern Europe or the Baltics. Or even in the United States.

One of them was female and not exceptionally tall, probably about five feet in height. She had an athletic build from what I could tell since her robe was more like a dress, fitting tightly against her body. The two men who accompanied her, however, were at least six-foot-five. They had slender builds, and their arms and legs looked a touch too long for their bodies. They were holding gold boxes decorated with various letters, an elven language I didn't know.

They lowered their heads as if to honor my presence. They didn't bow or kneel, but it was clear they knew who I was.

"I can sense the power within him!" one of the male drow exclaimed.

"I can as well," the other male replied.

The female walked up to me and put her hand on my arm. Her hand lingered there a while. "I can feel it too."

A sly, almost flirty smile spread across her face. "The sensation when I touch you tingles throughout my body."

Layla cleared her throat.

She wasn't the jealous type of girlfriend. Not at all. But I could tell that the way this drow was touching me bothered her. Layla hooked her arm around mine. "We're together, by the way."

I raised one eyebrow. I wasn't sure our relationship status was the most crucial issue at the moment, and Layla didn't have anything to worry about. Sure, this female drow was undeniably alluring, but a lot of women are attractive. That doesn't mean I'm interested in them. Not like that, anyway.

"I am Aerin," the female said. "These are my companions Haldir and Iston."

The two male drow nodded. I extended my hand to shake each of theirs, but they just nodded again in acknowledgment of my greeting.

"They don't speak to others unless granted permission," Aerin said.

"Permission?" Layla asked, raising an eyebrow. "How did you manage that? I mean, I've been trying to leash this one."

I grunted.

Aerin smiled. "The drow operate under the principles of matriarchy."

I cocked my head. "So, women are in charge?"

"Men are good for only two things: hard labor and providing seed for the womb," Aerin said. "Though we too have a prophecy that there would be one from the lesser gender, a human who rose to restore the proper order to all the world."

"To restore order?" Layla said. "Our prophecy dictated that he would save the elves and unify the peoples."

"Six of one half, a dozen of the other," Aerin said. "To restore order would unify the races."

"By order, do you mean…" I started, but she cut me off.

"I'm not speaking of matriarchy, Chosen One," Aerin said. "We recognize our ways are not universal."

"But I imagine it is much more efficient," Layla added.

"Indeed it is," Aerin said. "Were men in charge, I don't believe it would have been possible for our kind to have remained in quietude for so long."

"Egos," Layla added. "Theirs get bruised, and the next thing you know, they're fighting with each other."

I snorted. "Hey, I told you. I'm a lover, not a fighter."

"Correction," Layla said. "Most of them fight. Others are just insecure."

I stared at Layla blankly.

"Relax," Layla said. "I'm just giving you shit."

"So," I said, "you have been on Earth all this time. You can wield Earth's magic?"

"And we could sense it when another one, the chosen one, emerged and entered into communion with the elements." Aerin grabbed my hand.

Layla cocked her head and scrunched her brow. For a moment, I'd thought the two she-elves had bonded over their shared belief in female superiority, but the jealousy seemed to be creeping back in.

"What are you doing?" I asked.

Aerin turned my palm over and traced one finger from my

wrist to the tip of my middle finger. "Sensing your power. It is indeed destined that we must be together."

"Bitch, say *what?*" Layla asked.

"The prophecy is clear," Aerin said. "That he and I, the princess of the drow, must marry."

CHAPTER TWO

"The prophecy had to do with *me*!" Layla protested. "I'm the princess of elves! And we're already in love!"

Aerin cocked her head. "Your prophecy, your scrolls, the ones belonging to you and the other set given to the elven giants? They are but copies. We retain the originals, written by Taliesin himself."

"Taliesin?" Layla asked.

"Surely you know of him," Aerin said. "The druid-bard of the golden brow. The one who wrote the prophecy, the one who guided your ancestors to your world."

Layla replied, "We never knew his name."

"As I said," Aerin continued, "our prophecies are without alterations."

"Are yours sealed?" I asked.

Aerin nodded. "Indeed, and only one seal remains."

"See," Layla said, "the prophecy about being in love with the elf princess. That's, like, the second one."

"The third," Aerin said with a discernible hint of smugness.

"Whatever. The point is that he's fulfilled the rest after that one. He has the familiar, his cat. He destroyed the Blade of Echoes, and then there was the last one."

"The last one?" Aerin asked. "The sixth was fulfilled already?"

I nodded. "In New Albion, when I recharged their ley lines, I believe."

Aerin snorted. "That's not what the sixth prophecy was about. Do you not know what was written under the sixth seal?"

"Not exactly," I said with a sigh. Layla gave me the stink-eye. Our ignorance of the precise meaning of the final prophecy that Brag'mok said I was about to fulfill, the one he knew about when he told me to slam my fist to the ground and save New Albion, didn't say what we'd assumed it did.

If only he'd had a chance to tell us.

"Then how do you know the sixth prophecy was revealed?" Aerin asked.

"One of the orcs," Layla said. "Elven giants, sorry. He was with us at the time. He said he'd received word of it. We were in the middle of a battle, and he told Caspar what to do next. We trusted him, but we had to flee back to Earth before he had a chance to reveal the contents of the prophecy."

"Well," Aerin said, "I suppose it is a good thing we arrived when we did."

"Why is that?" I asked. "So you can tell us about the sixth prophecy?"

"He shall attain the power of another," Aerin said, the cadence in her voice indicating she was reciting it from memory. "And with it shall come not peace but a sword, and more blood shall be shed upon the worlds than has ever been in a single day since the worlds were hewn from the abyss."

I snorted. "Well, that doesn't sound good."

"I don't understand," Layla said. "Why would Brag'mok believe that justified you refusing to give the ring to my father and using it to recharge the magic of our world instead?"

I shook my head. "You said it yourself, Layla, when all this shit started. It's why you didn't want the Blade of Echoes to fall into the hands of the elven giants."

"Because they'd restore magic to New Albion," Layla said. "And with magic available again, the wars would continue."

I nodded. "Exactly."

"And now," Aerin said, "it seems that their war will soon spill over into our world. We must ensure that you are prepared, Chosen One. You must come with us."

Layla stamped her foot. "Come with you? Like hell!"

"You may join us as well," Aerin said. "That he and I are married does not exclude the possibility that you could use him for your pleasures, should I allow it."

I cocked my head. "Hold on. I'm not being used by anyone for any pleasures."

Aerin looked at me blankly. "You mean to tell me that you object to the idea of serving the desires of two female elves?"

"Well, when you put it like that…"

Layla backhanded me on the arm and continued to stare intently at Aerin. "He already fulfilled that prophecy, if I must tell you again, with *me.*"

Aerin smiled. "What must be, must be. Either way, we must work together if he is to be prepared to defend this world."

"We've been doing just fine," Layla said.

"Have you?" Aerin asked. "Tell me, Chosen One, with which of the earthen elements do you find the most cohesion?"

"The elements?" I asked. "I just focus and connect myself to the magic I sense all around."

"Because you were trained by one who learned to use magic in an alien world," Aerin said. "Here, the magic coheres to the five elements: air, fire, water, earth, and aether."

"Aether?" Layla asked.

"Spirit," Aerin said. "It is funny that the element you've engaged our chosen one in learning is the element you couldn't name."

Layla huffed. I couldn't blame her. This Aerin chick was, if nothing else, blunt. And she was overextending herself. I didn't care what she thought the prophecy said or how the drow understood it. From what I'd been able to tell, three races possessed these prophecies, and so far, not one of them shared a single understanding about what they meant.

It's not all that surprising. From my background studying theology, there were about as many different interpretations of the book of Revelation as there were denominations. Everyone had access to the same book. Everyone was convinced their interpretation was the right one.

At least as far as the Bible was concerned, all I knew was that good would win in the end. That was enough for me to find reading it worthwhile. I mean, in the real world, the good guys don't always win.

Read a little history. We are often left with the impression that good has typically triumphed over evil, but that's because the victors write the history books.

When it came to the elven prophecy, it struck me that all of them likewise agreed that somehow I would help forge a better existence.

Yeah, little ole me, who can barely convince church authorities to see eye to eye on much of anything. I was supposed to unite the peoples, all the races, across different worlds.

I'd seen enough to be convinced that I was the chosen one of the elven prophecies, but I was still a thousand percent clueless when it came to how I was supposed to do it. At least the drow wanted to help.

If they had a better grip on how to wield magic on Earth than Layla did, who were we to refuse their help because this drow princess was a little too forward about her intentions?

"We've come bearing gifts," Aerin said. "Artifacts set aside by the ancestors. Our people were charged to guard them with our lives until the chosen one was revealed."

"What sort of artifacts?" Layla asked.

Aerin looked around. "This crowd, they mean well, I think. But what we have to give is not for their eyes. And before we grant these gifts, we must put our chosen one through many trials."

I cocked my head. "What kind of trials?"

"Magical tests," Aerin said. "Meant to reveal for certain that you are indeed the one we have been waiting for. The trials correspond with each of the five elements and are conducted on separate nights."

"And what if I fail?" I asked.

Aerin shrugged. "Then I suspect we will all be quite disappointed. The signs are clear: the chosen one has risen. But all prophecies must be tested, for if these artifacts fell into the hands of anyone other than the one who was prophesied, it might mean the end."

"The end of what, exactly?" Layla asked.

"Of existence. Life itself. Not just the end of humanity, but the destruction of both of our worlds."

I nodded. "Good. So, no pressure, right?"

Layla put her hand on my back. "You'll be fine."

"And once it's confirmed," Aerin said, "we will be married."

"Like hell, you will," Layla said. "Over my dead body."

Aerin tilted her head to the side. "I hope it won't come to that."

"Suppose I'm not inclined to participate," I asked, "What would happen then?"

Aerin stared at me blankly. "If you refuse to undergo the tests, we will not give you the artifacts."

"Yes," I said. "I get that much. But what would the consequences of that be?"

Aerin said, "Without them, you will be ill-prepared to defend this world from the war that is coming. I hope you won't be so foolish."

I took a deep breath. "Good to know. What do these trials involve, exactly?"

"You must face each of the trials without any time to prepare, lest you find a way to manipulate the events and make yourself merely appear to have succeeded."

Layla grunted. "So, he just has to trust you blindly and accept that what you're telling him is true?"

"To be fair," I interjected, "that's what you were asking me to do when we first met."

Layla shook her head. "That was different, Caspar."

"How was it different?" I asked.

"Whose side are you on, anyway?" Layla shot back.

"Whose side?" Aerin interjected. "Why should you presume we are on different sides? Unless you, elf, are more loyal to your kin than you are to our hero."

"I'm always on your side, Layla," I said, "but Aerin is right. We have enough enemies as it is. Shouldn't we at least give this a shot and see if what she's telling us is true?"

Layla sighed. "I guess. Dammit, Caspar. Why do you have to make so much sense?"

I laughed. "What harm can come of it? If I fail their tests, it doesn't change anything. If I pass, maybe we'll be better equipped for when the elf shit hits the fan."

"Elf shit?" Layla asked, raising an eyebrow. "Isn't everyone's shit pretty much the same?"

"Your dad's shit," I said. "You know what I mean."

Aerin cocked her head. "You're a bit odd, aren't you, Caspar?"

I smiled wide. "You have no idea."

"For the record," Aerin said, "Drow shit glows in the dark and smells like cinnamon."

"Seriously?" Layla asked.

"No," Aerin said. "I'm fucking with you."

I laughed out loud. "See, Layla, she *does* have a sense of humor."

"Yeah," Layla said. "She makes poop jokes. She's a regular comedian."

I smiled and looked at Aerin. "So, these trials. How should we begin? I mean, presuming we agree to go along with your proposal?"

"We must begin in haste," Aerin replied. "Time wasted deciding to begin the trials is time lost in training you to wield these artifacts, and with them, the magic of the elements."

"And by haste, you mean what?" Layla asked. "Tomorrow? Next week? When?"

"The first trial must be conducted immediately," Aerin said. "It would be wise to prepare yourself. You need to be calm of mind. Clear of focus. Do what you need to do. We'll begin tomorrow."

I nodded. "Does it need to occur at any particular place or time?"

"Let us reconvene here tomorrow night an hour before midnight," Aerin answered.

"That late?" I asked.

"The drow revere the moon," Aerin stated. "We believe it offers protection to those who honor the elements. It is to your advantage if we conduct the trials at night."

"Protection?" I asked. "What sort of danger are we talking about here?"

"That depends," Aerin said. "If you are the chosen one, you will endure."

"And if by chance I'm not?" I asked.

Aerin pressed her lips together. "Then at least we'll know."

I nodded. Aerin hadn't answered my question. I'd asked what would happen if I failed twice. If I wasn't the chosen one, at least as the drow defined it, it wouldn't be good. I mean, if being the chosen one meant I would endure, then if I wasn't the chosen one, it could only mean one thing.

The trials would probably kill me.

CHAPTER THREE

"What a ho," Layla said as we left the meeting. The Order of the Elven Gate had recently purchased an old, defunct church building. I had to admit they'd fixed it up nicely. I'd never been in this particular church before since it used to be a Baptist church, and my denomination wasn't keen on interdenominational activities. Hell, it had taken a minor miracle to get my local church council to approve a partnership with the Methodists to operate an inner-city soup kitchen.

I laughed. "I don't think Aerin is a ho, Layla."

"Do you think she's pretty?" Layla asked.

"Of course not!" I said. "She's hideous."

It was a lie, and Layla knew it. I had over-corrected myself—I mean, Aerin was stunning—and Layla saw right through it.

"Shut up. You're attracted to her, aren't you?" she asked.

"Layla," I said. "Where is this coming from? Of course Aerin is pretty. So what? There are a lot of pretty women in the world."

"But not all of them want to marry you." Layla huffed.

I grabbed her hand. "I don't care what she said, Layla. I love you, okay? I don't love her. I just met her. And you need to at least consider this situation from her perspective."

Layla rolled her eyes. "What perspective could justify—"

"Think about it," I interrupted. "The drow have spent centuries guarding these artifacts for a time when a prophecy they'd held since ancient times began to be fulfilled. They see it happening, and they have their interpretations of what the prophecies mean. Aerin doesn't want to marry me for romantic reasons. She thinks she has to because her version of the eleven prophecy dictates it."

Layla sighed. "She could have been less direct about it."

"She thinks it's urgent, and she isn't wrong. We don't know how much time we have to prepare for whatever your father is going to do next."

"Hopefully, the Night Legion will buy us time," Layla said. The Night Legion was what the elven giants, who the elves disparagingly referred to as "orcs," called themselves on New Albion.

"Hopefully, they will," I said. "And since the fairies are on our side now, maybe they'll be able to stop your father. But if the sixth prophecy indicates that a war is coming and more lives will be lost in a single day of it than all the wars fought for centuries between the elves and giants, then what?"

"I get it," Layla said. "I suppose I'm acting a little jealous. I mean, I've disowned my family and betrayed my kingdom because I believe in you, Caspar. You're the chosen one. I don't need to put you through a barrage of tests to know it's true."

"But if I recall," I said, "that night when I was stabbed, when I overheard you speaking to your father through that crystal, even you were surprised that a human might be the chosen one."

Layla nodded. "We'd always assumed it would be an elf."

"Perhaps the drow have some assumptions about the elven prophecy that aren't entirely accurate also."

Layla put her hand around my waist. "I know, and you're right. But I still don't like this. I don't trust her."

"I don't trust her either," I said, putting my arm around Layla's shoulders. "But I don't have a good reason to distrust her, not yet.

And whether we like it or not, these drow are part of all this, and they could be powerful allies."

"Maybe," Layla said. "But we need to be careful."

I nodded. "I agree. And we will be. But don't we owe it to ourselves to hear them out?"

"I suppose you're right," Layla said. "She just rubbed me the wrong way."

"You guys ready?" Jag asked, jogging up behind us. "I assume you could use a ride back to your apartment."

I nodded. "Yeah, Jag. That would be fantastic."

My car was still out of commission, being in need of four new tires—a long story. I hadn't taken care of it yet for a variety of reasons, the biggest being that I just didn't have the time. And, with both Earth and fairy magic at my disposal, I now had a few other ways to get around town. Including, of course, the Metro as a last resort.

But Jag had come to my apartment to let us know about the arrival of the drow, and letting him give us a ride home was preferable to any of the other methods of travel at our disposal.

"So," Jag said, "that Aerin is pretty hot, don't you think?"

Layla grunted.

I cleared my throat. "I think I'm going to decline to answer that question right now, Jag."

Jag laughed. "Sorry. I mean, you're hot too, Layla. If it means anything, I'd do you both."

I cocked my head. "Jag, seriously?"

"Sorry," Jag said. "We still on for tomorrow?"

I nodded. "I don't see why not."

"We'll be at the gym first thing in the morning," Layla agreed.

"Are you going to take over Caspar's training again?" Jag asked. "I mean, now that you're back?"

Layla smiled. "You two seem to be working well together, and Caspar is making more progress with you than when I was training him."

"Cool!" Jag said, clicking his key fob and unlocking the doors to his Hummer. "So, what did you guys think?"

"About the drow?" I asked, climbing into the back seat. I figured I'd allow Layla to ride shotgun, but she climbed in next to me, which made me smile. We were still at that stage in our relationship, I suppose, when we preferred sitting side by side in someone's backseat while leaving the front seat vacant.

Jag nodded. "They kind of came out of left field, didn't they?'

"Just curious, Jag," Layla said. "What does the Order think about all that's happened lately?"

Jag replied, "We're reevaluating things, but there's a lot of disagreement about the position we should take."

"How so?" I asked.

"Until now," Jag explained, "we were focused on the inevitability of the new elven order. Some members are concerned that by helping you and the drow, we might put ourselves at odds with the New Albion elves' rule once they take over."

"*If* they take over," I said.

"Right," Jag said. "We were meeting tonight to vote on which side we'd take—our side or them—but then the drow showed up. I have no idea how that might change things now. I mean, I was prepared for what was probably going to be a schism in the order."

"The Order was going to split?" Layla asked.

"Probably," Jag said. "I mean, we're pretty evenly divided, and I don't see one side giving in to the other. It's not like we're disagreeing over trivial shit."

"It's kind of fundamental," I said. "I mean, are you going to help thwart the invasion or position yourselves to embrace it? Not a lot of room for compromise."

"Exactly," Jag said. "But don't worry about me. I'm totally on your side."

"Good to know," I said, smiling. "What about Fred? I mean, he's, what, the supreme leader, right? What side is he on?"

"Beats me," Jag said. "He's tried to stay neutral. He said it's his job to lead the whole Order. I suppose he doesn't want to be seen as the enemy if whatever side he takes doesn't prevail."

I nodded. "Makes sense, I guess. The safe position. Far be it from a leader to take a stand and lead."

"Caspar!" Layla snapped. "I don't think that's the issue."

"Whatever. Any sense at all, Jag, of how the drow showing up might change things?"

Jag thought for a minute. "It's hard to say. I mean, everyone is pretty taken with the new elves. I'm hoping it might help save the Order or at least cause the other side to reconsider. And if you pass these trials…"

"Wait," I said. "You are meeting to see this happen tomorrow, too?"

"Of course," Jag said. "We wouldn't miss it. And think about it, Caspar. If you pass these trials, if the whole Order sees what you can do, how could they not follow?"

I nodded. "I suppose that makes sense."

"He'll pass," Layla said. "I have no doubt about it."

"I mean, right now, the other side thinks you're a fraud. I think they're hoping to see you fail."

"Hoping?" I asked. "They realize that if I'm not the chosen one, it means humanity loses, right?"

Jag nodded as he turned the key in the ignition. "I think some of our original members, the ones who were here at the start, who were loyal to Hector… I mean, if these prophecies are true, a lot of people are going to die, right?"

Layla sighed. "Unfortunately, it looks that way."

"So you can see why some would prefer to see the elves come and simply take power?"

I shook my head. "They think the elven legion would march to Earth, and there'd be a peaceful transition of power?"

Jag nodded. "That's one of the purposes of the Order. I mean, from the beginning. To spread the message and prepare the government to be ready to cede power."

I snorted. "A group that a lot of people think is a fringe cult is going to convince the US government to just give up? Not to mention the rest of the world's governments?"

Jag nodded. "You don't know how extensive the influence of the Order is, do you?"

I shook my head. "I just figured you were a fringe group. I mean, who listens?"

"We have members in high places, Caspar. This is just one chapter here in St. Louis, but new chapters are forming all around the country. Even in Washington."

Layla and I exchanged glances. "Would we know who some of these members are?"

Jag nodded. "You probably voted for a few of them."

"So, this vote tonight," I said, "before the drow showed up. It wasn't just a vote for what this group was going to do?"

Jag shrugged. "Even if everyone in our chapter voted one way, there's no telling how the rest of the Order might go."

I sighed. "And if the rest of your Order doesn't see what happens tomorrow?"

"They'll see it," Jag said. "Haven't you ever heard of Facebook Live?"

"Shit," I said. "I'm going to be on a broadcast doing whatever the hell these drow are planning to put me through?"

Jag nodded. "Don't worry, Casp. I mean, when you succeed, you will change history."

I shook my head. "No pressure, then."

CHAPTER FOUR

"I can't believe I didn't see this before," Layla said as we walked back into the apartment. "I mean before Hector died. I figured he was just here to get the Blade of Echoes back to my father."

"It sounds like he was an ambassador," I said. "Like, an emissary sent to Earth to try to encourage the governments of the world to surrender in advance."

"That's what it looks like," Layla said. "But I can't believe it would have worked."

"Probably wouldn't have," I said, plopping down on the couch. "Not right away. I guess if we hadn't stopped your dad from marching his legions to Earth before, though, it wouldn't take long with all the magic you said they'd be able to wield to convince people in power that Hector had told them the truth."

Layla sat down beside me and rested her head on my shoulder. "Once again, I found out how little I was told about what my people were planning. They sent me to Earth to gather more information on human culture, they told me. If our world failed, we needed to be able to assimilate."

"Why wouldn't they just tell you the truth?" I asked as Agnus sauntered his way over and nuzzled my shin.

"Tuna. Tuna. Tuna. Tuna."

I reached down and scratched Agnus behind the ears. "Just a minute, buddy."

"I think it's because I appreciated so much about this world. I mean, not everything, but the culture, the music…"

"You brought our music to the elf kingdom?" I asked.

"A little. Mostly the classics. *Barbie Girl. Who Let the Dogs Out. Gangnam Style.*"

I snorted. "The classics? And you didn't mean Bach, Beethoven, or Handel?"

"Lord no," Layla said. "I didn't want to put everyone to sleep. Not to mention, they were looking for music that is influential."

I cocked my head. "You seriously think that *Who Let the Dogs Out* is more influential in our society than, say, *Beethoven's Fifth Symphony?*"

"Well, I mean, those songs teach the people about human values. Sort of."

I scratched my head. "I'm not sure the lyrics of *Barbie Girl* shed the best light on western cultural achievement."

Layla said, "I don't know; they sort of do. Well, it's not a cross-cultural masterpiece like *Gangnam Style.*"

Agnus nuzzled Layla's shin this time. He was like a child, parent-hopping and asking the second when the first told him no or wait a minute.

"Ehhhhhhhhhhh, sexy lady!" Agnus said.

We both looked down at him.

He stared at us. "Oppan can of tuna."

I snorted. "See what you've done? By mentioning *Gangnam Style*, you've got our cat making remixes."

Layla laughed. "I told you; it's a culture-crossing masterpiece, even bridging the gaps between humans and felines."

"What can I say?" Agnus asked. "Cats just wanna have fun."

Layla laughed. "Doesn't have the same ring to it as *Trolls*, or even 'Girls just wanna have fun.'"

I shook my head. "And it's not even true. Cats just wanna piss and moan!"

Layla scratched her head. "Not sure that lyric would fit the song."

"Excuse me!" Agnus interrupted. "Cat here. Still needs tuna. Open can now. Or else."

I stared at Agnus. "See what I mean? Pissing and moaning."

"It is written," Agnus said, locking his eyes on mine. "Thou shalt not put the cat to the test."

"It's the Lord, your God," I said, correcting my cat's intentional misquotation of scripture.

"What's the difference?" Agnus asked. "Give me tuna, or I shall smite you."

"You'll smite me?" I asked.

"Don't make me piss in your laundry again."

I sighed, stood up, and went to the kitchen. "I still don't know why you did that."

"As the heavens are higher than the Earth, so are my ways higher than your ways and my thoughts than your thoughts, declareth the lord your cat."

I shook my head. "I don't know how you got from misquoting bad pop songs to misquoting the Bible in two minutes."

"I still don't know what other music you think I should have brought back to New Albion," Layla said, ignoring my banter with Agnus. "I mean, if I brought back country, it would make this world seem like a sad, sad place. And if I brought rock music, well, it's a bit aggressive, don't you think?"

"I don't know," I said, twisting the handle on my can opener to open the tuna can. "I mean, you could have brought back less annoying songs. Maybe a diverse sample from important times in history. Like some Elvis or the Beatles. A little Sinatra. Something from Michael Jackson. Maybe Pink Floyd. Nirvana. I don't know. Just more variety. I mean, you seriously shared *Barbie Girl* with your father?"

"It's got a catchy tune!"

I shook my head as I dumped the tuna into Agnus' bowl and set it on the ground. "No wonder he wants to conquer us."

Layla shrugged. "You don't get it. I mean, the elves enjoyed it. You should have seen the royal court parade around the castle like supermodels when I brought them Right Said Fred."

I raised an eyebrow. "You're seriously telling me you brought *I'm Too Sexy* to New Albion?"

"*I do my little turn on the catwalk, I shake my little tush on the catwalk,*" Agnus said, dropping his voice a few octaves and wagging his hindquarters. I'd say he *sang* the words, but I don't think there is any actual singing in that song.

"You realize," I said, "virtually every song you shared with them, at least the ones you mentioned, were like one-hit wonders. Hardly anyone knows any other song that any of those groups ever released."

"It's not true," Layla said. "I also brought over MMMBop, and those girls had a lot of hits."

"No, they didn't," I said. "And they weren't girls; they were brothers."

"What about the Spice Girls?" Layla asked.

"Yeah," I said. "They were girls."

"No," Layla said. "Were they one-hit wonders, too?"

I cocked my head. "I don't think so, but I can only think of one song of theirs off the top of my head."

"*If you wanna be my lover,*" Agnus sang, his voice falsetto. His face was buried in his bowl of tuna.

"Just because you listen to weird nineties alternative all the time doesn't mean that your playlist would be the best choice to demonstrate the depths of Earth culture to my father," Layla said.

"On my list, I didn't mention nineties alternative bands," I said. "I had the King of Rock on there. The King of Pop. And no one has ever been bigger than the Beatles. Only Nirvana sort of qualifies as nineties alternative, but technically speaking, they are better classified as grunge."

"Again," Layla said. "All the musicians you mentioned are a part of *western* culture. My list was far more diverse."

"Not true," I said. "I mean, the Beatles had an experimental phase. George Harrison played the sitar."

"And how many of those songs do you remember?" Layla asked.

"Well, off the top of my head..."

"Exactly," Layla said. "But when I say *Who Let the Dogs Out*, everyone knows how to respond."

"*Who. Who. Who. Who. Who,*" Agnus said, still eating.

"Agnus," I said. "You're seriously singing a song about *dogs?* Isn't that sort of beneath you?"

"The whole song is a warning," Agnus said, licking his chops. "It also has a mystery to it. It's a true who-done-it. You can't stop listening because you want to find out. Who let the dogs out? Who committed the crime of the century!"

"They don't tell you in the end," I reminded him.

Agnus said, "It's a little postmodern. You're left asking yourself serious, profound questions. Who did it? Was it me all along? Did I let the dogs out? Is it about dogs at all? Perhaps, 'dogs' represents something deeper, an unleashing of carnal desire, of passion, or maybe gas. That song will blow your mind."

I shook my head. "No one asks those questions, Agnus. Usually, in the end, everyone is just glad that the song is over."

"That's what repeat is for!" Layla said. "Hey, Alexa, play *Who Let the Dogs Out!*"

I sighed. "Alexa, stop!"

"What?" Layla asked. "Don't you want to dance a little?"

I shook my head. "Not really. I mean, we have a lot of serious shit to talk about."

"I thought we settled it," Layla said. "You're going to kick these trials' asses. You're going to prove that you're the chosen one and that the drow are wrong about the prophecy. That you're not supposed to marry her."

I nodded. "Proving her wrong. Yeah, that's a great motivator. As if fighting over interpretations over obscure prophecies written centuries ago hasn't occupied too much of my life already."

"Then do it because you seem to think that having them on our side would be a huge help!" Layla said. "Either way, it's not like we can just blow them off."

"I'm not saying I shouldn't do it. But look, we just learned that this whole Elf Gate Cult is a lot larger than either of us ever expected. And they want to live stream this thing? What if someone from the church sees me on a video broadcasted by a cult?"

Layla shrugged. "Then they kick you out again."

I chuckled a little under my breath. "You realize I'm hoping that won't happen, right?"

"I get it," Layla said. "But the last we heard, the archbishop or whoever wasn't going to take action against you because after you healed all those folks, it wouldn't look good on their part to kick you out."

I nodded. "That's true. They're concerned about the public relations aspect of it all, but they're also questioning what I actually did. They think it might have all been a charade. If they see me participating in what will probably look like a magic show online, sponsored by a group they consider a cult…"

"Then wear a disguise," Layla said. "I mean, nothing says you have to look like yourself when you do the tests."

"A disguise?" I asked. "I don't know if I have much in the way of disguises. You've seen my closet. A lot of slacks and polo shirts."

"You don't have *anything* that could work?" Layla asked.

I thought for a moment. "I have a luchador mask that might work."

Layla stared at me blankly. "I have no idea what that is."

"They are masks usually worn by professional wrestlers in Mexico," I said. "Probably shouldn't wear it, though. Cultural appropriation and all. And it's uncomfortable as hell."

"Can I see it?" Layla asked.

I nodded and went to the bedroom. I'd had the thing since I was a teenager. My grandparents, at the time, wintered in south Texas. They used to make regular trips across the border and brought back all kinds of interesting trinkets from the local shops. This had been one of them. I didn't know why I'd held onto it all these years. Probably for sentimental value. I also had my grandpa's old Navy hat that he wore during the Second World War, a pocketknife he gave me when I was ten, and a collection of pesos.

The mask was primarily powder blue and had something like a red dragon across the face, the wings over the brow and the rest of the body curled around the nose and mouth openings. I slipped it on and looked at Layla.

Layla started laughing. "I don't know about that. They wear these when they wrestle?"

"From what I understand, it's almost considered sacred in the Mexican wrestling scene. I mean, if a wrestler is unmasked after a fight, it's supposed to be a major cause of shame. I don't think I should wear it."

"Why not?" Layla asked.

"Because it's important to that culture. I don't think it would be right."

"Fine," Layla said. "Do you have anything else?"

I shook my head. "Too bad it isn't close to Halloween. There'd be a lot of masks for sale."

Layla bit her lip. "What if it's more subtle, like glasses, a mustache—that sort of thing."

"Like those gags with a fake plastic nose, glasses, and thick plastic eyebrows?" I asked.

Layla laughed. "Of course not. Something that looks real. You'd still look like a normal human being; you just wouldn't look like yourself."

I shook my head. "I don't know. I mean, I'm not exactly a master of disguise. I don't know if we could pull it off."

Layla smiled. "Leave that to me. I have a few ideas."

"All right," I said. "I'm trusting you on this."

CHAPTER FIVE

Managing a double life isn't easy. This wasn't the first time I had to navigate two paths that were in opposition. Back before I got sober, trying to keep up on my ministry while bingeing most of my evenings into oblivion wasn't simple, and not just for practical reasons. It took an emotional toll. I never felt like I could be myself. I always had to hide something.

This was a bit different. Nothing I was doing was destructive. I wasn't abusing any substances. I wasn't hurting anyone. I was trying to help people, both as a minister and as the so-called "chosen one" of the elven prophecy.

It shouldn't have been a conflict. A lot of people want to save the world but don't bother helping the people they see who need it day to day. It's one thing to say you want to help society eliminate poverty. It's another to give a meal to someone who is homeless, or heaven forbid, have a conversation with them.

Part of me was inclined to give up the ministry. I'd had to put up with a lot of shit from the powers that be to maintain my preaching post at the Church of the Holy Cross.

But working with those people, bearing their burdens alongside them, praying with them, and encouraging them kept me grounded.

Literally, I mean, since I could fly—not a feat I was likely to perform mid-service any time soon. We were a church, not the Cirque du Soleil.

Ever since Layla came into my life, since I took that blade to my gut, the idea of saving the world or uniting peoples across worlds and races had been a little too much to wrap my mind around. I mean, simple breathing becomes difficult with that kind of weight pressing on one's chest.

When I went to the church, when I went to the soup kitchen, and I spoke to real people, when I opened myself up to the struggles and beauty of individual lives, it gave me strength. Without that, I wasn't sure I'd have what it took to save anyone, much less the world. I didn't know if I could motivate myself to save humanity, but I was motivated to save people like Doris, Cecil, and Grace, people I knew from my church and the soup kitchen ministry. Motivated to get up at the butt-crack of dawn to go to the gym to get into shape. They were the ones I had to keep in the forefront of my mind when I faced these tests, these trials, whatever they might be.

We took the Metro to the gym in the morning. Not a lot of folks on the bus in workout attire at that time of the day. A few folks were dressed for work. I identified some of them as they got on and off the bus. The khaki slacks and a red shirt: that guy probably worked at Target, or maybe it was the latest version of Jake from State Farm and I was in the presence of a celebrity. The black pants, white shirt, and green apron draped over the twenty-something girl's arm: I was guessing she was a barista. The man in grease-stained overalls was probably a mechanic.

These people had names. They had lives, things that would be turned upside-down if the elven legion ever made it to Earth.

I wanted to get new tires for my car, don't get me wrong. It would have made things a lot easier. But lately, I was noticing people a lot more than I ever had. To think that each of these people represented a whole life, that they had their own stories to tell, their dreams and aspirations, their unique stresses and anxieties. There was something beautiful about it when you sat back and thought about it.

Layla elbowed me in the gut.

"What the…"

"You okay, Caspar?" Layla asked. "You look like you're off on another planet or something."

I chuckled. "Nah. Been there, done that. I'm fine right here on Earth."

"You know what I mean," Layla said. "You seem distracted."

I nodded. "Just trying to keep things in perspective, you know? I mean, here we are, going to do our workouts again. Meanwhile, a cult has infiltrated our government, and I'm about to put on a show for them. What sort of show, who knows? And then there's the whole matter of the war on your planet. I mean, since your communicator doesn't work anymore, we don't have a clue how that's going short of waiting for the gate to open on the next full moon."

"What are you going to do about it?" Layla asked. "Working out will be good for you. Aerin said you needed a clear mind."

I nodded. "Exercise is always good for that. Might have to do a little yoga later today, too."

"How's that going since I was gone. I mean, when I left for New Albion, it wasn't exactly your favorite thing."

I nodded. "It's going about as well as it could, I suppose. I mean, I can stand on one foot now."

"Progress!" Layla said, smiling.

"But I can't bend like you," I said. "That whole thing where you put your leg behind your head…"

"Are we still talking about yoga right now?" Layla winked.

I laughed. "Yes. That, too."

"But I think I *am* a little more flexible than I used to be," I said. "I mean, I can almost reach my toes when I bend over now."

"Impressive," Layla said. "If you're ever in the mood to sing a round of *Head and Shoulders, Knees and Toes*, you'll be able to get through it."

"Maybe," I said. "I still might throw my back out in the process. I think that song is still a bit too advanced for me."

"Yeah, those children's songs are brutal," Layla said with a smirk.

"Some of them," I said. "But you should see me do the Hokey Pokey. I mean, I can shake myself about like no other."

"Brilliant," Layla said, chuckling through her words. "You'll be entering dance competitions before you know it."

"I might try that," I said. "After I win Mister Universe."

Layla smiled. "You'll have to beat Jag for that trophy. I don't know."

"Who am I even kidding? Jag made it clear that attaining levels of masculinity on par with his is impossible for old farts like me."

Layla rolled her eyes. "You aren't that old, Caspar. And I don't know I'd call what he is the ideal of manliness or anything."

"Wouldn't you?" I asked. "I mean, have you seen the size of his pecs?"

"If having a large chest is the measure of a man, then I'm more manly than you, Caspar."

"Ok, point."

"In my mind, being a man, if that's a thing you feel like you need to be, is about honesty, bravery, and things like that."

"And honor?" I asked.

Layla nodded. "And of course, having a large…"

"Hold on!" I said, interrupting her.

Layla was laughing so hard she snorted. "Why's it so important for men to measure how manly they are anyway?"

I shook my head. "Because we're all insecure thirteen-year-olds on the inside."

Layla nodded. "That explains why you still tell fart jokes."

"Says the girl who just made a joke about penis size?" I grinned.

"Exactly!"

"A lot of it has to do with our culture. As a boy, you're always being told to man up, to be a man, and the like. If something is girly, you're taught it's bad, at least for you. If you're called girly as a boy, it's somehow meant to be an insult."

Layla cocked her head. "Why would that be an insult? I mean, as a female, I find it insulting that you'd think that having traits associated with women is a negative thing."

I shrugged. "There's a lot of debate these days about how much of what we associate with gender is due to nature versus nurture. Like, is gender a cultural construct."

Layla cocked her head. "I never really thought about it that way. I mean, on New Albion, we had pretty strict rules and limits placed on females. Sounds like for the drow, it's the exact opposite."

I nodded. "Some people think it goes back to the days when humans had to hunt for and gather their food. Since men tend to be stronger, faster, and the like, it's assumed that they settled into different roles than women by necessity."

"Stronger and faster?" Layla asked. "Wanna wrestle?"

I smiled. "You have the advantage of a lifetime's worth of training to compensate for the biological advantages I probably don't have. You've been training, while I've spent most of the last several years eating cheese puffs and playing *World of Warcraft*."

"So, that was your off-duty life before I came into the picture?" Layla asked. "You've sort of mentioned it before."

"That's not the only thing I did."

"I should hope not!"

"I ate a lot of Twinkies and pizza, too. And until five years ago, I drank a lot of beer."

"But now it's all protein shakes and green drinks!" Layla said.

"Believe it or not, I'm starting to appreciate that Greenberry drink. I still don't have a clue what a Greenberry is, but I find myself craving one during the day. How weird is that?"

"Once your body gets a taste of whole nutrition, it's like your stomach craves things that have the nutrients your body wants."

"How'd you get to be such an expert?" I asked. "I mean, how much in the way of nutrition do the elves understand? And do you even have the same fruits and vegetables?"

Layla answered, "We have fruits and vegetables. Not the same ones, not exactly. Some are similar. A lot of them, I think our ancestors brought with them, but they've evolved due to the different nutrient profile in New Albion's soil, the climate, and whatnot."

I raised one eyebrow. "And is Greenberry something that grows on New Albion?"

Layla laughed. "I haven't a clue what Greenberry is, but you're right. That shake tastes like a freshly cut lawn the first time you drink it, but before long, you start to love it."

"Look what you've done to me," I said, shaking my head. "You've probably added five years onto my life already. I mean, presuming I don't die in these trials. Or at the end of your father's sword in the near future. If that happens, it'll be a waste being healthy."

Jag was waiting for us with a shit-eating grin splitting his face as we walked into the gym. "You two go ahead," Layla said. "I'm going to catch the kickboxing class."

"Wait," I said. "Kickboxing? I mean, if I'm trying to learn to fight…"

Jag snorted. "Fighting has nothing to do with that class. It's more like a shake your booty while shadow-boxing thing."

Layla said, "If you're in a fight, you really should be working it. What good is it to punch someone in the face if you aren't shaking your booty at the same time?"

I cocked my head. "All right. Have fun boxing the air."

Layla elevated her chin. "I'll make sure it knows who's boss. I mean, that's one of the elements, right?"

I chuckled. "I suppose that's right. Give the air hell. Soften it up so I won't have any problem if that's the element of the first trial."

"I don't think you'll have any problem with air." Layla shrugged. "You're an expert at breaking wind."

"I just don't try to hide it."

Layla kissed me on the cheek. "Have a good workout."

"You ever take that class, Jag?" I asked as Layla walked into the group exercise room.

Jag shook his head. "No. Watched it plenty of times. Not a lot of dudes in those classes for some reason."

"Must have something to do with the booty-shaking. I've never been able to figure out how to twerk."

Jag snorted. "I haven't tried."

I bit my lip. I couldn't say the same thing. I had been alone in my apartment in front of the mirror. It was before I could communicate with Agnus, an interlude in the air-guitar air-microphone solo lip-synching concert I usually presented to an audience of myself in the mirror. Needless to say, I couldn't so much as move my butt in rhythm, much less pull off a decent twerk. It's not like anyone would want to see that anyway.

"So, Jag. What's on the agenda for today?" I asked.

"We're going to add some HIIT training to your circuit."

"So I get to punch something between sets?" I asked.

"No, HIIT with two Is. High-Intensity Interval Training. Between each set, you'll be doing intensive cardio."

I snorted. "Cardio? I thought cardio was for pussies."

"What most of the people are doing here is. Just look at all those treadmillers barely breaking a sweat. No, what we're doing is one minute of full-on, push-yourself-to-the-limit, high-intensity moves. Then it's on to your next set, and you'll have to find the energy to push through it. This isn't pussy cardio; this is warrior cardio. No ass-shaking allowed."

I stared blankly at Jag. "All right, let's give it a shot."

"After we do your deprecations," Jag said. "Look right in the mirror and tell yourself how it is."

I nodded and stared at myself intently. "You suck!"

Jag laughed. "All right, but now tell the old you why he sucks. Sucking isn't bad. Some things I like to suck. Other things…"

"Jag, I'm not going there," I said. "And I haven't ever sucked on much of anything."

"It doesn't matter," Jag said. "It's about humiliating the old you into submission. Now, tell your old self what you suck!"

"You suck bananas!"

"Really?" Jag said, cocking his head. "How is that humiliating?"

"Fine," I said. "You suck toes!"

Jag laughed. "Really? You do that? To each his own."

"You said it didn't have to be real!" I protested, my hands on my hips.

"Dude, I'm not judging. You're into what you're into. Whatever strokes your jollies."

I sighed and shook my head. "My jollies? Seriously? Whatever. Let's just get this over with."

"Sure thing, Foot Boy," Jag said, shaking his head. "But that was the old you. The new you, the man who emerges from the cocoon of today's workout, will spread his wings. He'll be a warrior. A man. And he'll never suck on toes again. Instead, he'll suck on…"

"I told you," I said, interrupting him before he could say

anything more. "I was just coming up with something I thought I could say in public. I don't actually…"

"Look, man," Jag said, shaking his head. "Once the truth is out there, you can't put it back in the box. As I was about to say, after today, you'll only suck on lollipops."

I raised my left eyebrow. "Is that really what you were going to say?"

Jag shook his head slowly. "I was going to say fudgesicles. Or maybe bomb pops. But lollipops are much more manly, don't you think?"

I scrunched my brow. "Says who? When's the last time you saw a grown man with a lollipop?"

"I don't know," Jag said. "But I'm about to. After you crush this workout, we'll eat lollipops together. Like men!"

CHAPTER SIX

I collapsed in a pile of sweat. Thankfully there was a workout mat nearby. Usually, we used it for ab work. Today, it served to cushion my crumpled body.

That HIIT was some crazy SHIIT!

The weights were pretty standard—just as intense as ever. But then he had me doing burpees, jumping lunges, box jumps, battle ropes, and a few things I'm pretty sure he pulled out of his sadistic ass.

"You can do anything for one minute!" he insisted.

But these weren't normal human minutes. I swear, I think Jag has a magic of his own, some kind of mystic capacity to slow down time. Those were the longest minutes I'd ever spent in my life.

Full intensity. As hard as I could. My heart rate through the roof, and totally out of breath.

Then, no rest. Back to the weights.

We did that for a full godforsaken hour.

My heart was still racing as I laid there, my shirt so soaked in sweat I'd have to peel it off of my torso later.

"Damn!" Layla said as she walked over, her cheeks just a little pink from her kickboxing class. "You weren't playing around today."

"He's gone, isn't he?" I asked.

"For the moment," Layla said. "I think Jag went to the locker room. And from the looks of it, you could sure use a shower."

"I don't want to move…"

"Want a shake?" Layla asked. "I have the powder in my bag."

"Yes…please…"

Something fell on my face. It was hard.

I reached up to grab it.

"A Dum Dum?" I asked.

"Told you," Jag said as he approached my sweat-soaked self on the floor. "We'd eat lollipops together when you were done."

I snorted. "This is a Dum Dum. It's so small."

Jag cocked his head. "You prefer to suck on big things?"

Layla cleared her throat. "Okay, I'm just going to go make those shakes now, and you two can do whatever it is you're planning."

I shook my head, braced myself, and managed to slowly return to an upright, sitting position. "That workout was brutal."

"A little sugar right after a workout that intense is helpful. Causes a small insulin spike that helps your body absorb the protein in your shake."

I nodded as I unwrapped my sucker. "I'll just take your word for it."

Jag sat down beside me. We both faced the gym mirror, lollipops hanging out of our mouths.

"A couple of badasses," Jag said, nodding.

I snorted. "I've never sweated so much in my whole life."

Jag nodded. "You'll probably feel a little warm all day. That kind of workout turns up your body's thermostat. You'll be burning fat all day."

"Good to know," I said. "Any clue at all what's in store for tonight?"

Jag replied, "The drow have the whole place to themselves today. Haven't even tried to stop by."

"I just wish there was something I could do to get ready," I said. "Layla is going in a different direction when we leave. Said she has to get supplies for my disguise."

"We should probably stretch," Jag said.

"People do that?" I asked.

"The smart ones do. You work out like this, if you don't stretch, you'll have all kinds of problems. Right after a workout, your muscles are warm. More pliable. Best time to stretch."

"I'll take your word for it," I said. Jag extended both his legs in a v-shape in front of his body and leaned to one side.

I imitated him, feeling the pull across my lower back and hamstrings. Then, following his lead, I switched to the other leg.

Our lollipops were still dangling from our mouths.

"What flavor do you have?" I asked.

"Piña Colada. My favorite."

"What's mine?" I asked. "Butterscotch?"

Jag nodded. "I don't like that kind, so I gave it to you."

I chuckled as I tucked one leg under my body and tried to do whatever odd stretch Jag was doing. This one worked on my hips. It felt kind of good. "So, you just give me the ones you don't like?"

"Do you dislike it?" Jag asked.

"No, it's delicious," I said, slurping on my sucker as I talked.

"Then be grateful," Jag said. "I've been hauling these around in my gym bag for weeks."

I snorted and removed my Dum Dum from my mouth. "In your gym bag? The same one you throw your nasty gym socks in?"

"And my briefs," Jag said.

I gagged and, I think, threw up a little in my mouth. "And this sucker was in there all this time? I knew there was something funny about this butterscotch flavor."

"Mine tastes great to me."

I quickly grabbed my water bottle and gargled. Unfortunately, I didn't have a place to spit the water out, not in the middle of the gym floor. I pointed at the locker room, grunted, and stood up, the blood rush making the facility spin a little as I struggled to maintain my balance. Stumbling into the locker room, I spat the water into one of the sinks.

Jag came strolling in.

"Nice work today, Casp."

I was still rinsing my mouth out in the sink, one cupped handful of water after the next.

"Taste like my balls?" Jag asked.

I shook my head. "How the hell would I know? It tasted fine. It was just the idea, knowing that these were in the bag with your nasty socks and briefs."

Jag nodded. "It's all in the mind, bro. I mean, I had them in zip locks."

I grunted. "Still. Yuck."

"Mind over matter," Jag said. "Even if I rubbed your sucker on my crotch."

"You didn't?"

"No, I didn't," Jag said. "I'm not a total asshole. I didn't put your sucker there either. No worries, buddy!"

I shook my head. "I appreciate it."

"The point is," Jag continued to explain, "it's all in your head. It's only gross after you know the truth. That means if you change your thinking, you can get through it. Light weight, baby!"

"Like King Coleman?" I asked.

"You remembered!" Jag said, smiling. "When you look at a barbell, you don't let the weight on it intimidate you. You go after it. Tell yourself it's light, and somehow, it feels lighter."

I nodded. "I'm trying to master all this magic. A lot of it is in the mind, too. I have to visualize what I'm going to do. Somehow when I do that, my body just figures it out. Not exactly sure how it works."

"What I'm saying is more than that," Jag said. "I'm saying if you force yourself to believe something, it's almost like you can change reality. At least your experience of it."

"Maybe that will change my experience of this prophecy," I said, laughing as I followed him out of the locker room. "Layla isn't thrilled that Aerin thinks we're supposed to get married."

Jag was about to say something, but Layla showed up with our protein shakes and gave me mine.

Instead, Jag just smiled kindly and nodded, then tilted his head. "I don't think anyone knows for certain what is going to happen or what must happen. I mean, I was told when I was growing up that I was a small-framed boy. That was my lot, destined to a lifetime of being a pussy."

Layla laughed. "Looks like you defied nature, Jag."

Jag nodded. "I don't think that was it. I just learned how to give nature what it wanted so my body would naturally respond the way I wanted it to."

"Like steroids?" I asked.

Layla backhanded me on the shoulder. "Caspar!"

Jag smiled. "A lot of people assume that, but nothing I've done is illegal. The supplements I take help, but none of that is an excuse for hard work, learning how the body responds, and how my body reacts to training. You have to listen to your nature and give it what it's asking for. Some people see me and say I'm not natural. But what is natural?"

"That's a good point," I said. "Technically, it isn't like anything we have that we call artificial is supernatural. It has to be natural on some level. I mean, it all comes from the Earth somehow."

"Twinkies are not natural, Caspar," Layla added. "Stop trying to justify it."

She added, "That's not even what I'm saying. I just mean, why do we assume that sitting on our asses and getting out of shape is a natural body? The human body, or elf body, was never meant to be sedentary. We were meant to work. Doesn't the Bible say that too, Caspar?"

"Actually," I said, "it does. In Genesis. God told Adam and Eve to work the ground. To tend the garden of Eden."

"That's my point," Jag said. "I bet they had better nutrition, too. So to be natural, we have to force ourselves out of our artificial, easy lives. We have to work out, not because we have to put food on our plates, but because our bodies are designed for it. We have to feed ourselves properly because the food we buy, even our produce, is mass-produced and isn't natural the way it is. Supplementation gets us closer to what's natural than people usually assume. Our culture's lifestyle, doing nothing, eating fast food and drinking soda? That's not natural. But shakes and workouts? A few extra supplements to counteract the damage our lifestyles do? Much closer to nature."

I nodded. It was jarring to hear Jag get philosophical. If it didn't involve getting huge, shredded, or winning over chicks with a chiseled physique, I hadn't heard him discuss much that required deep thought. Not that those things are particularly ethereal subjects, but when it came to such matters, he knew what he was talking about. He had thought about it a lot. I guess I shouldn't have sold him short when it came to other matters. He'd joined the Elf Gate Cult for a reason, probably the same reason a lot of folks join religions. He was looking for meaning. For significance. Something to give him a purpose beyond crafting a swoon-worthy body and building bigger biceps.

"That's interesting," I said, smiling. "Hadn't thought of it that way before."

Jag nodded. "I don't think the idea applies just to exercise and fitness. It fits a lot of what we assume about how things are supposed to be."

I nodded. Jag was trying to tell me something about the significance of the prophecy and how Aerin and Layla understood it differently. How they each assumed what must be and what was destined to be by prophecy. Similar to how we assume that what is natural is whatever is most obvious or convenient based on our limited experience. At least, that's what I gleaned from it.

Not saying that Jag's idea wasn't helpful. It was, sort of. I mean, the elven prophecy came from an ancient druid, a fellow named Taliesin. What did he intend? Presuming the ones held by the elves, the giants, and the drow were all the same prophecy, there had to be a single meaning unless this Taliesin dude was wildly inconsistent. Maybe he just wanted to create relationship drama in the chosen one's life.

At least the elven giants hadn't brought me a princess to consider, too. I hadn't met any of their females yet, but even if they were smaller than B'iff or Brag'mok, they'd dwarf me. And with those massive bottom incisors that overlapped their upper lips, kissing one would probably be hazardous to my health. My dental health, at least.

Layla handed me my shake.

Jag slapped me on the back as I was taking my first sip. I almost spit it all back out.

"See you tonight, bro," Jag said. "If you kick that trial's ass the same way you did today's workout, you'll be fine."

"Thanks, man," I said, taking another gulp of my Greenberry shake.

"I'll meet you back at the apartment," Layla said. "I'm going to go pick up some supplies for your disguise."

"All right," I said. "I have to get ready for work anyway."

I still worked a part-time bartending gig at O'Donnell's pub, which was on the ground level of the building where my apartment was. It wasn't the best-paying job, and with everything else on my plate, I'd thought about giving it up. But since the O'Donnell family owned the building, as long as I worked there, I had free rent.

Not to mention, it was nice having a job that didn't involve saving people or saving the world, or doing anything of world-changing significance. All of us, I think, need a dose of normalcy to keep our heads on straight.

"We'll get you all fixed up after your shift," Layla said. "Don't stress it. I've got this covered."

I nodded. "Thanks, Layla."

I kissed her on the cheek as I went to the locker room to change. I had a few extra shirts in my locker for days like these when my sweat-soaked workout clothes just wouldn't cut it for the bus ride home.

Not that the Metro had a dress code.

But since my whole body smelled like a foot, I was trying to keep the other Metro riders in mind. You know, common courtesy.

By the time I made it to the locker room, Jag was gone and more than likely a set or two into his workout.

I walked past him on my way out of the gym. He was squatting what looked like at least five hundred pounds. I just shook my head. The guy was a beast.

I chugged the rest of my shake and went to the bus stop to wait for my ride home. The bus Layla was taking had already picked her up.

With my gym bag containing my nasty workout clothes slung over my shoulder and my shake in my hand, I boarded my bus.

"Reverend!" someone said as I walked down the aisle, looking for a seat.

"Cecil!" I said. "Didn't realize you took this route."

"Have a seat, Reverend," Cecil said. "It's good to see you."

CHAPTER SEVEN

"How's Grace doing?" I asked as I sat down.

"Fantastic, Reverend. Getting stronger every day. Barely needs her cane anymore."

I smiled. Cecil had shown up, to the chagrin of some of the church's members, at one of our services after hearing rumors that I'd healed one of our members. After he pressed me, by drawing on a little magic, I'd somehow managed to cure his daughter of spina bifida. After that, dozens of other members of the community had started crowding our pews. Not all of them wanted healings, but it had changed the dynamic of the congregation.

"I'm glad to hear it, Cecil," I said. "She's a special girl."

"You changed her life, Reverend," Cecil said. "And so many others."

"How's Shanda? Is your wife adjusting to all these changes well?" I asked.

"Now that Grace is better," Cecil explained, "she's been able to take a part-time job. We're saving up to buy a house!"

I cocked my head. "That's wonderful, Cecil. Congratulations."

"Praise the Lord, Reverend. I don't know where you came from or how you do what you do, but you've changed our lives."

I tossed my gym bag under the seat and folded my hands in my lap. Something about this conversation made me uneasy. Don't get me wrong. I was thrilled for Cecil and his family, but I was hardly the saint he wanted me to be or the holy man he was convinced I was. I was divorced. I was a recovering alcoholic. And not all of the church's members, much less the authorities in the church, were thrilled by the changes.

"I don't know what to say, Cecil," I said. "I'm excited for you, but I'm nothing special."

Cecil cocked his head. "You don't see it, do you? The hand of God on your life?"

I shook my head. "I'm a broken man, Cecil."

"Aren't we all?" Cecil asked. "I'm not so learned when it comes to the Bible, but didn't God speak through an ass once?"

I chuckled. "Yeah. Balaam's donkey."

"If God can use an ass to do his will, why do you think he wouldn't use you?" Cecil asked.

I scratched my head. "You know what, Cecil? That's brilliant. I hadn't thought about it that way before."

"All I know is that if God didn't use broken people, he wouldn't have much to work with, would he?"

I nodded. "Again, that's a great point."

"A lot of people are afraid of change," he said. "I know I am. I mean, it's scary to think about it. Owning a house? Really? Just last week, we depended on the soup kitchen for meals, and now we can put food on the table. Food we've paid for. And when we get into a new neighborhood, we can put Grace in a better school."

"And that change scares you?" I asked. "It's amazing. Don't give me the credit. You and Shanda, you've seized your opportunity. I'm thrilled for you."

"But will the new school accept Grace?" Cecil asked. "Or our new neighborhood? A family like us moving in next door?"

"What do you mean?" I asked.

"A black family," Cecil said.

I shook my head. "Honestly, I didn't even think about that."

"We have to think about it, Reverend," Cecil said. "Every day. I know a lot of folks, white folks, I mean, who are good people, say that they don't see color. But they do. Everyone does."

I bit my lip. "I can't imagine what it must be like."

Cecil waved his hand through the air. "It is what it is, Reverend. This is the world we're in. But don't think I'm not grateful."

I shook my head. "The world shouldn't be that way."

"I agree," Cecil said. "But even in the church, we aren't oblivious to the way the people there look at us."

"I'm hoping that involving them in the soup kitchen will help with that," I said. "But I'm sorry if they haven't made you feel welcome."

"I know you're taking some heat," Cecil said. "I'm sorry for that."

I shook my head. "You don't need to be, Cecil. It isn't your fault."

"Just know this, Reverend," Cecil said. "If your church won't have you, if they decide for whatever reason that it's too much, we'll still be there. Wherever you go, we have your back."

I smiled. "Thank you for saying that. It means more than you know."

We sat there in awkward silence for a good minute. There was so much about the situation with the church I hadn't had time to think about.

But I wasn't ready to write off that chapter of my life. I had gone into ministry to give people hope.

"This is my stop," Cecil said as the bus's brakes squealed. "First day, new job. Wish me luck!"

"New job?" I asked. "Congratulations, Cecil!"

Cecil nodded. "It isn't much. Just changing folks' oil. Fixing flat tires. But it's a step up."

I bit my lip. "You said tires?"

Cecil nodded. "Tire and lube."

"I've got a car in need of four," I said. "You don't happen to know if they have a tow service, do you?"

"Where's your car at?" Cecil asked.

"In the lot at O'Donnell's," I said.

"I'll take care of it, Reverend," Cecil smiled. "I mean, I can't cover the costs of the tires."

"Don't worry about that," I said. "But it would be amazing if your shop could help."

Cecil nodded. "Can't be a bad thing for me. Bringing them new business on day one? Sounds like a win-win to me."

"Thank you, Cecil," I said. "Truly. It helps a lot."

"I'll have a tow truck sent out this afternoon," Cecil said with a nod as he got off the bus.

I sat there staring out the window as the Metro took me to my stop. It's funny how when even the weight of the world is pressing down on your shoulders, a kind gesture can brighten your day. Sure, it wasn't like Cecil was buying me new tires, but I needed to get my car fixed. He had a solution, and he'd offered to help, even if it was just in a small way. To me, it was bigger than that. It was about more than about tires.

Cecil didn't have a car of his own, and he was offering to help me get mine fixed?

I didn't have a lot of spare money in the bank, and with fifty-dollar training sessions accumulating on my credit card, I wasn't enthused about buying new tires. I had procrastinated before dealing with it. Too much on my plate. It was a question of priorities. I had supernatural ways of traveling, after all. Being out of shape, though, could have more imminent life-threatening consequences for me than for most people. Still, I was getting tired of riding the Metro. I couldn't just fly or port anywhere. I needed my car. I would just have to figure out the cost, and I was grateful that Cecil would take care of arranging it.

CHAPTER EIGHT

I stood in front of the bookshelf in my apartment. I'd started listing books for sale once before. Amazon had an easy app that made it a breeze. All I had to do was scan the bar code and set a price, and they'd be listed in the used bookstore.

"Selling books?" Agnus asked as he hopped off the couch.

I nodded. "Need a little cash to get my tires fixed. Well, replaced."

"People buy this drivel?" Agnus asked. He wasn't one to mince words.

I looked at my phone. "This commentary set. The lowest price for any of them is fifty bucks. I think the series is out of print."

"Just don't sell your copy of *Everyone Poops*. It's my favorite."

I tilted my head. "You're now telling me that you read?"

Agnus head-butted my shin. "Not really, but I like the pictures."

"In *Everyone Poops*?" I asked. "All the pictures are of different animals pooping."

"Why do you even have that book anyway?" Agnus asked.

I chuckled. "Someone got it for me as a gag. It was an ordination gift."

Agnus wrapped his tail around his feet. "Humans are weird."

"You're the one who says you like the book, Agnus," I said, kneeling and retrieving the book from the bottom shelf.

"It's profound if you think about it," Agnus said. "Its whole message."

I shook my head. "There isn't much of a plot to it, Agnus."

"You're missing the point," Agnus said. "All those different animals, but when it comes down to it, we have things in common."

"Let me guess," I said. "That everyone eats…"

"And everyone poops!" Agnus agreed enthusiastically. "Even you humans who think you're so much better than the rest of us. At the end of the day—well, maybe not at the end of the day, but whenever nature calls—you do the same nasty the rest of us do."

I chuckled. "I suppose that's true."

"We could focus on our differences. Our superior intelligence, our refined senses, our innate beauty. But just because you're human doesn't mean you have to be insecure about all that."

I snorted. "You think cats have superior intelligence? I don't see any books on this shelf written by cats."

"You overcomplicate your lives," Agnus said. "It doesn't have to be that way, but humans are too innately simple to see it. The very fact that you don't realize our feline superiority proves my point. You're too obtuse to see the truth."

The television was on in the background. Agnus had the remote on the couch next to where he'd been sitting. "You were watching human television shows. What is it?"

"The History Channel," Agnus said. "Interesting that your histories only cover the things humans do. But look at this show. It's about ancient Egypt. It's inspiring."

"Mummies and pyramids inspire you?" I asked.

Agnus sauntered back over to the couch and jumped up. "They worshipped cats," he said. "It's incredible how advanced humans used to be."

I just shook my head. "You realize the ancient Egyptians used to poop too, right?"

"See!" Agnus exclaimed. "That's my point! Your histories gloss over all the important stuff!"

I laughed as I grabbed another book from my shelf and scanned it into my app. "Very true," I said. "I wonder what they did before they had sewer systems?"

"Disgusting humans," Agnus said, shaking his head. "They used buckets, then dumped it on the street. Even ancient cats knew better than that. They buried their turds in the sand."

"Sounds like cats haven't changed much through the centuries."

"Of course not!" Agnus said. "Because we instinctively know better than humans. People! Such vile creatures. The last show was about the black plague. You realize if they'd just had basic common sense sanitation in the dark ages, they probably could have avoided all that?"

"I think it was more complicated than that, Agnus."

"Not really," he said. "But that's my point. You humans make everything so damned complex. It's not a sign of intelligence. It's the opposite."

I decided to drop it. Agnus had the Cadillac of litter boxes. It used human technology to clean itself, sensing when the cat left the box and raking out the clumps. All because of human ingenuity. The one time I had threatened to sell his box and get a normal one, he'd raised all kinds of hell about it.

Still, since Agnus started communicating with me, I'd learned my lesson. There was no point in arguing with him or challenging his assumptions, especially when it came to the primacy of his species.

I'd have to list more books later. It was a good start. Not enough to pay for my new tires, but hopefully, a few bucks would come my way before my next credit card bill was due. It would offset the cost a bit.

I needed to take a shower before I went to work.

I double-checked my shampoo bottle. After a trickster fairy had dumped a bottle of Nair into my shampoo…well, I wasn't going to risk it. Not that I had a lot of hair left to lose. It was just starting to grow back in, and I didn't look great with a shaved head. I wasn't inclined to start the hair-growth process over. The shampoo was fine.

The shower was calming. I could have stood under the warm water for hours. Of course, it wouldn't last that long, but there was nothing as refreshing as a good shower after a killer workout.

I'd barely dried off and slipped into clean boxers when the front door opened.

That was fast.

"Layla?" I asked.

"It's me," she shouted across the apartment.

I stepped out of the bathroom and headed to the bedroom to get the rest of my clothes.

Before, I hadn't brought undies with me into the bathroom when I showered. But since Layla moved in and Agnus could speak, it felt rude to walk around the place naked.

Bachelorhood was over.

Layla walked into the bedroom right behind me.

"That was quick," I said. "You get everything you needed?"

Layla nodded as she threw a yellow plastic bag on the table. "Check it out."

I reached into the bag. "A twelve-piece set of fake mustaches?"

Layla nodded, smiling. "I had to get the full set, so I figured you'd have your choice."

"You think just adding a mustache will be enough of a disguise?" I asked.

"Trust me," Layla said. "When someone has a glorious mustache, no one sees anything else."

I slipped on a pair of jeans and a polo shirt. "You can pick. I don't care."

"Come on! You need to pick one that you're comfortable wearing."

I shook my head. "I don't think any of these fits me."

"That's the point," Layla said. "We don't want you to look like you!"

I grabbed the kit. There weren't any great choices. "I don't know, Layla."

"How about the Fu Manchu?" Layla asked.

I chuckled. "I don't want to look like Hulk Hogan."

"You won't. Trust me."

"Still, that's not the one."

"Here," Layla said. "This one is more subtle. It's called the Toothbrush."

I shook my head. "I'm not wearing a Hitler 'stache, Layla."

"Okay," Layla said. "You could just call it a Charlie Chaplin."

I shook my head. "No one sees that mustache and thinks of Charlie Chaplin. That Hitler asshole ruined the toothbrush mustache forever."

"Fair point."

"You just choose," I said. "It doesn't matter."

"All right," Layla said. "You're wearing the Handlebar."

I cocked my head. "Really? I'll look like a douche."

"You'll look like a douche with any mustache, Caspar. That's the point."

"Fine," I said. "But I'm not putting it on now."

"Of course not," Layla said. "Go to work. We'll get you fixed up after your shift."

CHAPTER NINE

I tucked my keys into my front pocket and my wallet into my back pocket before heading out the door and downstairs to the pub.

I just had to get through today's shift.

So much on my mind. Work would be a nice distraction.

I know working at a bar isn't ideal for a recovering alcoholic, but with Donna there—she ran the place and was also a member of my AA group—I had plenty of confidence. For the most part, it didn't faze me. Mixing drinks. Pouring beers. It was just a job.

And I didn't have any desire to drink. Not anymore.

Not as long as I maintained a fit spiritual condition. Not that I was together in that regard; I was questioning a lot about my beliefs. The whole prophecy thing had turned my worldview upside-down and inside-out, but I had faith. Even if I was uncertain what I believed, I still trusted that the God who'd taken care of me throughout my life, often despite myself, would see me through.

It was a simple prayer. I said it every morning. I didn't always kneel at my bedside or sit in front of my Bible, but I said these few words: "Lord, give me the strength not to drink today."

In more than five years, he hadn't let me down yet.

"Hey, Caspar," Donna said as I walked through the door. "A tow-truck driver is looking for you."

"Already?" I asked. I couldn't believe Cecil had arranged it so quickly. Just a couple of hours ago, he was getting off the bus to start his first day.

"I think he needs the keys," Donna continued.

I nodded and headed back out the door. The car was parked around the corner, so I hadn't even noticed he was there.

I gave the driver my Mitsubishi key and went back inside.

"All taken care of," I said.

"About time," Donna said.

I nodded. "Yeah, someone offered to help. Sort of a relief."

The shift went as well as could be expected. I didn't spill any drinks on any patrons, which for me was a win. For the midday shift, which was usually rather slow, it was fairly busy.

I was glad about that. It gave me a few hours without having to think about the trials, the prophecy, the church, or the mustache.

It was oddly therapeutic. I suppose we all need an escape.

Of course, the first thing I thought about as I climbed the stairs to my apartment was that Layla was probably preparing to glue a mustache to my upper lip.

Instead, I found the lights dimmed.

Candles lit all around.

And Layla bent over backward in a bridge on the floor.

"Yoga?" I asked.

"Shh. You're messing with my chi."

I snorted. "Elves have chi?"

"I've adapted the principles of yoga to our practice of ioga," Layla said. Since the elves had brought with them something comparable to yoga from the old world, which I was beginning to suspect they'd borrowed from the drow, who, based on their dress when I'd met them the night before, had probably been living in India for centuries.

"All right," I said. "I'll go make popcorn so I can watch."

Layla lowered her body to the ground. "I'm not doing this for your enjoyment, Caspar."

"Doesn't mean I can't enjoy the show."

Layla chuckled. "Why don't you join me?"

"I only do Tony Horton's yoga. When no one is looking."

"I've seen you do it," Agnus piped up. "You should see it. If we're talking about watching people do yoga, you in the mood for a little comedy, Layla?"

"Shut up, Agnus," I piped back. "It's not that funny."

"No," Layla said. "I think Agnus had a great idea. How about *I* go make some popcorn?"

I kicked off my shoes and laid down on my back.

"Shavasana pose doesn't count," Layla told me.

"Come on," I said. "Just lying still challenges the mind."

"All right," Layla said. "Then let's see if you can do it. We have about four hours before we have to leave. See if you can hold it the whole time."

"A four-hour nap?" I asked. "No problem."

"No," Layla said. "It's not a nap. In Shavasana, you're supposed to feel the world all around you. It's an awareness of the body and a heightened state of consciousness. It's why it's normally done at the end of a routine when you've had a chance to join your body to your mind through a variety of sequences."

I shrugged. "I'd just as soon skip to the end."

"All right. But while you're doing it, I'm going to put on your mustache."

"What?" I asked. "How can I focus my mind if you're gluing that thing to my face?"

"Total control over your body and mind," Layla said. "You told me this Shavasana stuff was easy."

"Fine," I said. "We'll do the routine, but we're doing Tony's video, not whatever brutal stuff you do."

"Better choice," Layla said. "That video is only an hour and a half."

"Yeah," I said. "But I usually fast forward through the balance poses."

Layla cocked her head. "Why do you do that?"

I looked at her blankly. "Because I can't do them. Duh. Rather skip past than crash into the floor repeatedly."

"You'll never learn them if you don't practice, Caspar. It doesn't matter if you stumble."

I nodded. "All right. Well, let's get it over with."

"Just wait," Agnus said. "When he tries to do crane pose, it takes a while before he gets there. But trust me. It's worth it!"

Layla giggled. "I'll start the popcorn."

"Hey," I said, slipping off my jeans and kicking them into the corner. "You were serious about that? I was joking when I said it."

"You were?" Layla asked. "That's a shame because I *was* serious. Let's see if you can focus with us watching you. Since people all around the world are going to be watching you tonight, you need to be ready."

I sighed as I walked back to the bedroom and put on a pair of knit shorts. I'd learned my lesson the first few times I did yoga. If I wasn't wearing elastic material, chances were I split my pants right in the crotch. This pair, though, had survived several rounds. They had more flexibility than I did.

At first, it was mildly distracting. I could feel their eyes on me as I made my way through a vinyasa and into warrior one. And them crunching on the popcorn? Irritating as hell.

But I tried to clear my mind and focus. That was what I needed to do. I wasn't sure what these trials were going to involve, but I needed to be able to tune out everything else. I had to focus no matter what happened.

Before I knew it, I was in the zone.

"That downward dog is pretty hot," Layla told Agnus. "I'd peg that."

"Not my type," Agnus said. "Anything with the word 'dog' in it is pretty vile if you ask me."

"You two!" I shouted. "Stop!"

"Focus, Caspar," Layla said. "We're just giving you shit. You were doing so well."

"What the hell does it mean, you'd peg me?" I asked.

"Google it," Layla said. "Looks like fun to me."

I snorted. "I can imagine. And no thanks. I definitely won't be Googling anything like that."

After that, I decided I just wasn't going to listen. I needed to be aware, but what I heard, what I saw—they were secondary to my basic sense of awareness.

I got back into the groove. I rocked the vinyasa sequences and got to the balance poses.

Tree pose.

No problem.

Royal Dancer.

I slew it.

Finally, Crane.

Balancing on your hands with your knees tucked onto your biceps. I'd been practicing. I know I said I fast-forwarded the balance postures, and if Agnus was watching, I did. But I did stop to give this one a shot because it seemed like one of those poses that once I got it, I'd accomplish something.

So far, I'd managed to get one foot off the ground. I used the big toe of my opposite foot to maintain my balance.

But this time, I was daring. I was going to give it a shot.

I slowly lifted my big toe off the ground.

Focus, Caspar.

I was doing it, but I couldn't think about that. I couldn't celebrate. I had to stay in the moment.

Then something buzzed.

I caught a green glow out of the corner of my eye.

Then it collided with my butt, which was in the air.

I tumbled onto the floor.

"Dammit!" I said.

"It's Ensley!" Layla said. Ensley was the trickster fairy who'd put Nair in my shampoo before. At the time, little did I know, as the fairy king, he'd had an alliance with King Brightborn, Layla's dad. But when push came to shove and Brightborn showed his true colors, he'd turned on him and helped me instead. He'd even left me with a dose of his powers.

Fairies were the only entities who could make gates between worlds and pass to and fro, provided they had a little help from a human or perhaps an elf or elven giant. It was a combination of fairy magic and typical Earth or elven magic that allowed gates to form.

If Ensley was here, it was serious.

Ensley perched on my knee.

"Urgent, urgent!" Ensley said. "The time is nigh! The redcoats are coming! The redcoats are coming!"

I cocked my head. "Ensley, slow down. What are you saying?"

"King Brightborn. Him and the legions. They defeated the elven giants."

"They what?" Layla asked. "The elves and orcs...giants, rather, have been at war for centuries. And in a matter of a few days, you're saying the Night Legion has fallen to the elves?"

"The magic you vested in the ley lines," Ensley said. "It revived New Albion. Mostly. But somehow, the elves had already cut off the ley lines. It only revived the magic in the region of the elves."

Layla added, "Which left the elven giants vulnerable."

"It was a slaughter," Ensley said. "We tried to slow them down, but the legion is well-trained. Our numbers were too few. We warned the giants, but you know how they are. Proud. They insisted on standing and fighting."

I sighed. "I can't believe it! Brag'mok?"

"I saw him fall with my own eyes," Ensley said. "I'm sorry, Caspar."

I clenched my fist. It wasn't just that the elven legion had won the war. I'd given them the power to do it, but I thought I'd saved their world. Instead, it was like I'd traveled back in time and given Hitler nuclear weapons. It was that horrible.

Layla squeezed my shoulder. "Well, we have about two weeks before the next full moon. At least we have that much."

I nodded. "Maybe Aerin will let us overlook these tests or whatever. I mean, given the circumstances..."

"Maybe," Layla said. "But I don't know. She seemed pretty adamant. If anything, she might expedite them."

"We have to try. And whatever they have to give, whatever they can teach me, we need to put all our personal feelings aside. At least for now."

Layla bit her lip. "I still don't trust her."

"I'm not going to marry her, Layla," I said. "My heart is yours."

Layla smiled. "It's not just that. There's just something about them, the drow, that itches me in the wrong way."

"Be that as it may," I said, "I think we have no choice. I'm not powerful enough to stop the legion if they make it through, and if this cult has the world's governments prepared to surrender..."

"We don't know that they do," Layla said. "Only that they intended to. Hector did, anyway, when he established their organization."

I nodded. "Maybe I need to do these trials after all, if for no other reason than to convince them that I *am* the chosen one. That humanity has hope. So they don't surrender."

"But if you can't stop them, Caspar, and you convince them to fight..."

I sighed. "More lives will be lost in a single day, they said, than in the history of all the world's wars. I know."

Layla nodded. "All right. Well, I believe in you. If they see your strength, your resolve, your ability the way I do, they'll have to be convinced."

"Surrender just isn't an option. I'm not going to allow our whole world to be overtaken by a tyrant king, No offense. I know he's your dad."

"No," Layla said. "You're right. He *is* a tyrant. And we have to stop him."

"Wait," I said. "Where the hell did Ensley go?" Layla looked around, and I did the same.

"Caspar," Layla said. "Where did Agnus go? That might be the better question."

"Oh, shit," I said, running to the bedroom. Agnus sat at the foot of the bed, his mouth full.

"Agnus!" I shouted. "Spit him out!"

"I thought fairies smelled bad to cats?" Layla asked.

"Yeah, so did I. What the hell, Agnus!"

Then Agnus looked at me. His eyes glowed green, and then he started heaving.

Uggghhh. Ekkkhh. Unnnngg.

Ensley flew out of his mouth like a bat out of hell before doing an about-face and charging Agnus head-on.

Agnus raised his paw and swiped him down like it was nothing.

"Don't make me use magic, cat!" Ensley shouted.

I quickly scooped Agnus up. "Dude, really?"

Agnus snarled. "They smell like shit, but taste a little bit like chicken."

"He's a friend, Agnus," I said.

Agnus sighed. "There are a few things about our species I must say I'm ashamed to admit. Our very few flaws. Our kryptonite."

"Wait," I said, pulling out my phone. "I'm going to record this."

"Your phone won't hear me, numbnuts. You only hear me because you're attuned to magic."

I sighed. "Yeah. Forgot. Still, what were you about to say?"

"There are a few things we cannot resist. One, laser pointers. Shoot one of those on the floor, and it's like something comes over us. We obsess over catching the damned things. Yes, I know it's impossible, but like I said, irresistible. And then, pretty much anything that flies. Something buzzes through the room, and we're immediately enthralled."

"I hate to break it to you, Agnus," Layla told him, "but those aren't secrets. Everyone knows about those things."

"What? Who told! That's top-secret stuff! No one is supposed to know."

I shook my head. "Just go on YouTube and search for cats and laser pointers. Cats and flies. You'll probably turn up hundreds of videos."

"Hey, everyone!" Ensley butted in. "I'm fine, by the way. Thanks for asking."

"Sorry, Ensley," I said. "Just trying to get the cat under control."

Agnus huffed, displayed his hindquarters, and mumbled something under his breath.

"What did he just say?" I asked.

Layla laughed. "Something about our insolence, I think."

I nodded. "He uses big words for a cat."

"Anyway," Ensley said. "Before I had to flee on account of that feline of yours, you said something about drow. Did I hear you right?"

I nodded. "Three of them showed up in town. Said they sensed my magic and they came with gifts for the chosen one. They want me to complete five trials, corresponding to each of the elements, to prove I am who they think."

"Curious," Ensley said. "The fairies, we are few in number, but if anyone was wielding magic on Earth, we should know it. And the drow, well..."

"Well what, Ensley?" Layla asked.

"We haven't sensed anything from them for a thousand years."

"How is that even possible?" I asked.

"Maybe the magic they are using," Layla said, "isn't of the Earth."

"A possibility," Ensley said. "If, for instance, they were drawing their magic from some other plane, perhaps the infernal or celestial realms, we wouldn't be privy to it."

"Infernal or celestial?" I asked. "You mean, like, hell or heaven?"

"Precisely," Ensley said. "Angelic power. It precedes this world."

"You don't think the drow are borrowing magic from angels, do you?" I asked, turning to Layla. "Seriously?"

Layla sighed. "I don't know what to believe."

I shook my head. "I swear, this magic shit messes with my worldview every other day. I didn't even know angels and demons had magic. I thought they had powers that were innate to what they were."

"Well, what do you think magic is?" Ensley asked.

I bit my lip. "Honestly, I haven't the slightest clue. Some kind of power or energy, I suppose."

"It's spirit," Ensley said. "Everything that has a spirit has magic. Not everyone can access it, but the capacity is there."

"But the drow said there is a magic that corresponds with each element. And spirit, or aether, is only one of them."

"Aether is disembodied spirit. Spirit without a container, if you will," Ensley explained. "I don't expect that it would make any sense to you. And that is not to say that the other elements do not have spirit in their way."

"You're telling me that water, air, fire—these things all have spirit within them?"

"And Earth," Ensley said. "Don't forget the Earth."

"So, animism," I said, shaking my head. "Another belief system my church condemns that I'm now hooked into."

"Animism?" Ensley asked. "I do not know this word."

"Me neither," Layla said. "Sometimes when he gets to talking religion, I just smile and nod. Makes him feel better."

I rolled my eyes. "You smile and nod a lot. Are you saying you do that when you don't know what I'm talking about?"

Layla shook her head. "Not a clue."

I chuckled. "Well, good to know. Animism is the belief that there's a spirit in all things. Spirits of place. Spirits of elements. Exactly what you were telling me a second ago."

"Sounds like your church is wrong again, Caspar," Layla said.

I snorted. "Don't tell them that. They think being wrong is like the unforgivable sin."

Layla retrieved her phone from her pocket and glanced at it. "We'd better get that mustache glued to your lip. We need to leave in about fifteen minutes if we're going to catch the bus."

CHAPTER TEN

"I look like Wyatt-fucking-Earp," I said, looking at myself in the mirror.

"I was going to say the Monopoly guy."

I narrowed my eyes. "His mustache is white."

"Okay," Layla said. "Fair point."

"At least Wyatt Earp was a badass Western sheriff. I can deal with that."

"You look like a douche!" Agnus piped up, peeking around the corner.

I looked at Layla. "Told you."

"Doesn't matter," she said. "The whole point is that you don't look like yourself."

"Funny how different a mustache makes someone look," I said.

Layla smiled with pride. "I told you I had this covered. Didn't need to be anything elaborate."

"Ensley," I said, "since I have a bit of your magic inside me, any chance you could teach me anything that might help with these trials?"

"Not really," Ensley said. "I could to a point. Teaching you to use this magic is sort of like you teaching a kid how to walk just because you know how to walk. You forget how you ever learned how to do it; you just do it. To teach it, I'd have to give that some thought."

I nodded. "Well, in that case, hopefully I can figure something out if push comes to shove. You coming along, at least?"

"Of course," Ensley said. "Wouldn't miss it. But just in case, I might play it a little coy. Watch from a distance until I know how these drow are going to react to my presence."

"Probably not a bad idea," Layla said. "There will be cameras there too."

"Ah, yes," Ensley said. "We don't show up well on cameras, though. Usually, we appear to be orbs, which people either mistake for ghosts or dust in the air."

"All right," I said. "I suppose you'll just port yourself there?"

"Don't even need directions," Ensley said. "I can sniff you out from a thousand miles away."

"See you there, buddy," I said. Ensley nodded, and in a streak of green light, he disappeared.

"Ready?" Layla said.

I nodded, turned, opened the door, and stepped outside my apartment.

POP! POP! POP! POP!

"What the?"

I looked down. There was a piece of bubble wrap under my welcome mat.

"Ensley!" I shouted.

All I heard was giggling in the distance.

I looked at Layla, who was smiling. "Nice to know he hasn't changed, right?"

"Hey, everyone!" Jag announced as we walked through the door. "The Iron Sheik has come to join us!"

I narrowed my eyes at Jag. "Iron Sheik? Seriously?"

Jag was trying to cover his mouth with his hand to hold back his laughter. "It looks glorious!"

I suppose being mistaken for a circa nineteen-eighties professional wrestler wasn't the worst thing that could happen. Hell, if the other chapters of the Elf Gate Cult thought the Iron Sheik had fulfilled the elven prophecy, it would be fine with me. All that mattered was that they believed *someone* had fulfilled it. That the chosen one had arrived. That humanity had hope. They didn't need to recognize me.

I looked around the room. The whole place had been rearranged. The chairs that had previously been set up in rows in what used to be the church's sanctuary had been moved to the perimeter.

In the center of the room were five large stones arranged in a circle, each much too large for anyone to lift by themselves.

Most of the people had congregated near the entrance when Layla and I walked in. Fred was among them. Layla and I waved at him, and he gave us a man-nod in response. You know, the way men casually acknowledge people while trying not to appear too enthusiastic. Because enthusiasm is for pussies.

Layla walked toward him, and I followed. Layla and Fred had worked together in the past, and he'd helped us with our Blade of Echoes switcheroo plan. It wasn't that long ago, but so much had happened that a few months felt like years had passed.

Fred was wide-eyed and enthusiastic.

"Isn't this thrilling!" he exclaimed.

"Almost as exciting as a renaissance festival," I said, smiling. This was the first time I'd seen him when he wasn't costumed as a faux king or a blacksmith.

Fred ignored my comment and looked at my companion. "It's a pleasure to see you again, Layla."

She smiled. "The pleasure is ours."

"These other elves. Who would have thought!" Fred exclaimed.

"Right. I certainly didn't expect it."

"They're so exotic, so regal!"

"They're all right," Layla said.

Fred smiled at her. "Not nearly as beautiful as you, my princess."

I snorted. Was the blacksmith/king/cult leader flirting with my girl?

Layla took it with stride. "Well, thank you, Your Highness!"

"Oh, they don't call me that here," Fred said. "I'm just the supreme leader."

"Supreme leader?" I asked. "Isn't that what they call that guy who runs North Korea?"

Again, he ignored my comment and focused on Layla.

"If there's anything I can do to make you more comfortable for the trial, Layla, please don't hesitate to ask."

"That's too kind of you, Fred. Thank you for the hospitality."

I would have gagged on my tongue if I wasn't trying my best to remain cordial.

"Where's Aerin and her boy toys?" I asked.

Before Fred could answer, they appeared from behind the stage, or what in our church, we'd call the altar area.

Aerin was wearing a long, colorful gown. It was translucent, and it didn't hide much. You could see everything. As she walked toward us, it flowed against her body, accentuating her undeniably alluring frame.

Layla elbowed me. "Eyes up, Caspar."

I cleared my throat. "I wasn't...ugh. Never mind."

"A pleasure to see you again," Aerin said, looking me up and down. "What's with the—"

"The mustache?" I asked. "Concealing my identity for the

cameras. Trying to avoid any unnecessary flak from people who might not appreciate my role in all this."

Aerin cocked her head. "Why would anyone—"

"Long story," I said.

Aerin nodded. "Very well. In that case, should we begin the first trial?"

"One thing you should know first," Layla added. "On New Albion, the elven legion has defeated the giants. We have reason to believe that my father will be marching on the Earth when the gate opens on the next full moon."

Aerin nodded. "In that case, we should begin in haste. And it would be wise to proceed through each trial, should you succeed, Caspar, as quickly as possible."

"Can we knock all of them out tonight?" I asked.

Aerin frowned. "This is not possible. These trials are more than a test. They are also, in a manner of speaking, a sort of training."

"Most of us, as it was with the druids of old, excel in one element. Perhaps two or three. But the chosen one must be a master of them all." Aerin licked her lips in a way that was oddly seductive as she spoke.

I cleared my throat. "All right. So, what do you need me to do?"

"Each trial," Aerin said, "will require you to subdue an elemental, a creature that represents each of the five elements. But the elements can only be subdued by magic that stems from one of the other elements. For instance, since you already possess a capacity to wield magic that corresponds with aether, the first element you will encounter will be water."

"So, aether trumps water?" I asked.

"In the beginning," Aerin explained, "the spirit, the aether, hovered over the deep. Spirit is the one element that existed before the waters were tamed."

I nodded. "I know that from the book of Genesis. I mean, I never thought about it that way, but it makes sense."

"Then tomorrow, should you prevail, you will encounter fire. If you subdue water, it will lend you its aid. Only with water at your side will you stand a chance against fire."

"And fire beats what, exactly?" I asked.

"Fire can char the earth, and earth can thwart the air. Then, together, with the remainder of the elements, you will face aether."

"I thought you said he already mastered aether," Layla piped up.

"He wields it in part," Aerin said. "But only because aether dwells within him as it does us all. He has not subdued it."

"So, this is like one big game of rock, paper, scissors?" I asked.

Aerin tilted her head. "I do not know this game."

"You know, Roshambo. Rock crushes scissors. Paper covers rock. Scissors cut paper."

"Paper covers rock?" Aerin asked. "That's weak."

"I agree," I said. "The game isn't logical. If you're coming at me with a piece of paper and I have a rock, I'd like my chances."

"If I understand this Roshambo correctly," Aerin said, "the principle is similar. The proper element must be selected to subdue the other. When all five are wielded together, you have every element at your disposal to master them all."

Layla nodded. "Level-five magic. It makes sense."

"Yes," Aerin said. "But these are not mere levels. No single element is greater than any other. Only when all five are mastered are you truly in full communion with the Earth."

I nodded. I had to be clever about my next question. I didn't want to tell Aerin about Ensley, but I felt like because he hadn't sensed the drow, I needed to probe a little more. "And you—the drow, I mean—you've been wielding these elements?"

"Some of us have accessed them, yes," Aerin said.

I nodded. "Well, a little while back when I was using my

magic, I attracted the attention of a trickster fairy. I imagine they've been hassling you for centuries."

Aerin smiled. "I suppose your fairy friend told you that he was unaware the drow still lived, did he not?"

I cocked my head. "How did you know?"

Aerin smiled. "We've devised ways to evade detection by the fae. We sense their movements, much in the way that we sensed your magic as you began to wield it."

"So, you don't wield infernal magic?" I asked. "Or angel magic?"

Aerin laughed out loud. "Of course not, but I'm not surprised that your fairy would assume as much. They are so convinced they are the sole guardians of the Earth's powers that they'd never admit the possibility that we've been able to avoid them all this time."

"How do you do that, exactly?" Layla asked. "Avoid being found out by the fae?"

"We do not wield the magic of the elements directly," Aerin explained. "We work with all of the elements through enchantments."

"That's brilliant!" Layla exclaimed. "I wouldn't have thought of that."

"What do you mean by enchantments?" I asked.

"Fairies only sense magic when a being such as you or me draws it from the Earth directly. But when an object is enchanted, we can wield the power of the elements since they are tied to particular objects."

"What sort of objects?" I asked.

"Like my blade," Aerin said, extending her hand. One of the two men standing behind her unsheathed a long, curved blade from his side and handed it to her.

She waved it, and something like flames sparked from its sharp edge.

"My blade is enchanted with fire," Aerin said. "When I use it, the power of fire accompanies it. But it is the blade rather than I that is wielding the element, even as I wield the blade."

"It's a loophole," Layla said. "But you're still limited in how you can use it."

"Indeed," Aerin said. "Different objects, if enchanted properly, evoke different aspects of the various elements."

"So, what's the advantage of enchanting a sword with fire?" I asked. "Isn't it deadly enough as it is?"

"Indeed," Aerin said. "But with fire, were I to strike you, the wound would cauterize on contact. It would wound you, but you wouldn't bleed out."

"Why would you want to do that?" Layla asked.

Aerin huffed. "I'd expect no less from an elf who was raised knowing nothing but war. It is meant to maim a foe but preserve their life. Unlike our elven counterparts on New Albion, we have no interest in killing."

"And these gifts you'd give me if I succeed in these trials...they are enchanted objects, too?" I asked.

"I cannot say," Aerin said.

"You mean, you won't say," Layla said.

"No," Aerin said. "I meant what I said. The boxes are, perhaps, enchanted, only able to be opened by one who wields all the elements. We do not know what they contain, just that these items were to be preserved and kept safe for the coming of the chosen one."

"Enchanting these elements has to require a certain amount of magic, I'd think."

"It does," Aerin nodded.

"And the fairies don't detect that?" I asked.

"We draw only on the magic that cohered within our spirits. We use that to enchant objects. It is minimal, but by projecting our spirit outside of our bodies, we can engage minimal quantities of magic."

"Enough to enchant an object?" Layla asked.

"Over time," Aerin said. "Does a master blacksmith craft a blade in a single hour?"

"He doesn't," Layla said, glancing across the room. Fred, the leader of this particular chapter of the Elf Gate cult, had worked as a blacksmith at the local renaissance fair. It was with his help that we'd crafted a forgery of the Blade of Echoes before I'd destroyed it. "A small blade takes several days."

"Precisely," Aerin said. "When enchanting an object, it takes time, and more than a few days."

"How long did it take to enchant your sword?" I asked.

"Nearly a decade," Aerin said.

"Dang!" Layla exclaimed. "That's an arduous process."

"It requires patience. Discipline. You'll find that when the drow want something, we have the patience to see it come to pass."

Layla grunted. I wasn't sure if Aerin was speaking of her previously articulated desire to make me her husband according to her interpretation of the prophecy, but that was how Layla took it.

Beyond being in love with Layla, I found I wasn't open to the idea of being Aerin's husband in a society that embraced female superiority. I was not inclined to assume a submissive role in a relationship. I preferred spouses to view one another as equals. I didn't ever want to become subby hubby.

I nodded. "All right. Any tips on what I should try against this elemental?"

Aerin smiled. "You already possess everything you need. I can say no more lest I cast doubt on the reasons for your successes. Should you prevail, of course."

CHAPTER ELEVEN

One of Aerin's two lackeys, Haldir or Iston, I forgot which one was which, approached with something shrouded by a blue cloth. Aerin took it in her hands and removed the veil. A blue orb rested in her hands.

Like a crystal ball.

"Behold," she said. "The element of water."

I nodded in response, then looked around. I wasn't sure where the cameras were. In the old days, you could find a camera because they had little red lights that lit when recording. But in the digital era, the camera could be anywhere.

Not like I planned to look at it and smile. Quite the opposite. If I knew where it was, I'd do my best to show it my better side more often than not.

I made eye contact with Layla, who smiled at me and nodded. Her way of communicating confidence in me, I suppose. Then I noticed Fred's bearded shit-eating grin right beside her. Of course, he was sitting with my woman. Fucker.

"The rules are simple," Aerin said, drawing my attention back to the matter at hand. "When I release the elemental, our subject must subdue it using only the magic he can wield. The elemental will not be able to pass beyond the circle of stones, so lest our subject is granted any advantages, he must likewise remain within the circle."

I put up my dukes for no other reason than I felt awkward standing there without so much as a wand or some kind of weapon at my disposal.

Sure, I had magic…sort of…but I felt naked. As if by punching a water elemental, I was going to accomplish something beyond washing my hands.

I assumed the thing would be pure water with intelligence.

I'd never seen an elemental, sort of like I hadn't seen elves, or giants, or fairies until recently. None of the mythic races met the expectations I had from growing up reading Tolkien. Real elves, apart from Layla, were the bad guys. The orcs, who didn't like being called orcs, were the good guys, God rest their souls. And the fairies. Well, I didn't have any expectations there, but I didn't count on them being expert pranksters or portal masters.

My knowledge of elementals was pretty much limited to video game lore. *World of Warcraft*, games like that. I doubted it was accurate. In the game, water elementals shot water at you, which hurt for some reason. Not sure if it was acid rain or what, but they weren't much more than good water-gun-battle partners.

For some reason, I doubted this elemental would be inclined to simply give me a shower.

Aerin dropped the orb she was holding, and it shattered on the floor. Someone was going to have to sweep that up later. Nothing worse than cleaning up glass. They'd probably find shards in strange places and stuck in the treads of people's shoes for months.

Then a strange figure, blue and luminescent, grew out of the puddle that had formed where the orb broke. By grew, I mean it got huge and kept growing.

I dropped my fists.

I thought I'd at least *look* ready if I was in a fighting pose. Compared to this massive thing, I just looked ridiculous.

Water is heavier than people realize.

Learned that when I had to swim to the bottom of Meramec Springs. You have to clear your ears as you go. Otherwise, you'll blow an eardrum. And they say that submarines can only go so deep without being crushed by the pressure of the ocean.

This elemental was sizable enough that if he just collapsed on me, I'd be done in by the pressure. Not like I knew for sure, but I wasn't about to test it.

I knew how to breathe underwater when I was attuned to magic. Learned that trick at the springs and while traveling the ley line from there to where the elf gate had formed at the confluence of the Meramec and Mississippi.

Maybe I could dive into this thing, then release my magic and blow it into thousands of droplets. I was sure I could envision an explosion of magic around my body. Maybe that would do it.

I took a deep breath and charged the creature.

I was so focused that the screams and cheers of the cultists who had gathered were muted. I could hear them, but I wasn't paying any attention.

I braced myself as I prepared to launch into the elemental's body, then I froze. Stuck! Stuck in place, like one of those nightmares where someone is coming after you, and you just can't move.

What the...

The creature was made of water. My body was mostly water. I started to sweat profusely. This creature was drawing the water out of my body. The damned thing was going to dehydrate me to death. Wouldn't take long because I'd sweated a shirtful of water and more earlier in the day and hadn't replenished my fluids.

My throat was parched. Ironic. There was a massive body of water not two feet in front of me, and I couldn't even drink.

You already possess everything you need.

Aerin's voice echoed in my mind. Was she telling me something that might help? Surely she had known this was going to happen, or at least, she knew it was a possibility.

So what did she mean by that?

What were we talking about before she said that? How the drow enchanted objects. How they got away with working magic without alerting the fae.

How did she say it worked?

By projecting our spirit outside our bodies.

Could I even do that? When I flew, it felt like that was what was happening, but my body always came along for the ride. If I'd been doing that by the magic of my spirit, the only element she said Layla had taught me to wield effectively, maybe it wasn't my body that flew, but my spirit.

Spirit, Aerin had said, preceded water. It was spirit that hovered over the face of the deep in the second verse of Genesis. Sure, in the Bible, it was the spirit of God, but it was His spirit, His breath, that was breathed into Adam's nostrils and brought him to life. The same spirit of God that was there in the beginning, taming the primordial sea.

I didn't know if it would work, but it was the only idea I had.

It seemed Aerin had been dropping hints as subtly as she could to help me. She gave me everything I needed to know because I already had everything I required to subdue water at my disposal. So I decided to fly, or to use the words in Genesis, to hover like a spirit.

A Madonna song came into my head. *Like a spirit, kicking elemental ass for the very first time.* Sure, my syllabification was off compared to the original, but it worked for me.

I tried to focus. I needed yoga focus. A Layla-and-Agnus-mocking-me-in-the-background-while-trying-to-hold-tree-pose level of focus. I envisioned myself flying out of my body and into the elemental's globular frame, and I visualized the elemental flowing into my body.

All the water absorbed through my pores into my mouth.

I opened my eyes, and I was standing in the middle of the stone circle alone. The elemental was gone.

CHAPTER TWELVE

People cheered. The whole place was filled with a roar. You'd think I was at a Cardinals game or something, and I'd just hit a home run. Maybe at a Chiefs game after a touchdown. It was loud. I didn't have a chance to take a bow.

I had to pee!

I took off through the crowd of cultists, even pushing past Layla, who was standing there expecting a kiss. I'd have to deal with that later. She'd understand.

Holy crap, I had to pee.

After absorbing that much water at once, it was no wonder.

Back when I used to buy CDs, I had an Adam Sandler comedy album with a track entitled *The Longest Pee*. It was just the sound of peeing, and it went on for like five minutes.

That's what this was like. I just kept going, like my manhood had turned into a fire hose and the entire city's water supply was hooked up to my bladder. Maybe that was how I'd take down the next elemental, the fire elemental. Pee on it. Probably not good for live streaming.

A green glow appeared beside me.

"Nice work!" Ensley said.

"Dude, don't creep on me at the pisser. It's weird."

"I'm not looking! I mean, I might have glanced."

I shook my head. "I can't believe that worked."

Ensley nodded. "At least I know how the drow evaded us for so long."

I nodded. "You're surprised by that?"

"A little," Ensley said. "Most humans, and elves for that matter, once they wield a little magic, can't exercise that sort of restraint. They use more and more until we have to get involved."

I nodded. "So it's legit? What Aerin said?"

Ensley nodded. "I think so. It's impressive, but I'll leave you to go bask in your glory."

I nodded.

I was *still* peeing. Then I stopped. Finally.

Then I felt the urge again.

I peed more.

Dear Lord, I thought. *When is this going to end?*

I must've been standing there urinating for a solid five minutes or more.

I stopped again.

This time the urge didn't return.

I shook myself, then I went to the sink to wash my hands because I'm not a disgusting human being. Not that disgusting, anyway.

I turned on the sink.

And water splashed all over my mid-section from my waist down my pants.

Someone had put cellophane across the sink.

"Dammit, Ensley!" I shouted.

I didn't see him, but I could hear him giggling. He was still here, hiding in the ether or whatever.

I looked like I'd just peed my pants.

I shook my head.

Nothing I could do about it.

Maybe no one would think anything of it. I was just in a battle with a water elemental, after all. Of course, I'd get a little wet.

I stepped out of the bathroom, and Layla lunged for me.

Then she stopped and took two steps back.

"Caspar!" Layla said. "You peed your pants!"

I shook my head. "It's just water."

"Sure it is," Jag said, stepping up behind me and slapping me harder than I'd like on my back.

"No, really," I said. "It's water."

I suppose I could have tried to duplicate my battle with the elemental. Maybe I could have absorbed the water from my pants, but the thought didn't occur to me until I was standing there in my humiliation.

"No worries, man," Jag said. "It's cool to pee your pants."

I chuckled. The second Adam Sandler reference in the last five-plus minutes. This time, from *Billy Madison.*

"You want to pee your pants with me?" I asked. "You know, as an expression of solidarity?"

"That's okay," Jag said. "I'm willing to admit that at this very moment, you're cooler than me."

I snorted.

"Congratulations," Aerin said as she approached. The rest of the cultists were gathered around, clapping. "If I were you, I'd practice wielding the new power that coheres within you. Figure out what you can do. You'll need it tomorrow."

"Thanks, Aerin," I said.

"And next time," Aerin added, "I'd suggest you bring a change of clothes."

"It's just water!" I insisted.

Aerin turned back toward me and winked, then walked away. Yeah, she knew it was water. But she was apparently willing to have a laugh at my expense with the rest of them.

"I'd offer you a ride home," Jag said. "But you know, pee. On my seats."

I shook my head. "I swear, Jag…"

"See you at the gym tomorrow, Captain Pee Pants."

I shook my head. "I'm never going to live this down, am I?"

"You won't," Layla said. "But I don't think peeing your pants is what people are going to remember."

"Layla!" I said. "I'm not lying. It *isn't* pee."

Layla shrugged. "Perception is reality, and this will forevermore be a part of the lore of the chosen one who rose in fulfillment of the elven prophecy."

I chuckled. "Yeah. He saved the world, they'll say. But remember that time he pissed himself?"

"So, you admit it?" Layla asked.

I narrowed my eyes. "Shut up!"

Layla was laughing. She believed me. I'm sure, anyway. But holy hell, it was embarrassing.

I made a mental note to buy a fly swatter for the next time Ensley showed up.

Don't get me wrong, he was an ally. But dammit, he was an annoying little bugger.

Despite all the embarrassment, though, I was still on an adrenaline high. I mean, I'd just stood up to a giant water monster, and I'd prevailed.

I don't know that it was a monster, exactly. More like a personification of water. Water can be a terrifying thing. In the Bible, when the waves crashed against the boat and threatened to sink it before Jesus went out to them by walking on the surface, the disciples were terrified. It was water that once flooded and destroyed the Earth. And if you've ever lived through a flood, you'd know how much damage water can do.

The ancients viewed the sea as a wily, unpredictable, hazardous place. Hell, from what I knew of the history, the off-kilter Roman Emperor Caligula had once waged war on Poseidon, the god of water, and returned to Rome demanding a formal triumph, a parade to show off his spoils of war, after the supposed battle.

Yes, I took my place now beside the craziest emperor in history. I faced off against the force that God Almighty once used to destroy the world. The power he'd used to thwart the Pharaoh's army during the exodus. Maybe my victory wasn't as dramatic. Maybe it ended with a touch of personal embarrassment. But I'd won.

It didn't take long, though, for the thrill to fade.

A sinking feeling settled into my gut as Layla and I boarded the bus.

"What's wrong, Caspar?" Layla asked.

I shook my head. "That thing almost killed me."

"But it didn't," Layla said. "I knew you'd win. You are the chosen one, Caspar."

"Maybe," I said. "But I sort of got lucky. If Aerin hadn't dropped the clues I needed..."

"I don't know what it was like," Layla said. "But there's a reason why the drow refer to these things as trials. They were never going to be easy."

"I know," I said, sighing. "But tomorrow, I have to face off with fire, and what if it's the size of that water elemental?"

Layla pointed out, "Now you have water to wield, right?"

I nodded. "If I can figure out how to use it."

"You have more at your disposal now than you did today. And the last I checked, fire doesn't stand up well to water."

"Yeah," I said. "But if the fire envelops me the way the water did today. If it gets that close before I can take it out, I won't survive long enough to put it out."

"Then don't let it get so close to you next time," Layla said. "You have to adapt your strategy to the strengths of your enemy."

I scratched the back of my head. "Perhaps you're right. I suppose we'll just have to take it one day at a time, right?"

Layla nodded. "Perhaps you should grab a meeting tomorrow. After the workout. Might help get you grounded, you know?"

"Grounded," I said. "The earth elemental comes later."

Layla smiled. "You know what I meant."

I pressed my lips together. "Dammit."

"What?" Layla asked.

"I have to pee again."

CHAPTER THIRTEEN

I was exhausted.

I needed to sleep.

But it seemed like every time I laid back down and started to snooze, I had to pee again.

So I sat there in bed with Layla, looking gorgeous as ever, at my side. Damn, I was a lucky man. Agnus was curled up at the foot of the bed, snoring more loudly than you'd think is natural for a cat.

I was also sweating profusely, but I wasn't hot.

It was like I'd absorbed so much water that my body was doing anything it could to shed it. It had to be a shock to the system, to go from the elemental pulling all the water out of me to suddenly having my body flooded with more water than should have been able to fit inside it.

I realize magic was involved, but what happened shouldn't have been possible.

Whatever.

I gave up trying to explain how most of this magic shit worked. That's why they call it magic, right?

But if I wasn't going to get any sleep, I figured I might as well try to experiment with my new abilities. I had less than twenty-four hours to get ready to face a fire elemental that was presumably on the scale of the water giant I'd just absorbed.

I grabbed a pint-sized glass from one of my cabinets and filled it with water.

I set it on the kitchen counter and stared at it.

The elemental was absorbed by me. Presuming I didn't piss the whole thing away, its essence was part of me now. At least, Aerin said it would be.

I stared at the glass. "Start swirling."

It didn't react.

Maybe it didn't respond to words. I don't know why I thought it might. So far, magic words had nothing to do with any of the magic I'd done.

I took a deep breath, closed my eyes, and tried to visualize the water in my glass spinning like a little whirlpool.

I opened my eyes.

Still nothing.

I wished Aerin had given me a few pointers, but she'd admitted that she hadn't wielded magic this way before. The drow used enchantments—spells, if you could call the enchantment process a spell—that required low power and long commitment. Layla wasn't familiar with elemental magic. It was tied to the Earth. Whatever the magic they'd taken from the Earth's ley lines and brought to New Albion was, it *wasn't* tied to elemental entities. Not like the one whose power I was supposed to have just harnessed.

There was one person I could ask. I half-dreaded what he'd do, but I expected he was hanging out somewhere nearby.

"Ensley?" I called.

I heard something fall over by my computer desk. I walked over to it, and my mouse was lying upside-down on the floor.

Ensley appeared on the edge of the desk with a green glow around his body.

"Well, you caught me," Ensley said.

I bent over and picked up my mouse. He'd affixed a piece of tape to the sensor on the bottom.

"Seriously, Ensley?"

"I know," Ensley said. "It's not my best prank, but I was getting bored. Glad to see you changed your pants."

I sighed as Ensley giggled, recalling the success of his previous practical joke.

Then I started laughing with him. "I have to admit, it was embarrassing as hell, but that was a pretty good one. I'll never know how you manage to pull these things off unnoticed. Did you have a roll of cellophane somewhere nearby?"

"A good trickster never reveals his secrets," Ensley said, smiling with satisfaction.

"Just stay away from my shampoo bottle," I said.

Ensley snorted. "Yeah, sorry about that one. I guess it was a little bit over the top. Get it? Over the top? Since it made your head bald?"

I chuckled. "So the fairy has tricks and jokes?"

"What can I say?" Ensley asked. "I'll be here all week."

"Any clue how I can use this elemental magic I gained tonight?" I asked.

Ensley interlaced his fingers and, extending his arms, popped his knuckles. "You've come to the right place, my friend."

"I tried commanding the water. I even tried visualizing it, like I did when I was fighting the elemental. But it isn't responding."

"That's because when you were battling the elemental, you were subduing it with your spirit," Ensley said. "Elementals do not operate as a projection of your will. Not the way your spirit does."

"So, the magic in the ley lines," I said. "Which element is that?"

"It isn't any single element," Ensley said. "It represents potential. It interacts with elements but is not tied to any of them."

"So, the elves on New Albion only use magic in conjunction with their spirits?" I asked.

"Yes and no," Ensley said. "That's what most of them learn. But during my time with the elf king, he had a whole collection of elementals. Almost like a zoo. I imagine he'd been sending elves to Earth for years to harvest them."

"Sort of like the crystal ball that Aerin had the elemental contained in?" I asked.

"Exactly that," Ensley said. "The elven legion has been training with the elementals to prepare for wielding their power when they invade this world."

"To control the weather?" I asked. "I mean, Layla already knew they could do that. How did she know that was possible if she didn't know that they accessed elementals?"

"I wasn't there," Ensley said. "So I can't say what she was told or taught. But I suspect she saw what the legions could do, albeit in a limited way, and presumed it was on account of different levels of mastery."

"So Aerin is right?" I asked. "The elves are less powerful than the drow?"

"Not necessarily," Ensley said. "The drow have almost no experience wielding elemental magic. They've studied it. They've captured elementals and channeled them into enchantments. But they haven't wielded magic directly, not on anything close to the scale the elves on New Albion are accustomed to using in war."

"So I could learn a lot from Aerin and Layla both," I said.

"Of course," Ensley said. "And do not underestimate the fairy magic I left within you."

"I've made a few portals," I said. "Still, when I use it, it feels unwieldy. Like, I can't be certain the portals I'm making are going to take me where I intend."

"That's a problem with your confidence, Caspar, not the magic or your ability to wield it," Ensley explained. "Why don't we work with that a little first. Maybe, then, you'll get a better grasp on how to wield the elements."

I nodded. "All right. What should I do?"

"Well," Ensley said. "I could possess you again and show you. Maybe if we do a few spells together, you'll feel more confident performing them yourself."

"Sort of like using training wheels?" I asked.

Ensley cocked his head. "I suppose that's an appropriate analogy."

"All right," I said. "Let's do this. But I'm in my underwear. If we're going to port anywhere public, I need to put on some clothes."

Ensley giggled. "Well, I suppose you saw that prank coming from a mile away."

I rolled my eyes. "Planning to trick me into porting into the middle of the freeway in my skivvies?"

"Actually," Ensley said. "I was going to put you on the stage at one of the local drag clubs in the Tower Grove neighborhood."

I laughed. "Brilliant. You know, I think I'll put on some pants anyway. You know, just in case."

"What?" Ensley asked. "Don't you trust me?"

I stared at him and shook my head. "In things that matter, sure. But when it comes to getting tricked? No, not even a little."

I snuck back into the bedroom, grabbed a pair of sweats, and quickly slipped them on. I was already wearing a t-shirt, so while I wasn't in my best, I wouldn't get myself charged with indecent exposure if Ensley redirected any of our portals.

"All right, buddy. Let's do this," I said.

Ensley nodded then, buzzing around me a few times, landed on my back, and with a brief, sharp pain, he dug himself into the back of my neck. Then a little tingle as he healed the wound after he entered.

"Okay. I'm going to prime you with a little of my magic. All you need to do once you're used to how it feels is bring it back to the forefront of your mind again. Do it a few times, and calling forth my magic will be as natural as moving an arm or a leg."

"Sounds good," I said.

I felt a warm tingle spread through my body.

"Feel that?" Ensley asked.

"I do," I said.

"Now think of a place you know well. A place you're familiar with enough that you can visualize it clearly. You don't want to accidentally port yourself into the middle of a wall or anything like that."

I nodded. I had to think of a place where I knew no one would be at this time of night. I visualized the sanctuary at the Church of the Holy Cross. Right in the middle of the chancel. "All right, I've got it."

"Now open the portal. Just visualize it in front of you. You've done this before."

I nodded and concentrated. A golden circle of magic appeared in front of me.

"Good. Now step through it."

I stepped into the portal and, after a brief sensation that felt almost like my body was dematerializing, it solidified again.

And I was standing exactly where I had visualized myself. The portal I just stepped through was still open behind me.

"Awesome!" I said. "It worked!"

"Now let's try again, but just move across the room. It's the sort of thing you might want to do when you're in the middle of a fight and you need to reposition yourself."

I nodded. I refocused. The portal behind me dissipated, and a new one formed in front of me. I jumped through it and reappeared at the opposite end of the aisle, near the exits.

I laughed. "That was easier than I thought!"

"Try it again. You need to do it enough that it's a reflex. Until it feels natural."

I duplicated the portal I'd made before and reappeared in the chancel.

Before Ensley could ask, I tried it again, appearing this time in the back row of pews.

I tried to move and couldn't. My butt was glued to the seat.

"What the hell did I just do?" I asked.

Ensley laughed from inside my mind. *You made a portal a bit too close to an object. Half your butt is stuck in the wood of the pew.*

"Well, shit," I said. "Can I get out without breaking this thing apart?"

Of course, but this time you need to create a portal and pull it over your body.

"How do I do that?" I asked.

The same way you made the portal to begin with. These portals are part of you. Part of the magic within you. Just pull it in again as if it were an extension of your body.

"Like moving an arm or a leg?" I asked.

Exactly!

My butt was starting to cramp, so I quickly formed another portal. Then, as weird as it felt, I pulled it toward me.

Careful, Ensley said. *You don't want to take the pew with you.*

I nodded. The portal moved toward me as I tried to pull it in, but it was shaking a little—almost like my legs moved after doing a set of squats.

I drew it into me slowly until I felt it barely envelop my butt cheeks. Then I pushed myself through the portal.

I reappeared in the chancel.

"You realize I'm not even channeling my magic to you now? You're doing this on your own."

I laughed. "Wow, this is pretty awesome."

"Now we need to practice using water, but first, port yourself to a larger space. Somewhere it won't matter if things get a little wet. Again, a place you can visualize."

I nodded. Forest Park was one option. I'd trained there with

Brag'mok. But there were a lot of trees. I didn't want to repeat my butt-blunder with the pew. I needed something more open, a simpler place I could easily picture in my mind. Then it occurred to me. I knew the place would be empty at this hour, and going there would be awesome.

"All right," I said. "I've got the perfect spot in mind."

"Let's do it!"

I formed another portal and jumped through it.

My body materialized on the pitcher's mound in Busch Stadium.

CHAPTER FOURTEEN

I cheered as I stood there, kicking at the dirt and looking around the stadium.

"Wahhhzooo!" Ensley yelled.

I laughed a little. "I have to admit, this is pretty fucking awesome. I've always wanted to stand here."

"I'm going to get out of your head. To work with water, you won't need me, and it'll probably be easier if I'm not in your head distracting you."

I nodded.

Ensley popped out of the back of my neck. Lord, it hurt when he did that. Just for a second, though. He quickly healed me and buzzed around the mound, his green glow casting its light on the perfectly manicured infield.

"The elemental is a part of you," Ensley explained. "When you used fairy magic, it had a distinct flavor. A feel to it unlike anything else."

"It did," I said, nodding.

"Try to remember how it felt the moment the water elemental was bound to your spirit," Ensley said. "You can use that sensation, that feeling, the same way you access fairy magic."

I remembered how it felt. It was like a refreshing, cool wave of energy had overwhelmed me. I didn't think much about it at the time since I was more focused on surviving, but I could recall the sensation. It was unlike anything I'd ever felt.

"I think I know the feeling," I said. "I can just bring it back again?"

"Of course you can," Ensley said. "You just need to reach into your spirit and let it out."

I was surprised at how easy it was. Once I could identify the sensation, it was right there. Hard to explain to anyone who hasn't felt it, but Ensley was right; it was part of me. Not just my body. It was part of my spirit.

"I've got it!" I exclaimed.

"Good," Ensley said. "With it, you should be able to sense any water nearby. You can use it, move it like you moved the portal over your body in the church."

"It's like it's everywhere, but nowhere in particular," I said, struggling to identify where the water was located.

"Water is in the air," Ensley said. "What you'd call humidity."

I nodded. "Always plenty of that in Missouri."

"Draw it together," Ensley said. "Tiny droplets in the air all brought together into a single body of water."

I reached out with my power, with the cool sensation that was still washing through my body. A small glob of water started to form in front of me.

It grew. Quickly.

Then a massive ball of water was floating in mid-air between the pitcher's mound and home plate.

"In moderation!" Ensley shouted as the glob of water continued to grow.

"I can't help it," I said. "It's like I'm either going to draw all the water around me or none of it."

"Release it," Ensley said. "The whole sensation in your spirit. Let it go."

I let go of the feeling, and the giant blob of water crashed to the ground, splashing all over me and soaking me from head to toe.

I shook my head. "I've never been good with moderation. Not with drinking. Not with much of anything."

Ensley flew around me and shook like a wet dog, water flying off of his body. "It'll take practice, Caspar. But you've got it!"

"I just don't want to flood any place where I use the magic," I said, shaking my head and wiping the water out of my eyes.

"Well," Ensley said, "you have to use common sense. You wouldn't use a flamethrower to light a candle. You wouldn't open a fire hydrant to take a drink. Consider your purpose. And if things get out of hand, you can always bail through a fairy portal."

"Or maybe port the element out of the place?" I asked, "if I can't master it? At least I'd survive that way."

"Sure," Ensley said. "Just like you pushed the portal over yourself, you can move a portal over others and move them on a whim. Just be careful. Make sure you can visualize where you want it to go. Best not to ever port anything anywhere that you haven't been, and certainly not to a place where you haven't been in a while. Things change. And if you think getting your butt stuck in a pew was problematic..."

I snorted. "My butt. Pew. That stinks!"

Ensley stared at me blankly. "Nice try. Stick to ministry. Leave the comedy to the experts."

I smiled. "I thought it was funny."

"Of course you did," Ensley said, "but as I was saying, just imagine if there was a human being there when you ported into that space. If you think the pew stinks, try porting yourself, or may the furies forbid, a giant glob of water or fire or anything else into another person."

"In that case, I could see where I was going, and I still got my ass into something of a tight spot."

"It's best to avoid trying to port yourself near any objects, and certainly not close to other people or animals. How do you think the minotaur was made back in the day?"

"The minotaur?" I asked. "That thing existed?"

Ensley nodded. "He didn't do it himself. It was another fairy. The human was messing with magic he shouldn't have, so the fairy ported his ass, and by ass, I mean his whole self, into a bull. The result? Minotaur. A prank taken a bit too far, even by my standards."

I pressed my lips together. "Too bad he didn't moooooooove out of the way in time!"

Ensley stared at me and shook his head slowly.

"Just stop, Caspar. Stop while you're ahead."

I smirked. "Yeah, because that guy lost his head and got a bull's in its place!"

"There you go again," Ensley sighed. "It's a shame you aren't a dad. You sure have the jokes for it."

"Maybe someday I will be. You know, after I've saved the world. Haven't talked to Layla about that. We haven't even crossed the marriage bridge yet."

"Sounds like that drow intends to marry you first," Ensley said.

I sighed. "She thinks the prophecy demands it."

"In my experience," Ensley said, "when it comes to matters of the heart, there isn't a magic on Earth or any world that can thwart it. And I've yet to meet a prophet who can predict a heart's desire."

CHAPTER FIFTEEN

Magic is exhausting. Doesn't matter what *kind* of magic it is. It takes a toll.

I didn't get a lot of sleep. It was three in the morning when I finally ported myself back into my apartment.

No sooner did my head hit my pillow than I was out like a light. Of course, I dreamed about water.

I was underwater. The whole ocean was forcing itself into my body. I saved California from falling into the sea on account of global warming.

Until I peed the whole ocean out again.

I'd saved the world just to flood it again. With my urine.

It was ridiculous, but I could swear it was real in the dream.

Probably the elemental spirit inside me working its way into my subconscious.

That might have been part of it.

Some of it was guilt. I'd tried to save New Albion, but what I did had led to the slaughter of the Night Legion, the elven giants. The prophecy indicated that in the process of saving the world, millions of people would die.

I'd tried not to think about it. How literal could these

prophecies be? But so far, despite my best efforts, every time I'd thought I spared the world, all I'd done was delay the elven apocalypse.

And now, if I succeeded in the trials, if I convinced the Elf Gate Cult to reject the elves, to refuse to submit when the legion arrived, what sort of savior was I? What good was it to save the world from elven rule if it meant so much bloodshed, so many lives lost?

No humans had died yet, but the giants…Brag'mok was my friend. He'd heard the prophecy. Had he known what was going to happen when he told me to blast earthen magic into New Albion's ley lines?

I'd hardly finished my world-devastating pee and I started to shake, or I was being shaken.

"Rise and shine, sleepyhead!"

It was Layla. For a moment, I was relieved. I hadn't destroyed the world after all. Not yet, anyway. But I was still tired.

I grunted, pulled my pillow over my head, and rolled back over.

Then I felt little bitty feet walking across my back.

"Agnus, go away!" I shouted, my voice muffled by my pillow.

He started pawing at the back of my head.

"Don't make me get out the claws," Agnus said. "Get up and give me some tuna."

"Ask Layla," I said.

"Caspar," Layla said, "we need to get ready to go work out."

"Work out, shmirk out!" I moaned.

"Last workout of the week!" Layla said. "You'll get a break tomorrow."

I sighed. Yeah, it was Saturday. I hadn't even given thought to the sermon I was supposed to preach the next day. I'd probably dig into the archives and recycle one from a few years ago. People didn't listen that intently anyway. What were the chances they'd even notice?

"Normal people don't work out on weekends," I said. "It was a long night. I need to sleep."

"You can sleep after the world is saved," Layla said.

"I need rest for these trials, Layla," I said, rolling over on my back, sending Agnus tumbling off my body.

He leaped back onto my chest, turned around, and sat on my chest. Swept his tail across my face.

"Dammit, Agnus!" I said, grabbing him with both hands and setting him to the side.

"Where'd you go last night?" Layla asked. "I woke up in the middle of the night and you were gone."

I sighed. "To the church. Then to Busch Stadium."

Layla furrowed her brow. "Why? In the middle of the night?"

"We needed a few places to go where there wouldn't be people. Ensley was helping me get a handle on fairy magic. Water magic, too."

"Did it work?" Layla asked.

"It did," I said. "I think I'm ready for tonight. Provided I get my sleep!"

"Sorry," Layla said. "If you no-show for your workout, you still have to pay Jag anyway."

"You said I should get a meeting in today," I said.

"Yeah, I did," Layla said. "*After* your workout!"

I sighed. "Fine. Maybe once I get my blood pumping, I'll manage to find a little energy."

"That's the spirit!" Layla said more enthusiastically than I was prepared to tolerate on short sleep.

I rolled over and grabbed my phone. "Well, shit."

"What is it?" Layla asked.

"Nothing," I said. "Last night was Friday. I was supposed to help Evelyn at the soup kitchen. She texted me to ask where I was."

Layla nodded. "It will be fine. Just tell her you had a personal issue come up. It's the truth."

I quickly typed the response that Layla had suggested to Evelyn and got out of bed. "Feels like that life isn't real anymore."

"What do you mean?" Layla asked.

"The church. Ministry. The soup kitchen. Even my bartending job. At first, that was what was real, but now with all this magic stuff and the prophecy, it's like that's everything, and the rest is just obligations."

My phone dinged. Another text. I checked it, expecting Evelyn's reply. Instead, it was Cecil. "And my car is ready now, too."

"Well, that's a plus!" Layla said. "No more Metro!"

"Right," I said. "Maybe I'll pick it up after the gym and before my meeting."

"You aren't excited to get the car back?" Layla asked.

"Just another obligation. Sort of like feeding the cat."

"Hey!" Agnus protested. He hopped off the bed and landed on all fours, then stared up at me. "I'm not just an obligation. I'm your familiar, remember?"

"He's right," Layla said. "He's a part of this prophecy too, so technically, he isn't a part of the normal, obligated life."

"You're right," I said. "Sorry, Agnus. I'm just a little cranky."

Agnus huffed and made his way to the kitchen. I stumbled in behind him, opened his can of tuna, and dumped it into a bowl. "Here you go. Chow down." I didn't have to say it twice. Agnus was on it, chomping his way through his food like he hadn't eaten since yesterday.

"Hurry up," Layla said. "We're already running late."

I nodded, sauntered back into the bedroom, and slipped into a fresh pair of workout shorts before putting on my shoes. "We'll make it in time."

"Probably not," Layla said. "We've already missed the first bus."

I sighed. "No, we'll make it. How many folks do you think are at the gym this time in the morning?"

Layla looked puzzled. "It's a Saturday, so probably fewer people than normal."

"Do they have your classes on weekends?" I asked.

"Yeah," Layla said. "But the first class isn't until ten o'clock."

I grinned. "Good," I said, looking Layla up and down. Damn, she looked great in yoga pants. "You ready?"

"Sure," Layla said, walking toward the door.

"Wait," I said. "I have another idea."

Layla cocked her head.

I brought fairy magic to the forefront of my mind, focused, and opened a portal in the middle of the living room. "I've seen you working out in that group exercise room enough times to visualize it. It should be empty right now. Let's go."

CHAPTER SIXTEEN

It wasn't the best workout. Not the worst, either. That would be the time I'd used magic to deceive Jag into thinking I could lift a lot heavier than I could, then had to pay him his fifty bucks, only to find out that he was a member of the Elf Gate Cult and had known what I was doing the whole time.

I don't know if it was because I was short on sleep or my mind just wasn't in it, but I was a little lethargic. Wasn't pushing myself as hard as I usually did.

Probably I was still overhydrated, courtesy of the water elemental.

Jag, on the other hand, was hyped up, which was annoying. I couldn't blame him. It *had* been pretty spectacular, what everyone saw the night before. Provided, of course, you weren't the one facing the water monster and nearly having your whole body turned into a raisin in the process, only to have it flooded a few seconds later.

He was now convinced I was some kind of superhero. That I was going to "kick the asses" of the rest of the elementals—not that elementals had asses to kick, but the anatomy of an elemental was beside the point.

THEOPHILUS MONROE & MICHAEL ANDERLE

More than that, though, Jag was sold on the idea the Order would be persuaded to support us by resisting the elven invasion rather than preparing to welcome King Brightborn as the new king of the world.

It's one thing to cheer on a hero from a distance. It's another to be a hero who doesn't feel like one.

As they'd say in AA, one day at a time. Not dying, I figured, was the first step. Couldn't do much to save anyone, much less the whole world, from six feet under.

"Give me your phone," I told Layla. She was going to stay for a group exercise class after I left to pick up the Mitsubishi and try to make it to a meeting.

"Why?" Layla asked.

"I feel bad about just disappearing on you last night. With all that's happening, we should probably keep better track of each other."

Layla unlocked her phone with her thumbprint and handed it to me. She had a picture of us with Agnus sitting between us with crazy eyes as her wallpaper. She'd taken it while we were sitting on the couch, watching I don't remember what. It was shortly after we met. After B'iff died, before everything went downhill and she had to go back to New Albion. Before the Night Legion fell to the elves.

We looked happy. Alert. Not as tired and worn down. Even Layla, while she seemed to keep her spirits up, had a constant look of exhaustion on her face. I'd probably aged a good year for every month that had passed since. Now that my hair was growing back, I could swear I had a few more gray ones than before.

I scrolled through her phone to find her app store and selected the one I was looking for.

"What are you doing?" Layla asked.

"This app is a 'find your friends and family' sort of thing. I'll add it to mine, too. From what I understand, it'll bring up a map and show us where we each are at any given time."

Layla cocked her head. "Well, that's a clever app. How'd you even know about it? Before me, it wasn't like you had anyone nearby to keep track of."

I chuckled. "In the church, we had a couple that was going through some shit. The wife suspected her husband was cheating on her."

"Well, was he?" Layla asked.

"No clue," I said. "He wouldn't admit it if he was. Anyway, they came to me to talk through their issues, and he was pissed that she'd put this app on their phones. Said she was using it to keep tabs on him."

"Why would he be upset about that if he wasn't cheating?" Layla asked.

"He thought it meant she didn't trust him," I said. "And, well, he was right. She *didn't* trust him. I just didn't know if she had good reason not to."

"He probably was," Layla said. "To get that bent out of shape over something that could prove his innocence."

I nodded. "You're probably right. But sometimes women who've been betrayed before jump to conclusions, too."

"She'd been cheated on before?" Layla asked.

"This was her second marriage. Before I was the pastor there, her previous husband was having an affair. I think she might have been so afraid of being hurt again that she couldn't trust him."

Layla nodded. "Well, I trust you. I don't trust Aerin."

"I wasn't trying to make a point about our relationship, Layla. I was just explaining how I knew about the app."

"I know," she said. "But maybe there's something to that. After my father betrayed me, I might be a little bit insecure. Can you blame me? A woman who looks like that? I think she could be taking out the garbage, and she'd look sexy."

I nodded. "Yeah."

"You agree with me?" Layla asked.

"Wait! I wasn't supposed to?"

"Of course not!" Layla said. "You're supposed to say, 'That's crazy, Layla! She's an ugly ho!'"

"So, you want me to lie to you about it?" I asked.

"That's not what I'm saying."

Layla and I stared at each other blankly for about a half-second. It felt like five minutes.

Then we both burst out laughing. "I'm not blind, Caspar. I know she's attractive, and I know you're a man. But I do trust you."

I scratched my head. "I know you do. This app will ease your mind if you're ever worried about me, and it'll do the same for me."

Layla nodded. "It's a good idea."

I gave her a quick kiss. "You taking the Metro home, or do you want me to swing back by here with the car after my meeting to pick you up?"

"I think I can find enough to do here while I wait for you," Layla said. "I've had enough of the bus!"

"I'll second that!" I said. "Though if it wasn't for that bus, I never would have run into Cecil on his way to work, so I still wouldn't have my car fixed. I suppose there's a mixed blessing there."

"There usually is," Layla said. "If you are willing to see it."

I kissed Layla again. I know I'd already kissed her goodbye once, but then we talked again, so the first one didn't end up being a goodbye kiss. The kiss had to be the last thing before we temporarily parted ways.

Because we were nauseating like that. To other people, anyway.

I couldn't port myself to the tire and lube shop. I'd never been there, so I couldn't visualize it. Chances were better than average that someone would see me if I did that anyway.

I could have waited for the Metro, but based on the bus schedule, the shop was close enough that I'd probably get there sooner if I walked. It was only a couple of miles away.

As if I weren't tired enough already. But as predicted, my workout had given me a temporary boost of energy. I could handle the two miles.

Have you ever had the sneaking suspicion that someone is watching you? Following you? Then you turned around, and no one was there? I could swear that someone was lurking around, ducking between buildings or whatever, keeping an eye on me.

I don't know how I knew. Maybe I was just being paranoid. I stood at a crosswalk and hit the "walk" button, then looked over my shoulder. No one was there. *Come on, Caspar. Why would anyone be following you anyway?*

I shook my head. Paranoia was only part of it. Not enough sleep was likely responsible, too. I walked a few blocks farther. Seemed like I was greeted by a red hand at every crosswalk.

I chuckled. Someone had taken black electrical tape and covered all but the middle finger on one of them, so it looked like the crosswalk light was saying, "Fuck you, you can't walk yet."

Then I heard a buzzing sound in my ear. At first I thought it was an alert to let me know the signal had changed to walk, but then Ensley appeared in front of me.

"Ensley!" I said. "We're in the middle of the streets. If someone sees you…"

"Worth the risk," Ensley said. "Keep walking."

"What are you talking about?"

"There's someone following you, Caspar. I don't know who. He's all in black."

"In black?" I asked. "Did you see his face?"

Ensley shook his head. "His face is covered too."

I cocked my head. "What do you mean, covered?"

"I saw a few men like that in King Brightborn's court. I think they were assassins."

"You can't be serious," I said. "Assassins?"

Ensley nodded. "Just pretend like nothing is wrong. Keep walking."

"But the elf gate is still closed," I said.

Ensley shrugged. "I don't know how he got here. Maybe there's a fairy traitor working with him. If there is, I'll have his head."

"You behead your traitors?" I asked.

"Doesn't everybody?" Ensley replied.

"No," I said. Then again, I didn't know what happened with traitors. I wasn't in a line of work to deal with traitors. Back-stabbers, sure, but traitors? That was high-level government-type stuff. Not my domain.

"Or," Ensley said, "it could be that King Brightborn had operatives here from before. Sent them when the gate was open."

I nodded. "Maybe. Should I port out of here?"

"Only as a last resort," Ensley said. "If you do that, he'll know you're on to him. It might force him to get more aggressive about his pursuit."

I nodded. "All right. I'll just keep walking."

I was only a couple of blocks from the tire and lube shop. If I could get there before the assassin made a move, I'd probably be in the clear.

I pulled out my phone.

"What are you doing?" Ensley asked.

"Texting Layla," I said. "I just put a locator app on our phones so she can keep an eye on things. And watch her back."

"Okay," Ensley said. "Good idea. But try to be subtle about it."

"Ensley," I said, "half the people out here are using their phones. It would be stranger if I didn't pull out my phone the whole time I was walking."

"Okay," Ensley said. "Fair point. I'm going to disappear again. Hopefully, he hasn't seen me."

I nodded.

Ensley's shape disappeared in a puff of green magic, but I was pretty sure he was still nearby.

I picked up my pace, not so much that it looked like I was running away from someone but enough that, having just checked my phone, it would seem like I was in a hurry. And I was. I only had about twenty minutes until my AA meeting was supposed to start.

Should I even go to my meeting? I thought. Probably. Who knew how long this assassin had been trailing me. Had he overheard me telling Layla I was going there? Had I even mentioned it? I wasn't sure. We'd talked about it before. Still, best to stick to my planned routine. That wouldn't send up any red flags.

Maybe Ensley would be able to figure out who he was and get a solid identification for him. If he was an elf assassin, chances were that Layla would know who he was. Maybe she'd know his strengths, his habits, his weaknesses.

I finally reached the tire and lube shop and stepped inside. The door dinged. Just being inside, I felt a little safer. If someone in all black with his face covered came through the door, I'd notice. The door would ding for him, too.

"Caspar!" Cecil said as I stepped through the door. He was at the front desk.

"Hey there! Here for the Eclipse."

Cecil nodded, reached behind him, and grabbed a set of keys. "Here you go!"

"How much?" I asked.

Cecil smiled. "Three-fifty."

"That's all?" I asked. "For a full set of tires?"

Cecil nodded. "I said you were a friend of the family, so they let me use my employee discount. You're getting them at cost."

I smiled. "Wow, Cecil. Thank you!"

"It's my pleasure," he said.

I reached into my pocket, retrieved my wallet, and handed him my credit card.

"See you at church tomorrow?" I asked.

"Wouldn't miss it, Reverend!" Cecil exclaimed, smiling.

I nodded and stepped out the door. It dinged on my way out, too. I looked around. No one was nearby, at least no one I could see.

I spotted my car waiting for me in the parking lot to the side of the building. I walked over to it as quickly as I could, got in, and locked the doors.

I checked my phone. Layla had answered.

Be careful. Still going to your meeting?

I texted back a thumbs-up because the phone offered it as a suggestion and clicking that was easier than typing yes.

Layla texted back.

I'll keep an eye on you on my phone. Come as soon as you can.

I drove away. Now that I was driving, I'd probably lose the assassin, but if he was trying to find me, he probably knew the spots I frequented. The gym. My apartment. The church. Even my AA meeting, most likely.

But I'd be able to put a little distance between him and me.

CHAPTER SEVENTEEN

I probably looked like a deer in headlights as I walked into my meeting. I couldn't stop glancing over my shoulder.

I didn't think Layla was in much danger. If King Brightborn had sent an assassin, it wasn't her he'd have killed; she was his daughter. Not that kings hadn't done worse to their children. King Herod, the one who'd had all the firstborn males slaughtered based on rumors that a new king had been born, had also killed his sons.

But every time he'd had a chance to go after Layla so far, he hadn't harmed her. He was focused on me; I was the threat. He could dissuade her of her belief that I was the chosen one after getting me out of the picture.

The assassin was trailing me. I was his target.

Usually, I had a chance to shoot the shit with some of my friends and fellow AA members before the meeting started. Today, when I walked into the room, they were already reciting the serenity prayer.

I quietly took my seat beside Rusty, my sponsor. It had been more than a week since I'd last made a meeting. I never went more than a week without attending one. I generally made two or three.

Most people, I suppose, wouldn't understand why, with so much going on, attending a meeting was a priority. For me, my sobriety was a matter of life and death, every bit as much as the assassin was who was on my tail. The truth of the matter was, I was lucky to be alive when I remembered the quantities I used to drink and the number of times I'd foolishly found myself behind the wheel while three sheets to the wind.

It was by the grace of God alone.

Ultimately, I think being sober today was more foundational to my faith than any dogma the church had ever taught me. When I was in seminary, I'd learned all the rational "proofs" of God. I'd studied the Bible in its original languages. I never doubted God's existence from the time I was a young child until now, but my belief had come by default. I believed because to me, it was more sensible to believe than disbelieve.

That was what my faith used to be. I believed in God because no one could disprove His existence. You can never disprove a negative proposition. It's basic logic.

But then I discovered I was an alcoholic. I kept things together for the most part and hid it well, but inside, I was a hot mess. I was drinking myself to death.

And I couldn't quit. Willpower didn't work. The church didn't help. Therapy didn't make a difference.

But the twelve steps of AA did.

As far as I was concerned, my sobriety was a miracle, more than the healings I'd done. More than any spell I'd learned.

Even if the assassin got me, the last five years were a grace I didn't deserve. If I hadn't found AA when I did, if I hadn't surrendered to the God of my understanding, I had no doubt I'd have been dead long before now. No assassin, no king, no one could take away my years of sobriety.

Today was a step meeting; the topic was the third step. To

make a decision to turn our will and our lives over to the care of God as we understood him.

The pronouns weren't important. Some of our members believed in goddesses. Some worshipped cosmic principles. Some were polytheists, and others were monotheists.

There were probably as many different ideas about God in our room as there were men and women sitting around the table.

But none of us had achieved sobriety by willpower. Every one of us, at least those of us who had spent any time in sobriety, had said the third-step prayer. We'd turned our will and our lives over to the care of our various gods.

But today, I had a grievance. As we went around the table talking about how God had miraculously gotten us sober, I had to admit that I still had questions.

"My name is Caspar, and I'm an alcoholic," I said.

"Hi Caspar," everyone responded in unison.

"In sobriety," I said, "I've strived to always do the next right thing next. I know I can't look too far into the future. I can't dwell on the past. All I can do is the next right thing and trust that God will work things out better than if I didn't. But I have to be honest. Lately, I've done the next right thing, and the shit has still hit the fan. The last right thing I did, thinking I was going to make a real, positive, difference in a lot of lives... Well, I'll just say I lost a friend lately, and if I hadn't done the right thing, he might be alive. What I did, while I thought it was right, devastated a lot of people. If even in sobriety I'm wreaking havoc in people's lives by doing the right thing, how can I ever know what the next right thing is?"

That was all I had to say. Of course, I was talking about Brag'mok. No one around the table knew the situation, of course. They didn't realize I'd effectively given a tyrant the power to commit genocide. And according to the prophecy, if I kept doing the next right thing, more bloodshed would follow.

I stopped talking.

"Thanks, Caspar," everyone said in response.

People aren't supposed to cross-talk in AA meetings. Everyone's supposed to share their difficulties and put their doubts and struggles out there. It was a way to get stuff off our chests. A way of taking hard issues and unhealthy thoughts and bringing them into the light. When we swallow this stuff—which I'd been doing ever since I heard about Brag'mok's death—it tends to fester in darkness. It grows. It becomes insidious. It threatens our sobriety.

So no one said anything to me directly, not in the meeting. But one of our old-timers, a man in his seventies named Doug, used his time to paraphrase a passage from the Big Book.

"I'm Doug," he said. "And I'm an alcoholic."

"Hi, Doug," I said, adding my voice to the rest of the group.

"All we can do," Doug said, "is what we think our God would have us do while humbly—and I emphasize humbly—trusting Him. Only then does He enable us to match calamity with serenity."

Doug cleared his throat and continued speaking. "I've had to learn that I never have the full perspective. I try to do what I think my God wants. Sometimes it works out. More often than not, it does. But not always. When it doesn't, I have to trust that I'm not in charge. I have to admit that if I'd done the wrong thing, if I'd followed self-will rather than doing what was right, things would likely be even worse.

"I don't have great eyesight, and I'm not just talking about my physical sight. God knows my vision isn't great, but I'm also incredibly nearsighted when it comes to spiritual sight. I see no more than two steps in front of me, but I have to trust that my God sees a thousand steps ahead. And I have to trust, like a blind man holding onto his seeing-eye dog—dog is just God backwards, after all—that my God will eventually see me through the journey.

"But suppose what I thought was the next right thing ended

up being the wrong thing? Well, in that case, I latch onto my guide dog again since I know he'll take me where I need to go a lot more reliably than if I'm walking blind. I've been there, walking blind, and I've walked right into walls and off my share of cliffs. I've even walked out into traffic. But my guide dog, who I choose to call God, will eventually take me to a better place."

I'm not sure what anyone else said during the rest of the meeting. I was still stewing over Doug's words. I don't think he had any real religious background. Certainly not any biblical education. But dammit, he had more faith than I ever did. And he was right.

I might have recharged the ley lines on New Albion. I might have inadvertently given King Brightborn the power to slaughter the giants. To kill my friend. But I wasn't the one who'd pulled the metaphorical trigger. I didn't kill anyone. When Cain killed Abel, was God to blame because he'd created the stone Cain had turned into a weapon? All I'd done was give Layla's homeworld a chance to thrive again.

King Brightborn had spoiled that chance. He'd taken what was good and warped it into evil.

I might take a blade to my gut the second I walked out of the meeting. I might not even make it back to my car. Maybe I wouldn't see Layla again, but as I left the room, I took hold of my guide dog again. I trusted God to lead me back to my car and from there to Layla, and then to complete the trials.

I had to trust the assassin wouldn't prevail, and even if he did, even if I died before I had a chance to fulfill the elven prophecy, I wasn't the author of the prophecy. I wasn't in charge. It would be fulfilled one way or another, with me or without me.

CHAPTER EIGHTEEN

I had a new vigor in my gait. A new confidence. I made it to my car without incident.

"You here, Ensley?" I asked as I pulled back onto the street.

My fairy friend appeared on my dashboard.

"All clear!" Ensley said. "You lost him, but somehow, he escaped me, too."

"So, still no clue who he is?" I asked.

Ensley replied, "He has to have access to some kind of magic. There's no other explanation. I was following him, but I think he must've known."

"I thought you could sense magic? That's how you tracked me originally."

"I can sense it if he's wielding Earth magic. Anything bound to the elements. Even if he utilized spirit, I'd know. But it was like he just disappeared."

"Like you disappear and reappear?" I asked.

"Except it wasn't fairy magic," Ensley said. "I'd know it if it was."

"The drow use enchantments," I said. "You heard how Aerin explained it. They're experts at evading the fae."

"It's possible," Ensley said. "But if he's using enchantments, they have to be insanely powerful."

I bit my lip. "Why would one of the drow want me killed? One of Aerin's lackeys, one of those males? Maybe they're dressing like Brightborn's assassins to deceive us."

"Maybe," Ensley said. "But I don't know how the drow would know what an elven assassin dressed like."

"Hector," I said. "Or another of the king's emissaries could have been in cahoots with the drow all this time. It's not impossible that at some point, they planned this together."

"I don't know," Ensley said. "I've never encountered anything like this before."

I nodded. "Think you can find him again?"

"I can try," Ensley said. "But like you said, the drow have avoided being found by us for centuries."

"Do what you can," I urged.

Ensley nodded and disappeared again.

Layla was waiting for me as I pulled up to the gym. I suppose she knew I was coming, thanks to the app.

She jumped into the car, and I quickly briefed her on what Ensley had reported.

"If it is the drow," Layla said, "the whole point of the trials might not be to prove that you are the chosen one. It might be to kill you. The water elemental almost got the best of you."

I sighed. "But I did survive, and Aerin gave me the clues I needed to do it. If she hadn't told me what she did, the thing would have killed me."

"Those two men," Layla said. "They might not be as obedient to her as they seem."

I shook my head. "But if that was their plan, why send an assassin after me now?"

Layla scratched her head. "Perhaps you were more impressive during the first trial than they anticipated. The assassin might be their Plan B."

"If I prevail again tonight," I said, "it's likely the assassin will get a little more aggressive in his pursuit."

Layla nodded. "True. Are you sure we can trust Aerin? Perhaps she wanted you to win the first round."

"Why would she do that if she's secretly hoping I'll die before the trials are over?"

"Perception is everything," Layla said. "The more you win, the more people are likely to be convinced you're the chosen one."

"But I don't understand why she'd want them to think that," I said.

"It's a common strategy in war," Layla said. "My father often gave the enemy, the giants, the impression they were winning even though he knew he had the advantage. That way, when he stole the victory in battle, it would be more psychologically devastating. If the enemy thinks they are going to win, their hopes are built up and then dashed again."

"The result being they're more hopeless than before," I said.

"Exactly," Layla said. "Maybe she's building you up just to strike you down. Let the cultists think you are the last hope for humanity, then the moment they start to think we have a chance to defeat my father's legions, you'll be killed. That way, you never were the chosen one. Give them the idea that there was never any hope."

"I don't know," I said. "That's an elaborate hoax. It's much riskier to do that when they could already have seen me killed."

"The Elf Gate Cult has a tall order," Layla said. "To convince the US government and the rest of the world to simply turn over control to my father. If all of them see you fall..."

"So, you think that Aerin is playing the long game?" I asked.

"Possibly," Layla said. "The drow are elves. If they think that my father's victory is an inevitability despite the prophecy, wouldn't it make sense to work with him from the start?"

"But they have a prophecy," I said. "They seem to be pretty convinced about it."

"Do we know that for sure?" Layla asked. "How do we know they're telling the truth about that? My father could have told them what the prophecy said, and they thought they could drive a wedge between us by seducing you and making us think you have to marry her rather than me."

"It would drive a wedge between us," I said. "And your father certainly isn't thrilled about our relationship."

"Right," Layla said. "All of this reeks of my father's doing."

"But we still don't know for sure," I said. "This is just a theory."

"Think about it," Layla said. "Ensley thinks the assassin might have been using an enchantment. The drow are superb enchanters. We don't even know what they are capable of doing."

"But Ensley also said he'd never seen anything like that before," I said.

Layla took a deep breath. "Which is to be expected since the fae weren't even aware the drow had been using enchantments all this time."

"So, are you suggesting we don't show for the next trial?" I asked.

"Not at all," Layla said. "If that happens, they'll suspect we're on to them. Not to mention, every time you win one of these trials, you get stronger. We still need that magic to thwart the elven legion."

CHAPTER NINETEEN

No shift at the bar on Saturdays. It was busier, and well, I was still an amateur bartender. I could make most of the drinks, but I still had to check my mix cards, and I wasn't especially quick about it. It was fine with me. I had no aspirations of climbing this particular career ladder or taking busier shifts.

I was grateful for that. Sure, I could have spent the day practicing magic. I could have done some yoga. But I needed sleep.

How could I sleep, though, when there was an assassin trying to take me down? You'd be surprised. Even when you're under intense pressure, even if your life is on the line, there's a point where your body just shuts down.

That's where I was.

I just didn't have any energy left. My head was pounding. It was only a matter of time before I'd start seeing double.

Assassin or not, if I didn't get some sleep, I wouldn't stand a chance against him if he came after me, not to even mention the fire elemental I was supposed to engage later that night.

Thank God for blackout curtains. It wasn't often that I took daytime naps. I had gotten the curtains mostly to block car lights and such. Today, I was grateful I had them.

Agnus, surprisingly, curled up beside me. I'd half-figured he'd spend the day in front of the television, but it was comforting to have him at my side.

Layla was standing guard.

While watching Netflix.

Not exactly Netflix and chill. More like Netflix and get ready to fight.

It was a good time for her to catch up on her rom-coms and polish her bow. If she had to use it, heaven forbid it wasn't shiny. That was the thing about Layla. She could kick ass if she had to, and she'd look amazing doing it.

I don't think I had any dreams. None that I could remember, anyway.

I was just out.

That was why I was shocked when Layla came in and turned on the lights.

"What the hell?" I covered my eyes with my hands.

"Time to go to the cult building for the trial," she said.

"Already?" I asked. "I just laid down."

"You've been sleeping for almost twelve hours, Caspar."

"What?" I asked. "There's no way!"

I reached over and grabbed my phone. Sure enough. It had been about ten in the morning when I laid down. Now it was five after ten in the evening.

"No sign of the assassin?" I asked.

Layla replied, "Nothing. But I almost finished a whole season of *How I Met Your Mother*."

I shook my head. "Isn't that the show with the redhead girl who went to band camp in the *American Pie* movies?"

"I think so," Layla said. "I've only seen one of them, though."

I snorted. "Would you believe I used to have a crush on her back in the day?"

"The girl from band camp? Seriously?" Layla asked.

"I think I still have the edition of *Maxim* magazine when she was on the cover. Somewhere on one of my bookshelves. I probably had a crush on her more because she was also in *Buffy*. I loved that show, too."

"Haven't seen that one yet."

I smiled. "We need to watch it together. It's awesome. At least, it used to be. You never know how older shows hold up over time."

"It's a date," Layla said. "If you can keep your hands off me long enough to get through an episode."

"No guarantees," I said, getting out of bed. "I suppose we need to put that damn mustache on again." Layla nodded and retrieved it from my dresser. Pulling it off the last time hadn't been pleasant. I wasn't thrilled about gluing the thing back on my still-tender upper lip, but it worked well enough, I suppose. No calls from Philip, my bishop, asking me about strange videos fighting water monsters. If he knew about it, I was reasonably certain I'd hear from him immediately.

I slipped on a pair of swim trunks.

"Why are you wearing those?" Layla asked. "You're fighting fire, not water this time. I don't think you have to worry about..."

"How do you fight fire?" I asked.

Layla's eyes widened and she nodded. "Of course. With water."

"Exactly," I said. "It isn't like I have any fire-retardant clothes. Probably something I should have tried to pick up today, but I thought sleep would serve me better."

"I'm bringing my bow," Layla said. "Just in case. I think we need to be prepared for anything."

"Chances are, whoever the assassin is, he'll be there."

"Especially if he's one of the drow," Layla said. "Then we *know* he'll be there."

I nodded. "But don't you think walking into the place carrying your bow will raise some red flags? You didn't have it last night. Why bring it now?"

"Already thought of that," Layla said. "I'm going to bring it and show it to Fred to see if he thinks he could forge me another one. As a blacksmith at the renaissance festival, he crafts all kinds of weaponry."

"Not a bad idea," I said. "And your quiver?"

Layla shrugged. "Same thing. If we're going to have to go to war eventually, I don't think it would be strange to ask if he could make me some arrows, too."

"All right," I said. "If shit hits the fan, though, you need to come to me. I can port us out of there, but I won't do it if you aren't with me."

Layla smiled. "We've got this, Caspar. Besides, I don't think the assassin is going to move on us there. If you win, though…"

I cleared my throat. "*When* I win, you mean? If I don't win, I won't have to worry about him. You know, on account of being dead."

"Not going to happen," Layla said. "These trials don't prove anything conclusively. And I still think the trials were invented by the drow as a trap."

"I don't know what to think," I said. "We do need to be cautious. We can't trust anyone, but we need to give Aerin the impression that we do. That we're on her side."

"No red flags," Layla said.

"Exactly."

CHAPTER TWENTY

We took the Mitsubishi. I could have ported us there, but we were keen not to let the drow, not to mention everyone else, know I had fairy magic. Maybe they knew already, but they didn't know I had a handle on it.

Brag'mok had taught me that in a fight, it was just as important to keep your strengths a secret as well as your weaknesses. If an enemy knows your weaknesses, they can exploit them, but if they know your strengths, they can prepare for them.

Layla concurred.

We were playing our cards close to the chest.

The crowd at the old church was probably twice the size it had been the night before. According to Jag, after the previous night's broadcast, several of the cultists from the chapter in Washington, DC had booked a flight. They wanted to see the rest of the trials in person.

"What's the deal with the hoodies, sunglasses, and masks?" I asked Jag.

"Politicians, I suspect," Jag said. "Folks you might recognize."

"Like, representatives?" I asked. "Senators?"

"Most likely," Jag said. "I wouldn't even be surprised if a few of them are part of the President's administration."

I snorted. "That's insane. I can't believe this little cult had garnered so much influence."

Jag shook his head. "When you have elves who can wield magic, like Hector, how many people can you recruit?"

"I suppose that makes sense," I said, looking across the room.

"There's Fred," I said to Layla. "Want to go show him your bow? Get that out of the way?"

Layla nodded. "You've got this, babe."

"Thanks," I said, giving her a quick peck. She moved across the room and took a seat next to Fred. Shocker. He'd saved the one next to him.

I know the guy helped us out with the Blade of Echoes, but he was getting on my nerves. He wasn't a real threat, just kind of a buffoon. And he wasn't the most attractive man in the world, so in terms of his flirtation with Layla, I didn't have much to worry about. Even if he'd been Brad Pitt, I'm not saying Layla would have hooked up with him or anything. Layla loved me. I was secure about that. But him being exceedingly ordinary-looking, if not trending toward ugly, gave me a little peace of mind.

When you have a hot girlfriend, you just have to acknowledge that other men are going to give her attention. I didn't have to like it, but it came with the territory.

I scanned the room again.

Then I felt a tap on my shoulder. The hand that touched me lingered.

I turned around.

Aerin was standing there, eyes wide, lips slightly parted. I was trying my best to remember there was a small chance this Jezebel wanted me dead.

I smiled back. "A lot of new people here."

Aerin nodded. "I can't say I'm thrilled by that. This Order has gained much influence in a short amount of time."

I nodded. "I know what you mean."

"Just make sure you win," Aerin said. "With so many of them looking, the stakes here are higher than I anticipated."

"I understand," I said. "I have to survive, but we also have to convince this cult to take my side."

"Our side," Aerin corrected. "We're in this together, Caspar."

I nodded. Was she bullshitting me, or was she genuine?

"Any hints this time?" I asked.

Aerin raised her eyebrows. "I presume you've had a chance to get a handle on wielding the element of water?"

I nodded. "It's not pretty, what I've been able to do so far. It isn't exactly subtle."

"We can work on refining your abilities later," Aerin said. "But when you encounter fire, I don't know that you can use *too much* water."

I chuckled. "I just hope none of these politicians think they're too good to get a little wet."

Aerin shrugged. "Well, they all came from the swamp anyway, right?"

I smiled. "For someone who has been off the grid forever, you have a pretty good handle on American politics."

"We've been in hiding, Caspar. But we weren't living under a rock. We have televisions, and would you believe it, we even have the Internet."

I laughed. "I suppose that makes sense."

"You should probably get into position," she said. "I'll be around soon with the next elemental orb."

I nodded and turned to go.

She pinched my butt.

I whipped back around with a shocked look on my face. "Aerin!"

The drow princess giggled. "Sorry. I couldn't resist. It's clear you've been working out."

I grunted and looked at Layla. She was still talking to Fred.

Thankfully, she hadn't seen it. Was Aerin really into me? Her little grope could have been a part of the ruse.

One of two things was true: she either wanted to marry me or kill me. From my time doing marriage counseling in ministry, I knew that those two things went together more often than you'd expect.

I stepped into the stone circle.

A hush fell over the crowd. I wasn't sure how many people were in the room. More than there should have been, considering a *fire* creature was about to appear.

Hopefully, everyone knew where the exits and the fire extinguishers were.

Aerin appeared, her two silent counterparts flanking her.

This time, she held the orb in her hands as she stepped into the circle.

"All of the elements," Aerin declared, "both give life and take it. Without water, none of us would survive, yet few of the elements can destroy a city or a civilization more rapidly than it can. But our hero has subdued it, and the power of water now resides in him. Tonight, we encounter another element. The discovery of fire sparked the birth of civilization, but fire is likewise deadly. Even the great city of Rome was once consumed by fire. This city too once fell to that element.

"Very few have ever mastered both elements. For water and fire to cohere in a single person requires exceptional strength and a resilient constitution. The one chosen by the prophecy as dictated by Taliesin, according to the oral tradition that has been passed on by the drow across the generations, must balance all the elements."

Oral tradition? I thought. These trials weren't dictated by the prophecy but by oral tradition? Prophecies are hard enough to understand, but to put one's faith in tradition? A sinking feeling settled into my stomach.

Why hadn't Aerin told me I didn't just have to subdue fire, I had to somehow balance it in my spirit or my body or wherever the hell I was holding these elemental powers?

Aerin had had time to talk to me about that. She could have said something, given me a clue about how to hold onto fire without the water that was already a part of me extinguishing it.

Apparently, there was now a third possible outcome. Maybe I wouldn't die, and I wouldn't prevail. I'd beat the element but fail to absorb it. I'd fail the prophecy and live.

I suppose if that happened, I would not be a threat anymore. Maybe the assassin, who wanted me dead, would lay off. Not the worst outcome.

But it would also leave me without the power I would need to face the legion.

Part of me thought I could just drown the elemental out the moment it appeared. Be done with it. Move on with my life, and with Layla's help, find some *other* way to kick her father's ass, or his and his army's collective ass. What the hell is a collective ass, anyway?

My brain is a strange place to be sometimes.

But who was I kidding?

I had to face an elven legion, one that could wield all five elements. I needed the ability to counter each of them. I needed fire as much as I needed water.

Aerin raised the orb high so everyone could see it.

She was wearing gloves. I expected it was hot as hell.

Inside the globe, it looked like a small inferno was raging.

Not sure how it could burn in that thing without oxygen.

This wasn't common fire, though. It was fire itself—the elemental, the spirit behind the energy that *is* fire.

Aerin dropped the orb, and it shattered into a million pieces.

I braced myself and brought the spirit of water to the surface… I started gathering all the water I could from the air.

But the elemental didn't form into a single blazing creature as the water elemental had.

Instead, it divided into a thousand tongues of fire.

I imagined it must've been like that at Pentecost in the book of Acts.

But these flames weren't dancing over people's heads, giving them the ability to speak in different languages.

They were swirling around me.

A giant water blob like the one I'd made at the stadium might not cut it. If I released it and it hit the ground, it might extinguish some of the flames.

I wasn't sure what else I could do, though, other than form the blob and force it to hit the ceiling. If I dropped in on the floor, the water would scatter, but if it burst on the ceiling. It would make it rain. Sort of.

Hopefully, I wouldn't extinguish it completely.

One of the tongues of fire landed on my arm.

It hurt like hell.

I slapped at it, extinguishing it almost immediately.

When I'd fought the water elemental, it wasn't like all of the water *was* the elemental. It wasn't its essence. Otherwise, I would have peed it out. But the elemental had gathered water, even as I did by wielding its power. If the elemental could survive in the globe without oxygen, maybe it would be able to withstand water, too.

Might be another thing if the elemental spirits collided inside me, but I'd worry about that if or when I managed to subdue it. I focused my water powers.

A giant glob of water formed over my head in the middle of the stone circle.

I forced it to the ceiling, and a deluge of water, not like rain but rather a giant canopy of water, crashed down on the whole room.

People screamed.

Apparently, getting wet was more frightening than the notion of the building burning down.

One by one, the flames went out, all but one.

"Just you and me, buddy," I said as I stepped up to the single flame.

It grew.

It expanded and enveloped my body. It *hurt*!

But I wasn't burning.

I inhaled, and the flames leaped into my mouth.

I've never had issues with heartburn, so I was not sure if that was what I was feeling.

But the inside of my chest was hot, like I'd just swallowed a ghost pepper.

I exhaled, and steam poured out of my mouth.

Water meeting fire produces steam.

I pressed my lips together.

The room fell silent.

Had I extinguished it? Had the water spirit inside me killed the fire elemental?

I recalled that sensation. That burn, could I draw it out?

I sensed the cool power of water and pushed it to one side of my body, then I felt the warmth. It was there!

I extended my arms, my palms turned up.

A ball of water appeared in my left hand.

A ball of fire exploded into my right.

The room erupted in cheers.

I closed my palms, and the magic of both elements disappeared.

CHAPTER TWENTY-ONE

Conquering fire had been surprisingly easy. It was surprising because I had expected it would be harder to beat than water. Fire just seemed scarier. Weird, because drowning is just as frightening as the prospect of burning to death, but flames are more frightening if only because fire *spreads.* One drop of water spilled on the carpet won't do much of anything. A single spark can catch and engulf a house or worse.

It was going to be another short night. Aerin had said these trials had to take place at night, but come on. It gets dark well before eleven.

I wasn't tired. A twelve-hour midday nap tends to do that for you, even though I had wielded multiple forms of magic. For some reason, it didn't take the toll on me that absorbing all that water had the night before. If anything, I felt invigorated.

Church used to mean an early Sunday morning, but since we'd started going to the gym so early, Sunday mornings felt like sleeping in.

"Up for a game of Twister before bed?" I asked.

"Twister" was code for something else.

Wink, wink. Nudge, nudge.

Layla knew what I meant.

Sure, I probably should have worked on my morning sermon, but I'd picked one from Pentecost five years ago. I figured the whole tongues of fire thing would be ironic. I was the only one who'd get the joke. The rest of the church would probably wonder why I was preaching Pentecost out of season.

Our denomination had a prescribed set of readings for every Sunday, a lectionary. The idea was that with everyone hearing the same Scriptures, it was like all Christians would be hearing the same Word. Well, those who were part of our church. A way of affirming our unity—the mystic reality of the church that transcends time and space.

Yeah, cool thought. No one attending on Sunday cared, so I wasn't going to feel bad about selecting an out-of-season homily for the day. It was just too fitting.

On Pentecost, tongues of fire had descended upon the twelve; they had already replaced Judas at that point. Then, three thousand folks who heard them proclaiming the gospel got baptized in one day.

That was fire and water, just like me. The correlation was too good to pass up.

Layla and I had our fun. For once, both of us won, which wasn't a guarantee. Sometimes I won, and she was left insisting on an instant rematch. Not that I was ever opposed to that, but you know, Twister can be exhausting. I'd need a good fifteen minutes or so to prepare. I mean, I'd only played Twister with two women in my entire life.

Well, excluding those I couldn't remember from my drinking days. Those three or twenty women didn't count. What happened in the stupor stayed in the stupor.

Besides, I'd asked for forgiveness for all I did or might have done.

Before Layla and after my divorce, I was a born-again virgin. That's my story, and I'm sticking to it.

A Twister virgin, that is. Obviously.

Of course, our game was interrupted. Agnus had figured out how to open doors when he was a kitten. I'd intended to get a lock on my bedroom door, but until Layla, I hadn't had any reason to keep him out, so I'd forgotten about it.

Before I could hear him talk, it hadn't even occurred to me that I'd ever need to. Something about being able to communicate with my cat made all sorts of things most people wouldn't think twice about doing in front of their pets seem oddly awkward.

Agnus leaped, grabbed the doorknob with his front paws, and swung his body to turn the knob. The door popped open, and he pushed it the rest of the way with his forehead after he dropped back to the floor.

Layla and I were in the throes of Twister, and Agnus was walking around the room, serenading us.

"Bow chica bow wow! Chicca chicca chicca waaaooowww!"

Layla and I looked at each other and laughed. I had no clue how Agnus knew the kind of music that was supposed to accompany this sort of thing.

It struck me that I should probably check my credit card bill. Who knew what he was buying on demand when I wasn't around?

We had to force ourselves to tune him out, which wasn't as difficult as you'd think.

I was so enthralled by Layla's near-perfect body that circus clowns could have busted into the room, juggling, and I'd have managed to ignore them.

Until we finished. Then, of course, I'd call the police. Because what's creepier than clowns?

We laid in bed. I was on my back. Layla curled up next to me and put her head on my chest.

I was at peace.

CHAPTER TWENTY-TWO

Layla was coming to church with me for the first time. I didn't know how people would react seeing her ears. They'd assume she was a member of the Elf Gate Cult. One more thing one of my concerned members would contact my bishop Philip about.

Of course, Philip had met Layla. I think he even suspected we lived together—a major *faux pas* for ministers—but he never said anything about it. I also knew Philip had been directed by the archbishop, the president of our denomination, to keep an eye on me. After my healings made the news, it became widely known that I didn't fit the mold my denomination expected of its ministers. If anyone made a stink about my relationship with Layla? Well, if the news got to the archbishop, there wouldn't be much Philip could do to protect me.

At this point, though, I realized that not bringing Layla to church was just delaying the inevitable. What was I waiting for? I wasn't ever going to break up with her. The church would either accept our relationship, or they wouldn't. Delaying bringing her wasn't going to change anything.

And with the assassin out there, probably more motivated

than before to take me out now that I'd completed two of the trials, I wasn't going anywhere without her. It was safer that way.

Of course, bringing her bow with her to church probably wouldn't go over well, but we weren't about to leave that behind. Sure, Layla was competent when it came to hand-to-hand combat, but if this was one of the elven legion's assassins, that was his expertise.

She was good, but not that good. Her expertise was as a marksman. If the assassin showed up, she was better suited to take him out from a distance.

So we left early. If we got there before anyone else, she could stash her bow and quiver in my study for the duration of the service.

It wasn't hard to differentiate between the regular members and the influx of new attendees who'd come in the wake of the recent healings. And as people arrived, it became clear that, once again, we were going to set an attendance record.

The regular members were now in the minority. All of them wore church-appropriate attire, most of the women in dresses, the men in suits or at least shirts and ties.

A few of the newcomers were dressed similarly. Different folks, depending on their history with church, had different habits when it came to choosing their Sunday best. For a lot of the people who came, their best was a well-worn pair of jeans and a t-shirt.

Fine by me.

I don't think God cares how we're dressed.

Layla took her place in the front pew. No one realized she'd come with me, but being seated in the front, she could easily move through one of the doors that led to my study and retrieve her bow if necessary.

I simplified the service on account of all the visitors. Our typical liturgy was difficult to follow for those who hadn't been raised with it. No one wanted to be stuck flipping back and forth between pages of a hymnal, trying to figure out where the hell we're at the whole time they're in church.

Rather than go through a series of responsive readings, canticles, and pre-written doctrinally approved prayers, I began with a simple invocation and a casual extemporaneous prayer before our organist led us in singing *How Great Thou Art*.

We had a short scripture reading after that, then another hymn, and then I preached.

I printed out the sermon that I'd intended to use. I could have read it verbatim. A lot of ministers did. Heaven forbid you got some of the words wrong, that you were misunderstood, and might inadvertently communicate something that didn't perfectly match our dogma.

But at the moment, it felt too wooden, too cold and stoic, to simply read the homily.

Instead, I left my manuscript on the pulpit, stepped down from the chancel, and walked among the people while I preached.

The message was about fear and how the early Christians were transformed almost overnight by their encounter with the risen Christ. The same men who hid in locked rooms after the crucifixion were now, on Pentecost, out in public and preaching to people who'd come from all over the country on a pilgrimage to Jerusalem for the festival. Less than two months earlier, Jesus had been crucified. Now, these previously timid disciples were preaching in the open.

Had they known what was going to happen? Did they realize the Holy Spirit was going to send fire from heaven and allow them to speak languages they'd never learned?

God did what He had to do because no one was an outsider for these early ministers. No matter one's tribe, or race, or language, they all heard the message of hope Peter delivered that Pentecost, and there was nothing the authorities could do to stop it.

It hit home. We had a diverse gathering for the first time in my ministry. We couldn't be timid or afraid because things were changing. I'd once been a timid minister too, but I'd recently been baptized with both water and fire.

That was not something I touched on in my message, but it was on my mind. There was no place for fear any longer. I had to believe that what was foretold would be fulfilled, no matter who might threaten me for it.

Even if it was the religious authorities. Or an elven assassin.

I wasn't the same person I used to be. No one who'd encountered the risen Christ in the New Testament was either.

I had transformed in ways I didn't yet fully understand, and with three more trials awaiting me, I'd change more.

When you're a preacher, you generally get an idea about how well your message was received when people are shaking your hand on the way out. I knew which members just said it routinely every week.

"Good sermon, Pastor."

There were others who reserved their compliments for the occasional message that struck a chord.

For the first time in I don't know how long, even the most conservative and reserved members expressed their appreciation.

So did the visitors, none more than Cecil, who had his wife Shanda at his side and their daughter Grace between them. The girl was walking without so much as the aid of a cane. They didn't shake my hand; they hugged me.

A hug? Not used to that level of enthusiasm, but it was encouraging. Awkward, of course. Man-hugs are always a little weird. I don't know why; maybe it's a cultural thing. Men don't hug each other very often.

Only Doris regularly hugged me after service, and this Sunday was no exception.

But as she hugged me, as we stood there at the entrance of the church, the double doors wide open, I saw him.

Across the street, all in black, his face covered like before.

Layla had been lurking in the church. I'd planned to introduce her as my girlfriend, but when I looked for her, I didn't see her.

I quickly closed and locked the door after the last person exited.

I ran through the door to the side of the chancel and to my study.

Layla's bow was gone. She'd seen him too. I checked my phone. Nothing.

I called Layla. No time for texts.

She quickly picked up.

"He's here, Caspar."

"I know, I saw him."

"I'm going to try to lure him inside."

"Where are you, Layla?"

"Just outside," Layla said. "I don't think he's seen me. Not yet."

"Be careful, Layla."

"Just be ready, Caspar. He's going to come after you. I'm going to try to make my way to the balcony. I'll take him down before he gets to you. Just make sure I have a clean shot."

"I love you, Layla."

"Love you too."

She hung up. This was the plan. Like it or not, I was going to face the assassin in my church.

"Ensley!" I shouted. If he was floating around nearby, he'd show up.

He didn't.

Of all times for him not to be lurking around and watching. Where the hell had he gone, anyway?

No water magic. No fire magic. Not in the church. I couldn't target it precisely enough.

If Layla was going to lure him inside, though, I needed to unlock the doors.

BANG!

The assassin kicked the door open as I made my way back to the chancel.

In his hand was a familiar blade; it looked just like the Blade of Echoes.

Then he charged me.

CHAPTER TWENTY-THREE

I stood there, holding Layla's phone. I just stared at it. She'd never made it to the balcony.

Somehow I'd managed to survive an expert assassin, but he didn't know I'd mastered fairy portals. I didn't know how he'd manage to get down from the Arch where I'd sent him, but I wasn't going to waste any time.

Layla had suspected the drow were behind it. While I didn't know for sure they'd be there, there was only one place to look.

I formed another portal and visualized the steps outside the former church where the Elf Gate Cult gathered, where I'd faced the first two trials.

I used my newly acquired water magic to shoot a blast at the doors of the building. I could have used fire, I suppose, but I didn't want to burn the place down. Water provided more than enough force to do the job.

"Where is she?" I demanded.

"Caspar, what are you…" Jag put his hand on my arm.

I shrugged it off. "Don't push me, Jag."

"I swear I'll flood this whole damn place! Or burn it down! Burn it down and then flood it for good measure!"

"Caspar," Aerin said, approaching me cautiously. "What are you talking about?"

I rolled my eyes. "Don't pretend you don't know. One of your little subbies here must've done it. No wonder he had to cover his face."

"Caspar," Aerin said, "these men have been in my company since we arrived."

I shook my head. "You're lying. One of them came after us. Tried to kill us. And they took Layla!"

"It was not one of the drow, Caspar," Aerin said. "I will not deny that she presents a peculiar challenge to me, given my intention to see the prophecy fulfilled. The drow are patient."

"Again, words. Things you've told me. How do I know anything you've told me is true?"

"Caspar," Aerin said, taking my hand. It trembled as she held it, I was *that* furious. "Why would I make such a move, even if I *were* inclined to do it, before you finished the trials?"

I sighed. "I don't know."

"I want you to succeed. I'm hoping you will prevail. This is not only your world. Do you think I want those other elves to take over our home?"

I took a deep breath. "I suppose not, but what other explanation is there? The gate to New Albion is still shut. No one could have come or gone from there to here."

Aerin shook her head. "Tell me, can these elves communicate between realms even when the gate is shut?"

I bit my lip. I remembered how Layla used to communicate with her father before she learned all he was up to. I recalled how Brag'mok used a similar crystal to keep tabs on what was happening back in New Albion. "Yeah. I mean, I'm pretty sure."

"And has the gate been open even once since King Brightborn discovered who you are?" Aerin asked.

"It has," I said, lowering my head. "You think this assassin, or whatever he was, had been here all this time?"

"Think about it, Caspar," Aerin said, intertwining her fingers in mine. I instinctively pulled my hand away. She raised her hand to my cheek instead. I cringed. "If the elven legions are preparing an assault and you represent the greatest threat to thwart their intentions, wouldn't it make sense to attempt to remove you from the picture?"

I snorted. "Just be thankful I used water rather than fire to break through that door."

Aerin smiled. "You're more like the drow than you know. You are at heart a peaceful man. Even with a more destructive power at your disposal, you chose water."

I stomped my feet. "I think they might need to call a water remediation company."

"Not necessarily," Aerin said. "This water didn't come out of nowhere. You drew it from the air."

"Yeah," I said. "It's always humid in St. Louis."

"You can draw it out of the carpets, too."

I shook my head. "How do I... Even if I could, I'm in no frame of mind."

Aerin grabbed my hand and pulled. "Come with me."

I followed Aerin into a small room behind the stage, where I imagine the preacher used to stand when this was still a church. She closed the door behind us.

The room was filled with couches in oranges and greens. They looked like they'd been made in the seventies, probably donations to the church that used to be here. And to think, perfectly good couches just left behind?

Yeah. No one would want these monstrosities.

"Sit down, Caspar," Aerin said.

I sat on one of the couches. I sank in a good two feet the second my butt hit the cushion. I grunted. These couches were ugly *and* uncomfortable.

Aerin opened what looked like an old chest and retrieved a folded cloth.

It was an ornate blanket, similar to the material used for Aerin's dresses.

"I'm fine," I said. "I have water and fire now. It's like an internal heating and cooling system."

"I'm not retrieving the blanket to make you comfortable, Caspar," Aerin said. "At least not exactly..."

Then Aerin shook it and dropped it.

Layla stood there with her bow in her hand, smiling at me.

I tried to leap off the couch, but I was sunk too low and clumsily fell back into it.

Layla laughed, walked over, and took my hand, helping me up.

I hugged her. I clung to her like my life depended on it. In a way, it did. When I thought she was gone, it felt like a part of me was missing.

"I don't understand!" I said.

"Aerin saved me," Layla said.

I cocked my head. "Aerin? But why?"

"Someone in our midst *is* trying to kill you, Caspar. I don't know who, but I've been tracking him since we arrived in St. Louis."

"Was he trying to kill you, Layla? Before he confronted me in the church?"

Layla said, "I don't know. He was coming after me, but Aerin showed up, like, out of the blue. I'll tell you what; she knows how to handle a sword."

I shook my head. "And she just took you?"

"She used this enchanted rug," Layla said. "She threw it over me. I thought she was trying to kidnap me."

Aerin rolled her eyes. "Your girlfriend had this distorted idea that I was in league with her father."

I bit my lip. "Yeah."

"But whoever the assassin was, I think he was trying to do exactly that."

I shook my head. "So you took her and left me to fend for myself against the assassin? That asshole could have killed me!"

"I know you have fairy magic, Caspar," Aerin said. "You had a way to escape. She didn't, and the assassin was going to get to her before she'd have a chance to come to you. I had to intervene, and I trusted that given what we've seen from you so far, you'd be able to handle a single assassin."

I snorted. "I ported him to the top of the St. Louis Arch."

Layla laughed. "You what?"

"It had to be something I could visualize," I said. "I've seen that thing so many times."

Aerin interjected, "He'll have no problem escaping that; he has magic. But it wasn't a bad move. He'll have to regroup before he comes after you again."

"Wait," I said. "How did you know I have fairy magic?"

"The same reason I could sense you wielded spirit magic. We, the drow, are sensitive to all kinds of magic."

"Then you know what the assassin is using?" I asked. "Because Ensley, the fairy who has been helping me, didn't have a clue."

"He wouldn't," Aerin said. "Because the magic the assassin is wielding? It's not of this world."

"Is it from another place, like New Albion?" I asked.

"It's not from the physical world at all," Aerin said. "You believe in angels and demons, do you not?"

I snorted. "You're talking about infernal and angelic magic?"

Aerin nodded. "I don't know who this assassin is. I fought him off, but he's concealed his identity. But whoever he is, he's dealing with a dangerous power."

"Do you think he was sent by my father?" Layla asked.

"I cannot say," Aerin said.

"How in the world do we deal with someone who has demonic power?"

Aerin cocked her head. "You're a minister, are you not? Isn't this your wheelhouse?"

I snorted. "I've never exorcised a demon. We don't do that sort of thing, or not routinely, anyway. We aren't trained for it."

"I see," Aerin said. "But if you were to exorcise a demon, how would you pull it off?"

"By the power of the Holy Spirit, I imagine."

Aerin nodded. "We must proceed through the trials. You must embrace aether."

"My spirit won't be enough?" I asked.

"Humans can cast out angelic power," Aerin said. "The power of demons and that of angels is the same. They are not essentially different; only their loyalties differ. But for a human to command an angel or a demon requires a lot of focus. Typically, those humans who have done it have had to use rituals. And it usually takes more than one person and might take several attempts spanning days, if not weeks."

"If I subdue aether, if I can wield the element itself…"

"Then you'll stand a chance," Aerin said. "I don't know how this assassin acquired the ability. But you can be certain he will make another attempt on your life before you subdue aether in the final trial."

I shook my head. "I still don't understand why you saved Layla. I thought you were trying to steal me from her."

Aerin smiled. "I am not petty, Caspar, and it's clear you love her. If something happened to her, what shape would you be in to face the legions? I still believe we are destined to be together, but like I've told you many times, the drow are patient. I would rather your relationship run its course and we come together at the proper time than force the prophecy into fulfillment."

I nodded. "Thanks. I think."

"I have news for you, Aerin. Don't get me wrong, I appreciate all you've done, but I think you have the prophecy wrong. I'm not letting my man go anytime soon."

Aerin smiled and nodded. "Only time will tell which of us is correct."

CHAPTER TWENTY-FOUR

We still had trials to complete. Earth. Then, air. Finally, aether.

I didn't expect to be here now, ready to complete the next trial. I'd barely had a chance to practice using fire.

And I didn't have my mustache.

Well, I'd tackle the rest of the trials, one after the next, as myself, Caspar Cruciger, reverend or not. If the church condemned me as a witch or a cultist, or heaven forbid, a heretic, so be it. I could live without my career.

I couldn't live if I was killed.

I know. In addition to being Captain Pee Pants, I was Captain Obvious as well.

But I also couldn't live if the assassin managed to abduct Layla.

My life with Layla was more important than my job.

Maybe no one would know. Or maybe they would. At this point, I wasn't going to worry about the risk. Come what may, I had to face these trials as soon as possible.

What was the worst that the church could do to me?

Fire me?

Not the way they used to.

It had been a few hundred years since the church burned their heretics.

Even if they tried, fire and I were, like, best buds now, and I still had water at my disposal. You know, just in case.

The church didn't fire heretics the same way anymore. Now, the worst they'd do was defrock me, strip me of my ordination. Kick me out of the denomination.

The church couldn't hurt me. It wasn't my job, being a minister. It was just something I did. It wasn't who I was. I don't know if I would have felt that way a few months ago. I used to think that if the powers that be ever blackballed me, it would be the end of life as I knew it. I'd be left wandering through the world like a ghost without a purpose.

But I had been suspended from the ministry before. I still woke up the next day. The world still turned. My heart continued to beat. By the time I came back to the church, Layla and I were together. I'd started to find purpose in other things.

I'd learned that I could adapt. God, grant me the serenity to accept the things I cannot change. That's the first part of the serenity prayer in AA, but that's not all of it. There's also the bit about asking God for the courage to change the things we have the power to change. Experience had given me enough wisdom when it came to the bullshit in my denomination to know the difference. I wasn't going to change the denomination, but I could still, minister or not, make a difference in people's lives. And I could change myself.

Maybe no one would see the video. Maybe they wouldn't recognize me. How many people were watching these trials, anyway?

I didn't have to ask.

"So, Casp," Jag said as I walked back into the entryway. "You okay?"

I nodded. "Sorry about that earlier. I thought at the time that someone abducted Layla."

"I get it," Jag said. "If someone ever took Layla from me…"

I raised my eyebrow. "Jag, seriously? You're still fantasizing about my girl?"

Jag shrugged. "I fantasize about a lot of women. Probably almost as many as fantasize about me."

I snorted. "Right."

"So," Jag said, "I hate to complicate things further, but the first two trials were streamed, right?"

I nodded. "To the rest of the Elf Gate Cult."

"Yes," Jag said. "But someone didn't click the private stream box."

I cocked my head. "How many people are watching these videos?"

"Well," Jag said. "The last I checked, the last two nights had more than a million views."

"A million?" I asked. "Combined between both of them?"

"A million each." Jag refreshed his phone. "Closer to two million now."

"Well, shit," I said.

"I'm sorry," Jag said. "I have a mask in my bag that you can wear."

"A mask?" I asked.

Jag grabbed a duffel bag from the corner. He unzipped it and pulled out what looked like a Donald Trump mask.

"Seriously?" I asked. "Trump?"

"Make our cult great again, Caspar."

"Why do you even have that?" I asked. "No, the better question is, why do you have it with you?"

"Because I was waiting for the opportunity to tell that joke, but now it's spoiled. I guess I don't need the mask anymore. It's yours if you'd like."

"Two million people?" I asked.

Jag nodded. "Probably more. The views are pouring in by the minute."

I shook my head. "I'm not going to wear a mask."

"I get it," Jag said. "Trump is controversial. And you need to unite…"

"It's not that," I said. "Has nothing to do with the former President. It has to do with me. I can't wear a mask anymore. I can't find balance, the balance I need to subdue the rest of the elements, if I'm living two different lives. I'm doing this tonight as myself, come what may."

Aerin knew what had happened. She'd saved Layla. She knew we'd have to finish the trials sooner rather than later. This was why Jag and a few of the other cultists had gathered. The door swung open. Now Fred was here, too.

"Oh, good," I said. "The supreme leader has arrived. Now it's official. We can get started."

Layla backhanded my shoulder. "Be nice, Caspar."

I nodded at Fred. "Glad you could make it."

Fred nodded back, then fixed his eyes on Layla. "Glad to see you're safe. I was worried when I heard."

I grunted. *Bite your tongue, Caspar.*

Layla just smiled at Fred. "I just wish we knew who it was."

Fred nodded. "I'm sure he'll reveal himself again. But right now, we need to get the trials underway."

The place felt different without so many people, more like it was for the first trial. There were a fair number of cultists, but not the intimidating crowd that had gathered the night before. This was unscheduled. All those Washington politicians would be disappointed. Oh, well. Screw 'em.

They were going to live stream it, anyway. They could have fixed it. They could have made this one private, but I was done hiding. I was sick of pretending for the sake of the church. I was who I was. What was happening was happening.

If I had learned anything in AA, it was that I couldn't leave things about me hidden in the dark anymore. I couldn't manage a double life.

After these trials, I'd either be dead, or the world would know who I was. Probably even my congregation. The archbishop, too.

They'd either accept me—the real me, all of me, including my identity as the chosen one of the elven prophecy—or they wouldn't. Simple as that.

I could live with the consequences, but I couldn't live with the lies. I couldn't stay sober while putting on a façade every time I stepped into the church to preach.

They'd probably excommunicate me. Again.

But this was my truth. My faith had not changed. Sure, it had been challenged. Everything I'd faced had raised more than a few doubts. But I was the same person I'd always been. The only difference now was that I knew who I was, and I wasn't going to hide it.

Not anymore. Not ever again.

I stepped into the stone circle to face the element of earth. I remembered what Aerin had said before: fire could char the earth. I brought the power of fire to the center of my consciousness, and the familiar burn spread through my chest. I was ready.

Aerin stepped into view, again flanked by the two drow. This time, each of them held an orb.

"Due to unexpected circumstances," Aerin said. "Our hero will face the remaining three trials in succession. Should he prevail over them all, we will all know today that he is indeed the chosen one predicted by the ancients.

"First, our hero will encounter the element of earth, then air and aether one after the next, with a brief moment for our candidate to rest between trials.

"Earth, like the other elements, is a source of life. Together with fire and water, earth provides food to nourish the body. But like the others, earth can be devastating. Quakes, as often as flood or fire, can and have demolished civilizations. Should our hero prevail, he will subdue a power that both gives and takes life."

Aerin dropped the orb, swirling with green energy, to the floor.

Then another shattered.

The drow holding the orb of air froze in shock. A blade like the Blade of Echoes protruded from in his chest as two elementals–one of earth, the other of air, formed into massive monstrosities in front of me.

"No!" Aerin shouted.

Then the final orb shattered, broken in the hands of the third drow, who likewise had a blade in his chest as he fell to his knees. A translucent elemental, aether, formed beside the other two.

Aerin unsheathed her sword and charged after the one who'd thrown the blades.

I turned.

It was Fred! He was the assassin! How in hell...

Layla sprang to her feet, her bow in her hands, and fired an arrow at him.

He pulled another blade that resembled the Blade of Echoes from his belt and swiped her arrow out of the air.

Aerin brought her blade down toward him, but Fred parried before raising his fist in the air.

"Long live the king! All hail Brightborn, Emperor of Earth!" With a cloud of purple magic around him, he disappeared before her blade could hit its mark.

I turned back around.

The three elementals were approaching my position.

"Fuck!" I shouted. How the hell was I going to take down three at once?

"Remember the order!" Aerin shouted.

"Roshambo," Layla added.

I nodded. Three threats, but I could only subdue them in the proper sequence. I had to start with earth.

And I had to do it before the others did whatever the hell they were going to do. If the water elemental could suck out all the water out of my body, could earth crush my flesh? Could the air elemental take my breath away? Lord only knew what aether could do. Separate my spirit, my soul, from my body, perhaps?

I wasn't about to chance any of the three.

I unleashed a torrent of flames on the earth elemental. Of all the relationships between elements, this was the one I was the least certain of. Fire was to earth as paper was to rock. The rules of the game said it was supposed to prevail, but it didn't make a damn bit of sense.

Sure, fire could char the ground, but throwing dirt on fire will put it out much the same way water would.

It was going to take a hell of a lot of fire to bring earth down.

Thankfully, I didn't think I could produce anything less than maximum power anyway.

I threw my fist forward, pushing the burning sensation from my chest through it.

Once the fire magic hit the air, it was a lot hotter than it was inside me. Must've been because it hit oxygen.

My flames engulfed the earth elemental.

He stopped, dropped, and rolled, which snuffed it out. Sure, its shape was a little darker than before, but it was still coming after me.

It got hotter with air.

Maybe with more air, a wind, the fire would burn more intensely.

Thankfully, there was a great source of air: the air elemental.

"Hey, Breezy!" I shouted before drawing the cool sensation of water into my frame. I knew water wouldn't hurt it. At least, I didn't expect it to, but who likes to get wet? Maybe I could piss the thing off.

I gathered as much water from the humid air around us as I could draw, and with pure force of will, forced it at air.

A giant Sea World-sized splash–the sort that gets you if you sit in the front row for the Killer Whale show–enveloped air's form.

Then it came after me.

That's right, Breezy! This way...

Everywhere it went, it was like a big tornado. It moved with such force that it was tearing up the floor tiles on its path.

I just had to get it between earth and me.

I brought fire back to the forefront. I had to be ready.

Thank God I'd been working out. I had to run harder than I ever had before. Those HIIT workouts were paying off.

Air moved fast. I just needed one shot.

And since earth moved slowly, the slowest of all the elementals I'd seen so far, I wasn't too worried it would catch up with me first.

I ran around the perimeter of the stone circle until I had air in the perfect position between earth and me.

Then I unleashed it. A blast of flames hit air and turned into an inferno before engulfing earth.

The elemental rumbled as it was overwhelmed by flames.

I had to not only beat the thing, I had to absorb it. But I couldn't shower it with water. I would probably wash it away.

Erosion and whatnot.

I took off after it.

"Shit!" I shouted. Aether had gotten in the way, and I got a little too close to it. For a half-second, my spirit was shocked out of my body.

"Caspar!" Layla shouted as my ghostly self floated upward.

I glanced at her. She did ground me.

Then I focused and forced myself back to my body, but I made a pit-stop at earth. I didn't know if I could absorb it better as a disembodied spirit than with my body, but maybe...

The charred pile of dirt was too hot to touch with a body, but I dove through it. I felt...whatever made up an elemental spirit and grabbed it before charging back to my body.

It was exactly like flying; I just had to visualize where I was going. Only this time, my body wasn't forced to go along for the ride.

I pulled it into my body, along with the rest of my spirit.

It's jarring to be yanked out of your body, even more so when going back into your flesh. And now I could feel earth. I don't know how to explain it. It was a heavy, gritty sensation.

No time to waste. I didn't have a clue what I was doing or how it would form, but I forced it out of me toward air.

Nothing poured from my fists, but the floor beneath my feet started to shake.

The five stones around me took flight. How could I control this? The same way I had moved a fairy gate or the blob of water before.

I tried it, and it worked. Go, me.

I threw the stones at the air elemental, stacking one top of the other. They slowed down the tornado just enough that I thought I could get to it. There was a golden glow of some sort inside. That had to be it.

I grabbed it, and the second I touched it, it was absorbed into my skin.

The water elemental had made me pee by absorbing all that water. I sincerely hoped this one wasn't going to force me to break wind with a similar frequency.

It didn't, at least not yet. I felt an airy sensation in my body, almost like breathing pure oxygen, untainted by the atmosphere, from a tank.

I recalled the words from Genesis: *When God made man, the Lord breathed into the creature, forged of earth, the breath of life. And man became a living creature.* I knew Hebrew. He became *nephesh*, a living spirit.

So I released air at aether. Nothing much happened.

Then I inhaled, and air brought aether. It brought spirit with it and poured into my nostrils.

Spirit was different from the other elementals. I just felt more alive. More aware. More stable.

After aether joined them, the elements came to life. I didn't even have to focus; they were just there, no longer subduing each other but in union. A union I had caused.

When God commanded the first man and woman to exercise dominion over all creation, this must've been what He meant. Not a burdensome, oppressive, or exploitative rule over the Earth and all her elements, but a communion with them. A harmony. A balance.

All at once, the room erupted in cheers. None was louder than Jag's, who, by the sheer size of his lungs, released a joyful roar.

Then Layla was on me, and her arms wrapped around me. She kissed me hard, right in front of everyone. In front of the live stream. Everyone.

Talk about PDA.

I didn't mind. I kissed her back.

"I give to you," Aerin said, raising her voice, "Caspar Cruciger. The chosen one, in fulfillment of the ancient elven prophecy. And likewise, Princess Brightborn."

CHAPTER TWENTY-FIVE

"That was kind of you, Aerin, announcing me as a princess."

Aerin smiled. "The people of this world, the humans, know little of the prophecy, but I know what must be fulfilled. Until then, it would do no good for me to attempt to force the issue. We must work together."

"Your friends," I said. "The two drow. I'm sorry, Aerin."

Aerin nodded. Tears welled in her eyes. "They weren't talkative, not to others, but they were good men. Obedient men."

"Not easy to find," Layla said.

I grunted. I was trying to be respectful. You know, cross-culturalism. "Again, condolences on your loss. If there's anything I can do..."

"You need to focus on what lies ahead, Naayak."

"What did you just call me?" I asked.

"'Naayak.' In Hindi, it means hero. It is what we have always called the chosen one, and today you have proven yourself, Caspar. You are Naayak."

"Do I get my presents now?" I asked.

"Caspar!" Layla exclaimed. "Don't be rude."

"Since when are you worried about being rude to the drow?" I asked.

"I don't know," Layla said. "Maybe since she saved my life? Don't get me wrong. He's still mine."

Aerin nodded. "Perhaps he is, but time will reveal all. And Caspar, you are correct. You are entitled to the gifts that have been prepared. I cannot tell you what they are, not precisely. All the elements must combine to open them. And as you know, we have not wielded magic directly for centuries."

"Right," I said. "Only enchantments."

"Do we need to live stream this too?" I asked.

Aerin shook her head. "They have seen what they must. I can only presume Fred was hoping you'd fail the trials. He'd hoped your death would be broadcast to the world and our prophecy would be discredited. That must've been his Plan A. Going dark assassin and taking you out, probably Plan B."

"Didn't work out for him," I said. "Either plan. At least not yet. I'm not sure he's moved on to Plan C yet."

Layla shook her head. "He was always so kind to me."

"Of course he was," Aerin said. "I now believe it was his intention to deliver you to your father all along. A token to prove his loyalty."

"He chose his side, and he wasn't thrilled with my success so far."

Layla sniffed. "But he helped us with the Blade of Echoes."

"Did you see the daggers he was wielding?" I asked. "They weren't just blades, they were steeped in magic. Whatever kind of magic he'd used. I think he agreed to forge the false blade for you so he could study its properties and make something to bear whatever magic he was using."

"I will retrieve the presents, as you called them, now," Aerin announced.

She stepped out, and a few minutes later she returned, her face white and shocked.

"Aerin," I said. "What is it? You look like you just saw a ghost."

"The two prisms, the ones containing the ancient gifts of Taliesin. They were open!"

"Open?" Layla asked. "How is that possible?"

Aerin shook her head. "The prisms could be opened by one such as Naayak, who wields all the elements, but they could also be opened by a group of sorcerers representing all the elements."

"I'm assuming Fred did this," I said. "Did he have help? How in the world did he pull this off without you noticing? I thought the drow could sense magic. That's how you found me originally."

Aerin groaned. "They must've done it in the middle of the trials. There was so much other magic in the air that we didn't notice."

Layla nodded. "Fred did get up and leave in the middle of the last trial."

Aerin nodded. "I suspect that was how he did it. And there is more. There is an inscription on the lid of each of the boxes describing what it contained."

"Which was?" I asked.

"Two crystals, divided, that when brought together would bestow the power of angels upon the one who held them."

"That's what Fred was doing," I said. "He harnessed angel power."

"And it seems he enchanted blades with it," Layla said.

"The blades *were* enchanted," Aerin said. "But only with earthen elements. Again, he had help."

"And if he had help," I said, "he's not alone."

"There must already be elves on Earth," Layla said. "I don't know when they came."

I held out my hand and drew in fairy magic, then formed a portal back to my church. Didn't have any business in the building, but I'd left my car there.

"Leaving so soon?" Aerin asked.

"I acquired this ability when Ensley possessed me, for lack of a better word."

Layla looked stunned. "When we were in New Albion, my father had been possessed by fairies, too."

I nodded. "I can't believe we didn't see it, but he never had to wait for the full moon for the gate to be thin. He could come here all this time."

"And it seems," Aerin said, "the only thing preventing it was that he'd hoped Fred could do him a service in advance. Enhanced by angel power, he intended to use him to eliminate you before he marched on Earth."

Layla shook her head. "It makes sense. I just can't believe... I don't know what to believe about the depths my father would go to anymore."

"The elven king knows the prophecies," Aerin said. "He knows his chance of success is greater if you are removed from the picture, Naayak."

"But now that I've succeeded and proved myself in the trials, and I'm stronger than ever..."

"He is not going to wait until you've had a chance to practice with your newfound powers, Naayak. I fear the invasion is imminent."

CHAPTER TWENTY-SIX

Where the hell was Ensley? It just didn't seem right that he'd mysteriously be absent when the shit started to hit the fan. The same Ensley who'd followed me obsessively, who'd spotted Fred on my tail (before we knew it was Fred) and helped me figure out how to wield elemental and fairy magics wouldn't just up and disappear.

I could only think that one of two explanations was likely: Ensley was either occupied with something of the utmost importance, something so crucial that he thought it better to allow me to face the assassin without his aid, or he'd been taken. Fred, maybe, but certainly by someone allied with or sent by King Brightborn.

It wasn't hard to imagine why Brightborn would abduct Ensley. Maybe he was struggling to create portals, even if he could access fairy magic, without Ensley's guidance and aid. Or maybe he couldn't make portals large enough to bring his whole legion through.

I suspected Aerin was right, and the invasion was imminent. I wasn't going to assume anything about Brightborn's capabilities, with or without Ensley.

Then again, Brightborn wouldn't need Ensley. There were other fairies on New Albion, Ensley's subjects. He was the fairy king, and if he needed to, the elf king could capture one of them. And it would be easier than conducting a fairy abduction on a world he didn't presently inhabit.

I picked up the Eclipse at the church, then drove back to the apartment.

Layla and I were still in shock about Fred. It wasn't that I liked him, not even a little. Hell, he hardly acknowledged me, and now I knew why. It wasn't just because Layla was with me. It wasn't petty jealousy. He didn't dare look me in the eye because one, he thought I was a false messiah who'd led the king's daughter astray, and two, because he was trying to kill me. If he looked me in the eye, he'd have to acknowledge me as a human being. He'd have to learn something about me. I mean, I don't know much about killing folks. It's not my jam. But I knew that in the military, they often went to great lengths to depersonalize the enemy and distance the soldier from the foe's humanity to lessen the burden of guilt many soldiers felt after taking a life.

Fred's flirtations with Layla? They were either a pretense to justify why he was giving me the cold shoulder, or he just couldn't resist hitting on a hot elf. He thought elves, rather than humanity, were the future, and by playing the buffoon, he'd picked up details about our daily habits.

Sure, finding us at the church had been obvious. Everyone knew I was a minister. My healing service had made national news.

But Fred wasn't gone. If he came after us again, he'd have to be subtle. Especially since, defying the odds, I'd completed the trials and hadn't gotten myself killed in the process. He might have thought the elementals would do the job for him, but now I was stronger than ever before, and I knew about the magic he'd stolen from the drow—the angelic power.

I don't know if it was the adrenaline of the trials still

flowing in me, an extra dose of energy from three new forms of magic I'd added, or a simple sense of helplessness. I'd completed the trials. Fred and Brightborn clearly wanted me dead, but I'd defied their plans. Still, it seemed like they were two steps ahead of us. Angel magic? What the hell, or heaven, was that, anyway?

One day at a time. One magical hurdle at a time.

In AA, we celebrate every victory. You get a coin for twenty-four hours sober. You get another one for thirty days. Sixty days. Ninety Days. Six months. You get one every year. Each celebration isn't an end. It's a milestone, and it's worth celebrating.

That was what we were going to do tonight. I'd worry about Fred, the elves, and all that shit tomorrow.

This wasn't about celebrating my success in the trials, though that was part of it. It was about celebrating us. A few hours earlier, I had been scared to death that Layla might not be alive at worst or had been kidnapped and brought back to New Albion at best. Now she was in my arms, unscathed.

Tonight was about us.

I looked around the living room. Good, Agnus was snoozing on the couch. We had a little privacy for once.

"Up for a game of Twister?" I asked.

"I'm always up for that," Layla said. "Provided everyone wins. The way we play it, I'm all in favor of participation trophies."

I smiled. "It's not about winning and losing. It's about having fun. But I don't know about trophies. The figures they'd put on top. Can you imagine?"

"I don't need a trophy to know I've already snagged the prize," Layla said, grabbing my hand and pulling me to the bedroom.

We lay in bed, catching our breath. Layla rolled over and put her arm across my torso, and I held her tight.

"When I thought you had been taken today," I said, "I don't know if I've ever been so afraid."

"What were you afraid of?" Layla asked. "Did you think the assassin had killed me?"

"Maybe," I said. "I figured there must've been a second one. Since I'd dealt with him and then I saw your phone there, I was thinking the worst. He'd either killed you, I figured, or had thrown you in a hole to force you to lotion yourself."

"To lotion myself?" Layla asked.

"It puts the lotion on its skin, or it gets the hose again," I said, adopting the scariest tone I could muster.

"Let me guess," Layla said. "You're quoting a movie."

"*Silence of the Lambs,*" I said, laughing. "We'll have to watch it someday. You know, after all this is over."

"I take it that it isn't a rom-com?" Layla asked.

"Heavens no," I said. "Probably the creepiest movie ever made, aside from the live-action version of *The Lion King.*"

Layla laughed. "That's not creepy!"

"Of course it is," I said. "I mean, the movie was, like, a Discovery Channel documentary narrated by Disney songs."

"I agree. It didn't hold a candle to the original, but I wouldn't call it creepy."

"I don't know," I said. "Animated talking animals seem normal somehow, but when they are real animals, it's creepy."

"Says the man who has a talking cat," Layla said, chuckling.

"Fair point, but at least he doesn't try to serenade me to the tune of *Can You Feel the Love Tonight.*"

Layla giggled. "Hakuna Ma-ta-tas."

"I don't think…"

"It means nice boobies!" Layla said, laughing at her joke.

I laughed back. "Well, I wouldn't disagree! You certainly resemble that particular remix."

"Thanks!" Layla said. "I figured you'd agree, considering the way tonight's Twister game played out."

"I didn't have a choice! The game dictated right hand, right boob. If I didn't do it, I'd have to forfeit."

Layla laughed. "Someday we'll have to try playing a real game of Twister."

I shook my head. "With your flexibility compared to mine, I don't think I'd stand a chance. Besides, I don't own that game. But I think I have a game of Operation somewhere. You know, in case you're up for playing doctor some time."

Layla laughed. "If you touch me the wrong way, I'll just shout, *BUUUUZZZZ!*"

"No loss," I said. "Because then it would be your turn."

"I think I'd win. So far, I haven't found a wrong way to touch you."

"What can I say? I'm easily pleased."

We laid there in silence for a few minutes as I stroked her hair. I heard her start snoring.

Only Layla could make snoring cute.

I gently moved her off my chest and tucked her in beside me.

I still wasn't tired, but I laid there, my arm across Layla's body, just holding her.

I knew I loved her, but I didn't realize I was *in* love with Layla until I thought I'd lost her.

I didn't care what Aerin thought she was waiting for. I knew that when my relationship with Layla ran its course, we'd end up married. There was no other end-game here. I just couldn't imagine living without her.

CHAPTER TWENTY-SEVEN

My vibrating phone woke me up. Two little buzzes every text message. I could have silenced it, but with all that was going down, if something happened and either Jag or Aerin needed to reach me, I wanted to know.

I rolled over and checked my phone.

It was Philip, my bishop. I sighed.

"What is it?" Layla asked, rubbing her eyes.

"A bunch of messages from Philip. Says we need to talk."

"Think he saw the stream of the trials?" Layla asked.

"Someone did," I said. "I was a pretty hot topic in the denomination after the healing service."

"A hot topic?" Layla asked.

"Yeah," I said. "I've mostly been ignoring it, but apparently, about half the denomination wanted me censured after the healings made the news."

"And the other half?" Layla asked.

I shook my head. "It's not that simple. At least half of the other half was indifferent. Good ministers focus on helping the people in their churches, and those folks don't care much about denominational issues. If I had any supporters at all, it was a minority."

"And if anyone, even a single person who was aware of the controversy, saw you complete the trials?"

"I'm pretty sure Philip is trying to contact me to let me know I've been suspended again, if not excommunicated outright."

"Such bullshit," Layla said.

"I concur," I said before calling Philip back.

"Hey, Caspar," Philip answered after a single ring. "You home right now?"

"Coming to pick up my keys to the church?" I asked.

"We're not having this conversation on the phone, Caspar. I owe you more than that."

"Try to make it fast," I said. "I have a lot going on."

"So it seems," Philip said. "I'll be there in half an hour."

I hung up. Funny that smartphones still say hang up when you click the little red phone icon. Not like the kind we used to have, back in the day. Those were the good old days. Life was simpler. At least, in retrospect. Of course, I was a kid, and life is simpler in childhood. Part of me wished I could go back. I don't wanna grow up, I'm a Toys"R"Us kid.

You know, back when Toys"R"Us existed.

Reminded me of another song, not a jingle: *Ch-ch-ch-changes.*

If only I could turn back the clock to a simpler time when the only people who believed in elves were children, and those elves didn't fight wars or have aspirations for world domination. All they did was make toys for good little boys and girls.

And yummy cookies.

Layla and I quickly got dressed, fed Agnus, and drank Greenberry superfood protein shakes.

There was a knock on the door. It was my bishop.

"I'm sorry, Caspar, but this is beyond anything I can defend."

I nodded. "I get it. Suspended, or…"

"Excommunicated."

"Not even conducting an investigation this time?" I asked.

"Nothing to investigate," Philip said. "It's all on the video."

"What are they saying?" I asked. "How are they explaining what happened?"

"There are two theories right now. Either it's an elaborate Hollywood-scale hoax and you're involved, complicit with the cult's agenda, or it's demons."

I snorted. "Demons? Really?"

"A diabolical deception," Philip said. "Demons masquerading as elves and sorcerers, intending to deceive God's people."

"Of course," I said. "Because anything that doesn't fit inside our little boxes of possibility must be demons. A convenient way to dismiss and condemn things they don't understand."

Philip nodded. "For what it's worth, I don't share their opinion."

I scratched the back of my head. "What do *you* think happened last night on that stream?"

Philip replied, "It doesn't matter. But I know you, Caspar. I don't think you'd get involved in something like this without good reason."

"Everything you saw was exactly as it appeared," Layla said. "Caspar isn't a heretic. He's a hero."

Philip looked at Layla. "You're an elf?"

Layla tucked her hair behind her ears. "These ears don't lie."

Philip bit his lip. "And is there an elf king planning to attack the world?"

Layla nodded. "I'm sorry, but it's true."

Philip put his hand on my shoulder. "You may not be a pastor anymore, Caspar, at least not in our denomination, but I still believe in you. I don't know how much it means, but my prayers will be with you."

I nodded. "It means more than you realize."

"I can't fix this for you, Caspar," Philip said. "And I'm genuinely sorry it had to end this way."

"It's fine, Philip," I said. "But can you promise me one thing?"

"What's that?"

"Don't change. Don't stop preaching hope. Because of what's coming, the people need hope. Just make sure the people at Holy Cross are served well by a minister who will give them that."

"The archbishop has asked me to personally assume your ministry," Philip said. "He wants to make sure that any errors you taught are addressed."

"Good," I said. "That is comforting to hear. I know you'll do right by them."

"I'll make sure the soup kitchen ministry continues, too," he said.

I nodded. "Thank you, Philip."

CHAPTER TWENTY-EIGHT

Layla rubbed her hand up and down my back. "You okay?"

I smiled. "I'm great. Strangely enough, I feel free. By putting the nail in the coffin of that part of my life, I'll never have to sit through another council meeting. No more debates over trivial bullshit."

"Just not the best time to have to start job hunting," Layla said.

I shook my head. "I still have the bartending gig, so we won't be homeless. And if we are hungry, I know where a great soup kitchen is. May have to cut back on those sessions with Jag, though. Fifty bucks a pop?"

Layla shrugged. "You can always work out with me."

"Or with Tony Horton." I smirked.

"I think you'll like the workouts with me better," Layla said, smiling slyly.

"Oh, really?" I asked. "Do you have a name for your routine?"

"I was thinking 'sexercise.'"

I grinned. "You're right. I don't want to do that with Tony Horton."

"We'll get back to the routine later," Layla said. "Right now, though, I think we need to focus on stopping my father. Since Aerin said that Fred needed magic corresponding to all the elements, we know there are at least a handful of elves he's working with."

I shook my head. "I just wish I knew what happened to Ensley. I could use his help tracking them down. Fairies can sense when someone's using magic. He must've known something was up when they unlocked those boxes."

"But you saw him after Fred already had that magic," Layla said. "If Ensley knew, he would have said something then."

"That makes sense. Aerin had them under lock and key all that time. They had to have done it when she wasn't around, and as far as I know, she has been in that cult building since she arrived in town."

"The first trial," Layla said. "Aerin was occupied conducting the trial of water. With all that magic swirling in the air, maybe a small amount in the back room used to open those boxes wouldn't be enough for Ensley to notice."

"But Fred was sitting with you the whole time," I said. "So it must've been other elves from your dad's legion. They'd have to be sneaky as hell to get back there, open the locks and the magical boxes, and escape without being noticed."

"I don't think they were common sorcerers or legionnaires," Layla said. "They had to be operatives or assassins. And Fred didn't accidentally dress the same way as an elven assassin on his own. Someone was teaching him, training him."

"Great!" I exclaimed. "Just what we needed. As if having one assassin on my tail wasn't stressful enough."

Layla frowned. "One assassin I can handle, provided he doesn't take us out when we aren't expecting it, which is possible. These operatives do their best when you don't know they're there. But multiple ones? At least most of the operatives aren't any more powerful magic-wise than level two."

"Well, that's a relief," I said. "Puts the magical advantage in our column."

Layla nodded. "Yes, we do have that, but it's not good news. If it was two assassins who together wielded all five elements, we'd have a challenge of three, including Fred, not to mention figuring out how to deal with the magic he has."

"So, how many assassins do you think we're dealing with?"

Layla shrugged. "At least three. I can't imagine any of them being able to wield more than two elements. Most of them, I expect, only wield one. We didn't have all the elementals on New Albion, so whatever abilities they've acquired probably aren't refined."

I snorted. "You mean, like my magic?"

"Right," Layla agreed. "But you've already used your abilities in a combat scenario. Sort of. I don't think the assassins are going to rely on those abilities to take us down. They have years of training in subterfuge and killing. That's what we need to be concerned about. We probably shouldn't go anywhere our view might be obscured."

I scratched the back of my head. "That pretty much rules out anywhere and everywhere, Layla. There's always an alley to duck into. I don't know where we could go in the city that we'd be safe."

"Our best chance is to draw them out to fight," Layla said. "Let them think we're bringing the war to them."

"How are we going to do that?" I asked.

"We bring the war to them," Layla said.

"With me and what army?"

"Do you think Aerin is a drow princess but doesn't have a legion of her own to command?"

I tilted my head. "I hadn't thought of that. We could bring a whole legion to the elf gate! But how am I going to open it without Ensley?"

Layla shrugged. "The same way you blew it open before."

"When I destroyed the Blade of Echoes in the source?" I asked.

"Big problem there; we already did that. No more Blade of Echoes."

"That happened because the magical surge it caused when you did that blew the gate open. You still have magic, more than ever. You might be able to overload the ley lines."

"If I do that," I said, "there won't be anything to prevent your father from coming through at any time. At least if he's using fairy gates, he has to work to manipulate them and force them to do it. As far as we know, he's only been able to send a small contingency of operatives to Earth."

Layla nodded. "He's planning to come here one way or another. If we force the issue, we draw him through when we're ready for him."

"It shifts the element of surprise in our direction."

Layla nodded. "He's expecting us to rest on our laurels. Sure, he's been planning this forever. But Plan A was clearly for you to be eliminated before sending his legions here. Now you're a bigger threat than you were before."

"I'm only going to get better at wielding these powers. If he's smart, he'll attack sooner rather than later."

"True," Layla said. "But if I know my father as well as I think I do, even though he's lied to me my entire life, I'm not sure he's given up on Plan A yet."

"You think he's still going to try to take me out before he attacks?"

"Think about it," Layla said. "He sent Fred after you. *Fred.* Sure, he has acquired magic that we aren't sure how to confront, but he's still Fred. He hasn't spent his whole life training as an assassin. And if we're right, if my father has other assassins already here."

I sighed. "If we're going to try to bait him to launch his assault now, we're going to need help. We need to figure out who's really on our side. Not just the drow. Jag said the cult was divided. Did my success in the trials sway anyone? If so, how much help can we expect? If the legion can wield the elements, it might not be enough for me to just neutralize what they try to do. We still have to beat them back."

"It's not enough to not lose the war," Layla said. "We have to be sure we can win it."

CHAPTER TWENTY-NINE

I texted Jag to meet us at the Elf Gate Cult building. He was probably at the gym, but he knew we weren't going to work out today. That sort of went without saying, but I had no doubt he'd be there.

I was surprised to find out he wasn't. He was at the Elf Gate church already, and he said it would be a good idea for us to make an appearance.

After clarifying that the center area, the place where I'd fought the elementals, was clear and that I wouldn't inadvertently portal us into someone's body or one of the stones that were now piled in a column in the middle of the floor, I cast a portal.

Layla and I showed up in the middle of the room.

A small crowd had assembled. Not as many cultists as had been there the night before, but the out-of-towners—the Washington contingent—was there.

The second we appeared, we were greeted by raucous applause.

I looked around. No more masks. No more disguises. I recognized more than a few of the faces. Several senators, Republicans and Democrats both. It isn't often you can convince them to unite behind any cause, but these senators, at least, were united in their belief that ceding the government to elves wasn't a great idea.

I'd seen the Defense Secretary on television too. I think he was a general. I couldn't remember his name. I don't follow politics that closely. I used to, but my sobriety is important, and watching too much political news is enough to send anyone on a binge.

"Caspar! Layla!" Jag called, jogging over to us. For a big man, he could move. Unlike other bodybuilders who wobbled around the gym, their bodies so bulked up that they could barely walk like normal people due to a lack of stretching, Jag made flexibility a priority.

I grinned. "So, it looks like the folks from out of town didn't leave after they missed the show yesterday."

Jag shook his head. "They were mildly disappointed that things didn't happen according to schedule. But for the most part, they're pleased with the result."

"For the most part?" I asked.

Jag shrugged. "Our side won, Caspar. Those who were undecided swayed our way. But others? Well, sometimes people don't change their opinions no matter what evidence slaps them in the face. They just dug in their heels and left."

"Loyal to Fred?" I asked.

Jag nodded. "I don't know where he is, but I'm guessing they've followed him."

"Where's Aerin?" I asked.

Jag shrugged. "She left when you did."

"Where did she go?" Layla asked.

"I haven't the slightest clue," Jag said. "All she said was that she had to go prepare."

I nodded. "Understandable. It would have been nice to coordinate our efforts, though. I suppose she didn't say when or if she'd be back?"

Jag sighed. "Not a word. But hey, I'd like to introduce you to someone who'd like to talk to you."

I followed Jag to the man I'd recognized as the Secretary of Defense.

"General Breeland," Jag said. "I suppose you don't need an introduction."

"Caspar Cruciger," Breeland said, extending his hand. "It's a pleasure."

I shook his hand. "The pleasure is mine, General."

"We need to talk," the general said. "Is there a place where we can speak privately?"

"This way," Jag said. We followed him to the room with the out-of-style couches.

The general sat on one of them, looking surprised when he sank in farther than he'd anticipated.

I laughed. "Sorry, General. Should have warned you about that."

"It's fine," he said. "Might need a little help getting up again, but it's sort of comfortable."

I nodded and took a seat on one of the other couches. Layla sat beside me.

"The President believes the threat from the elven legion is real," the general said. "And he's inclined to offer whatever aid you might require."

Layla and I exchanged glances. "That's a relief to hear. Is he talking about the military?"

The general nodded. "As I said, whatever aid you might require. Including Secret Service protection."

I snorted. "The Secret Service? Really?"

"You're a valuable asset, Caspar. We can't risk any harm coming to you. Just say the word, and it can be arranged."

"I think that might be a good idea," I said. "We're pretty sure the elf king has assassins here to take me out."

"Would you accompany me to Washington?" the general asked. "The President would like to speak to you in person."

I bit my lip. An invitation to the White House? How could I decline?

"I'm not sure we have the time for that," Layla added. "My father's legions could launch an assault at any time."

"And you're certain he'd attack here, in St. Louis?"

I cocked my head. It hadn't occurred to me that the elf king would attack anywhere else. This was the epicenter of everything that had happened so far. Then again, if I was going to attack another world, would I start where the only person who had a chance to stop me lived? Or would I try to evade him at all costs?

"It's a fine point," Layla said. "Under normal circumstances, I'd be inclined to agree that you might have other assets in other parts of your country that he'd prioritize. But I've seen my father's wars my whole life, and he almost always attacks the enemy's strength first."

General Breeland pressed his lips together. "Perhaps, Layla, you're the one we should speak to at greater length. Our intelligence regarding your father and his capabilities is virtually nonexistent. All we know is what the elf who founded our chapter in Washington told us."

"Let me guess," Layla said. "Hector said you wouldn't stand a chance."

"When facing conventional threats, our military is second to none. But if we've learned anything in the war on terror and the wars we've fought abroad for the last couple of decades, it's that when it comes to unconventional methods of battle, our usual methods are not as effective as we'd like."

"My father has capabilities that even I am not aware of," Layla said. "I'm afraid he's hidden a lot from me. He used me to gather intelligence on this world while hiding his true intentions."

"That might still be useful," the general said. "Sometimes, just as important as knowing the enemy's capabilities is to know what the enemy knows about yours."

Layla shook her head. "Even in that respect, I'm afraid to say, I might not be as much help as you hope. I know what I've reported over the years about your world, but most of what I've shared has been cultural. Tidbits about this world's people, the values Americans and other people share. He knows as much about your military and the wars you've fought as the common citizen might. I cannot account for whatever Hector might have shared before he died."

General Breeland smiled wide. "We have that covered. Do you think any of us seriously accepted his proposal of surrender?"

Layla sighed. "I don't know. You realize they can manipulate the weather, right?"

"So we've been told," the general said. "But it seems your fellow elves underestimated American resolve. I'll simply say we were more open than we'd normally be with him. We talked quite a bit with him about what we might or might not be capable of."

"Why would you do that?" I asked.

"Oh, we didn't tell him the truth about much," General Breeland said. "When you're at a disadvantage in terms of the information you have about an enemy, the second-best thing you can do is make sure the information they're gathering is inaccurate."

"So, you gave him disinformation?" I asked.

"Of course we did," General Breeland said. "Many of the cultists who feigned loyalty to the elves were doing exactly what we wanted them to do. They shared information liberally and gave him the impression they were his allies. All the while, very little of what they told him will prove useful."

I scratched my head. "We were thinking we could maybe lure him here sooner than he intends. I might have a way to open a portal to New Albion."

The general nodded. "I still say you should come with me to Washington. The President insists."

"Even if it leaves the city vulnerable?" Layla asked.

"We can have you in Washington and back in less than a day," the general said. "I am not at liberty to tell you more than what the President has allowed me to share, particularly not here. We can't be sure who might be listening, but the Oval Office is secure. And I think you'll find what he has to share with you exceedingly helpful."

CHAPTER THIRTY

I hadn't ridden in a limousine since my senior prom. That one didn't compare to this one.

Thinking back on it, I felt a little bad for the limo driver we'd hired for the night. After hanging out the sunroof acting like imbeciles, we got pulled over and warned by the cops that if we didn't behave, our night would be spent not at the school dance but at the local city-sponsored criminal resort, aka jail.

And we didn't even tip the driver. We were just teenagers being morons. I didn't envy that driver's job.

No such antics this time. I expected that standing up and spreading my arms over the sunroof, shouting, "I'm the king of the world" wouldn't go over well with the general.

The whole king of the world thing, besides being reminiscent of the movie *Titanic*, wasn't funny at the moment, given the circumstances. Layla's father was intent on becoming exactly that.

This limo had much less of a party feel to it. Sure, there were drinks. The seats were comfortable. It had that new car smell that everyone loves, and rather than being accompanied by my high school buddies and their dates, or mine (who, the last I'd heard, had married a postal worker and had five children), we were sitting with the Secretary of Defense and two congressmen.

Senators Flumer and McDonnell. I didn't know much about them except that they were usually on opposite sides of every issue. Even now, they weren't talking much.

The ride was awkward, and it didn't get much better when we boarded the government jet. At least the limos that met us in Washington split us up. The senators had their limos waiting, and Layla and I joined the general in a third limo to take us to the White House.

I thought that the general probably didn't get this kind of armored car escort all the time. When Breeland had mentioned Secret Service protection, he hadn't been joking.

It was all weird to me. I mean, who was I? Until now, I was mostly insignificant from the government's perspective. Just a common preacher who paid his taxes, tried to follow most of the laws, and stayed to himself.

Now, it seemed, I was Asset Number One. Were they even going to let me go back home to my apartment after this? Agnus would be pissed if he didn't get his evening tuna.

A whole cadre of black-suited, sunglass-wearing agents surrounded General Breeland, Layla, and me as we exited the limo. We followed them through a series of doors unlocked by one of the agents who was communicating with someone through an earpiece, entering passcodes on doors, and passing through a bunch of other security measures.

We were all frisked and taken through metal detectors and body scanners, the sort they had at airports so TSA agents could creep on you naked even though you were clothed.

It seemed silly since Layla and I could wield magic. They'd all seen just how much magic I could wield the night before. Now that I thought about it, I presumed these Secret Service agents weren't surrounding us for my protection but for the President's.

I'd only ever seen one President in person, and that was

before he was President. Then-candidate Obama had held a massive rally on the grounds of the St. Louis Arch back in 2008. I was just a seminary student at the time, but even I couldn't help but be captured by his charisma. I stood there with the rest of the crowd, holding "Change You Can Believe In" signs and shouting "Yes, We Can!"

I was about to stand face to face with the current President. Butterflies churned in my stomach. What would I even say? Probably something uncalculated and dumb since I tended to do that when I was nervous.

We stepped through the door.

The President was sitting at his desk in the Oval Office, but I didn't see him since a much larger and imposing figure was in my line of sight.

When we stepped into the room, he stood up. I couldn't believe it!

"Brag'mok?" I exclaimed, tripping over my tongue. "I thought you were dead!"

CHAPTER THIRTY-ONE

Hugging a giant is risky. You know, given the likelihood of being squished.

"I thought you were dead!"

"So did I," the giant said. "It's a long story."

"Apologies, Mister President," I said, turning to the man I'd expected to meet. "I just…I thought he was dead!"

The President laughed as he stood up, a wide smile on his face. He was a little taller than I'd anticipated. Television can be deceptive when it comes to height.

"Caspar Cruciger," the President said, shaking my hand before turning to Layla. "Princess Brightborn, I presume?"

I nodded. My nerves hadn't settled, and I was still floating on Cloud Nine since Brag'mok was alive.

"Take a seat," the President said. "*Mi casa es su casa.*"

I smiled. "Literally, right? The White House is the people's house, isn't it?"

The President nodded. "Which was why I said it."

So much for my half-hearted attempt at light humor. I suppose when the joke was exactly what someone intended and not a joke at all, it loses its effect.

I stood awkwardly for a second before realizing Layla had taken a seat on one of the leather chairs around his desk.

I took the hint and sat down.

"Again," I said. "Apologies, Mr. President. I guess you're used to people being nervous when they meet you, but I'm still shocked by all this."

Before the President could speak, a green glow formed to the right side of his face, and Ensley appeared, perched on the President's shoulder.

"Ensley?" I asked. "You're here, too? Where have you been?"

"Helping this oaf of a giant come back from the dead!" Ensley said. "Technically, he wasn't dead."

"But you said you saw him fall."

"I did," Ensley said. "But my subjects healed him before his spirit departed from his body. When they came to Earth and found me, I didn't have any time to waste. I had to get to him and bring him back here. To Earth, I mean."

I just sat there shaking my head. "I'm sorry. I'm speechless right now. You two have been in Washington all this time?"

"They arrived late last night," the President said. "Caused quite the stir. A giant of a man and a pixie."

"Fairy," Ensley corrected.

"Apologies," the President said. "A giant and a fairy appeared out of thin air at the foot of my bed. I'd never heard the First Lady scream so loud!"

I laughed. "I can only imagine the ruckus that must've caused."

"I would have pressed the emergency security button next to my bed," the President said. "But Ensley here had somehow managed to superglue my hands to my thighs."

I chuckled. "Sounds like him."

Ensley just smiled and shrugged.

"Eventually, I'm sure the hair will grow back on my thighs," the President said, shaking his head.

"You're lucky it's just your thighs," I said. "He put Nair in my shampoo bottle once."

The President winced. "Nair? Seriously, Ensley?"

"I have to say, Mister President. Your reaction to the presence of a giant and a fairy was remarkably calm."

"You'd be surprised the things you encounter in this job. Ever heard of Area Fifty-One?"

"Of course," I said. "What's there, anyway?"

The President snorted. "I could tell you, Caspar, but then I'd have to kill you."

I laughed. Then I noticed the President wasn't laughing with me.

"Seriously?" I asked.

The President stared at me blankly for two long seconds, but he couldn't hold back his shit-eating grin. "I'm sorry, I couldn't resist. You should've seen the look on your face!"

"So, there aren't alien spaceships there? And you aren't secretly in talks with little green men?"

"Not at all," the President said.

I laughed.

"They aren't so little and not exactly green. I'd call it more chartreuse. But calling them tall, lanky, otherworldly chartreuse hominids doesn't have the same ring to it."

I cocked my head. "Really?"

"I'm fucking with you, Caspar," the President said.

"So, are you saying that there are, or aren't aliens that you know of?"

The President grinned. "It's classified."

"Of course it is."

"Back to the task at hand," the President continued. "I've learned quite a bit from Braggie here."

"Brag'mok," my giant of a friend said, correcting him.

"Your kind not much on nicknames?" the President asked.

"'Your kind?'" Brag'mok replied. "What's that supposed to mean?"

The President winced. "I didn't mean. I'm sorry. That must've sounded prejudiced."

"I was going to say racist," the giant said.

The President tapped his fingers on his desk. You could've cut the tension in the room with a knife.

Then Brag'mok burst out laughing. "I'm sorry! I couldn't resist. As you'd say, Mister President, I was fucking with you."

The President tilted his head, then started laughing. He was so tickled he slapped his hand on his desk. "I like this guy! I have to say, people who come see me, they're always so formal, so anxious. It's easy for me to take advantage of that. I do so much of the fucking, it's nice to get fucked sometimes. Fucked with, rather. That came out wrong."

CHAPTER THIRTY-TWO

The whole experience was surreal. I had just sat with the President of the United States and a friend I'd thought was dead and another who had been missing, along with the elf princess I was in love with. We discussed how to thwart the plans of an elf king from another planet who intended to take ours over.

They didn't prepare me for this shit in seminary.

General Breeland stayed behind after our discussions to talk over plans and recommendations. Brag'mok had already been through a series of interviews with various members of the President's team, and they wanted to follow up with Layla and me individually.

Those interviews were not as delightful as our encounter with the President. He had been surprising, almost unusually normal. I'd expected him to be the politician I'd seen on television, campaigning, answering questions from the press and the like, but there was a crassness to him in person that was oddly charming.

Couldn't say that about the black suits who interviewed us afterward. They behaved precisely the way you'd expect of someone who worked in government and was accustomed to keeping corn cobs up their ass.

I knew the sort. None of them were like that in their daily lives, but this was their second life, the place where they wore a façade. They had to act like people they weren't because that was what was expected.

Kind of like being a minister. The constant pressure to watch your mouth, to appear semi-happy even when you aren't, the false piety and pseudo-Christlikeness that only showed up during official church business. Such was my life before. And such was, in my experience, the life of most pastors—and apparently, government officials.

Sure, the façade they had to wear was different. Closer to assholiness than being Christlike. No false happiness or joy, but a perpetual air of formality that left me with the impression that their emotional intelligence was closer to that of Schwarzenegger's Terminator than to real humans.

The Secret Service folks stayed near us at all times. I still suspected they weren't as concerned about protecting us as with protecting others and the President in particular from us.

And I was the only one who was a citizen. The rest of them, Layla, Brag'mok, and Ensley, were illegal aliens.

I expected ICE agents to show up at any time, but to deport them to where exactly? Instead, before we left, we were told they'd been granted temporary asylum. They were refugees, and particularly in Brag'mok's case, I doubted they were inclined to simply release them into the community. But they also took the threat of invasion seriously. This wasn't the first time they'd considered it. It had been on their radar as a matter requiring high-security clearance to discuss ever since Hector had shown up and founded the Elf Gate Cult.

They sent a guy named Darrishaw with us. He was the primary contact between us, the Secret Service, the President, the military, and anyone representing the government. I didn't know

Darrishaw's first name. He was just Darrishaw, a handsome man, clean-cut and only slightly more personable than the rest of them.

I prodded him on the flight. Ensley could have ported us back, but the flight provided an opportunity to get to know this Darrishaw fellow and try to sort out how the government planned to help us. All I learned was that he was a former Navy Seal who had served in Iraq and Afghanistan. I asked him about his family, and he said he had one. I suppose that when you're dealing with threats and assets like us, you keep your personal life out of it.

"The general has requested a demonstration of your abilities," Darrishaw said during the flight. "Will that be possible?"

I snorted. "I'd like a demonstration of my abilities too. I just got them. I don't know what I'm capable of."

Darrishaw pressed his finger to his ear. Someone was listening and giving him feedback on the other end.

"Besides," Layla added, distracting Darrishaw from the voice in his head. "If you still want us to attempt to lure the elven legion here, we need to move before my father does."

He extended his index finger in the universal though unofficial sign for "wait just a second." He took a few steps away, just outside of where we could hear. If he was trying to avoid being heard by us, fat chance. Ensley was on it.

But when all Darrishaw ever said was "yup," and "uh-huh," and "yes, sir" to whoever was on the other end of his earpiece, it was virtually impossible to know what he was being told, even with Ensley sneaking around in the ether.

"The President agrees," Darrishaw said, walking back over to us. "It would be better if we struck sooner rather than later."

"Preemptive war?" I asked. "Not expedient politically."

Darrishaw answered, "It's only preemptive if we commit the first act of aggression. We have no stated treaties with the elves and they aren't covered by international law, and ideally, whatever happens will remain off the official books."

I nodded. Sounded like deep-state shit. Off the books. Of course, he was right. Our plan wasn't to attack the elves, it was to lure them here. They'd only come if that was what they'd intended all the while. The elves would be invading the US, not the other way around, though strictly speaking, I'm not sure the President wouldn't have preferred we launch an assault on New Albion. But without a satellite to provide a lay of the land or to guide US missiles, a preemptive strike would have to be on foot, boots on the ground. The elves might not have firearms, but they didn't need them. The sort of magic they used to wage wars was far more devastating, and the elves knew a little about human military tactics. The US government knew next to nothing about elven war.

"The President has ordered troops to back up your position," Darrishaw said, flashing me a satellite map on his phone. "Are these the proper coordinates?"

I nodded. "At the confluence of the Mississippi and the Meramec."

"The general recommends that we keep our distance. Best not to be seen. We'll engage when the enemy is exposed and most vulnerable."

"Assuming this works," I said. "We still don't know King Brightborn will make his move if we open the gate."

"He'll do something," Layla said. "We can be sure of that."

"If the elven king suspects you are opening the gate, he'll likely think you're doing it to destroy it like before," Brag'mok said. "The fairies he's been manipulating, forcing to help him under pain of death, are limited. They've only been able to forge portals large enough to bring three or four through at a time."

"If that's the case," Layla said, "he'll make a move soon. If he thinks we might be trying to seal the gate, he won't waste any time."

"But I didn't close the gate," I said. "When B'iff sacrificed himself, the magic blew the thing wide open. It didn't close."

"But what if you do the opposite? Say, rather than overwhelming the ley lines with magic, you draw from them and extract as much magic as possible."

I shrugged. "Can I even do that?"

"I'm not certain," Brag'mok said. "Elemental power is not well understood on New Albion. We have those who can wield it, but we always believed it was just a difference in how the individual engaged the magic. We didn't know that different kinds of magic run together through the ley lines."

I shook my head. "I wish Aerin was here right now. She'd know what to do."

Layla nodded. "I never thought I'd say it, but I agree. We could use her insight about now. Where the hell did she go?"

I shrugged. "Probably went dress shopping."

"Not funny, Caspar." Layla shook her head.

"I was joking, Layla. You realize I'm not marrying her no matter what."

Layla asked, "What if we're wrong and she's right? What if you have to in order to save the world?"

I rolled my eyes. "A prophecy is a sign of things that will come to pass. I can't imagine any scenario that would require a marriage to get a strategic advantage over your dad."

"That's not necessarily true," Brag'mok said. "King Brightborn's primary objective is to conquer Earth, but if he suspects you've spurned his daughter for another and she returns to him in remorse with something he could use, that could work."

"What could we possibly give him that he'd want?" I asked.

"Me," Ensley said. "If I go with her, the fairies he's using will follow my command. We could bring his legions here."

I was puzzled. "Why would I have to marry Aerin to make that happen?"

"King Brightborn is in communication with his operatives

here," Brag'mok said. "If your wedding is public like your trials were…"

"He'd have reason to believe you did reject me," Layla finished.

I grunted. "I can't do it. I'm not marrying her. I'm not marrying anyone other than Layla."

Layla cocked her head. "You want to marry me?"

"Of course I do!" I said.

Layla smiled a little. "I suppose I knew that, but hearing you say it is good."

"Besides," I said, "Aerin isn't here, so the point is moot."

"I'm just saying," Brag'mok said. "It isn't strictly true that there might not be a strategic reason to do as the drow intends."

"What is going on?" Darrishaw asked, moving toward our group. "Are you reconsidering the plan?"

"Not at all," I said.

"It's just a possible Plan B," Brag'mok added.

"More like a Plan Z," I snapped. "Too risky, altogether unacceptable, and we don't even know where the people we'd need to pull it off are. So to answer your question again and more emphatically this time, there have not and will not be any changes to the plan."

"Understood," Darrishaw said. "I've been told that you should expect a small contingent from the National Guard there within the hour. Two at most."

I cocked my head. "An hour? That's fast."

"The President has deemed this a critical matter of national security. You'd be surprised how quickly we can mobilize, and he's had this in the works since we left DC. He wants this handled quickly, discreetly, and forcefully."

"Forcefully?" I asked.

"To leave the enemy no doubt that we mean business and are more than capable of defending ourselves," Darrishaw said.

Layla winced. She didn't say it out loud, but I could tell from the look on her face that she wasn't convinced a small contingency of the National Guard would be enough.

I wasn't either. How forceful would that be when King Brightborn intended to bring a legion to Earth that he believed could dominate the world? But Darrishaw also made it clear that the President wanted this handled discreetly. I suppose a large-scale mobilization would be anything but discreet.

But I had to wonder if they underestimated Brightborn. If I couldn't stop him, how long would they insist on discretion? It wouldn't be long before the elves forced the issue into the open. Then everyone would be asking, if the President knew this was coming, why didn't he do more to stop it at ground zero?

CHAPTER THIRTY-THREE

When the plane landed, a military convoy was waiting for us. It was a step down from the limousine and armored car escort we'd had before. I'd given Darrishaw the location: the confluence of the Meramec and the Mississippi, which was also the confluence of the ley lines.

There was one major problem with Plan A. I wasn't sure how to channel pure magic into the ley lines. Step one: overcharge the lines, blow the gate open. Step two: pull magic out of them to give Brightborn the impression I was trying to close the gate.

The first part was to give him the opportunity. The second was to let him know it was only available for a limited time.

But elemental magic? What I'd done so far had brought the elemental powers to the forefront in me. Then I had manipulated the elements that were already there using that power. I had fairy magic, of course, and I could make portals. With Ensley's help, I could probably make one directly to New Albion. If Brightborn's assassins had done it with lesser fairies, we could do it too. But this wasn't a temporary portal. It was an intersection of ley lines that, together, had been manipulated by ancients to create a permanent connection between Earth and New Albion.

It wasn't originally done here in St. Louis. The ancient druids, who later evolved into elves, and the giants came from what was then known as Albion, now Britain. Somewhere in Wales, I think. At some point, another gateway was forged that connected New Albion to the confluence of ley lines here in St. Louis of all places.

I couldn't draw pure magic out of nowhere, but I could use the magic inside me to engage the magic in the ley lines. Earth magic was the magic of the elements. With all five at my disposal, as I stood at the confluence of the ley lines, I could sense a connection.

I'd engaged the magic from the ley line beneath the Meramec before, but not the Mississippi, which was the stronger of the two. I'd have to draw magic from both sides and force it into the confluence, where the gate usually formed.

In theory, if it caused a surge like what had happened when B'iff died and the Blade of Echoes was cast into the source at Meramec Springs, it should blast the gateway open.

Then it would push all the magic away like Moses parting the Red Sea, only I'd have to push the magic in four directions. Just enough to weaken the gate, to tempt the elven king to move before he was prepared.

Presuming he wasn't prepared already.

I couldn't say I was sold on our plan, but it was the best option we had. I just didn't like the idea that so much depended on what Brightborn decided to do.

What if he realized we were bluffing?

I didn't know if it would even work. I couldn't keep the confluence devoid of magic indefinitely. The ley lines would eventually force magic back to where the gate was forged.

"Ensley," I asked as the shocks on the military transport vehicle we were in bounced me up and down, "this gateway was originally forged through a partnership between fairy and human, correct?"

"Originally, yes," he said.

"Is there any reason we couldn't just seal the gate permanently? If we could just close it, why would we need to blast it open?"

"Because my father has other ways to get here," Layla reminded me.

"Indeed," Ensley agreed. "He still holds enough of my kin that even if he has to portal three or four legionnaires at once, eventually he could get his whole legion here."

"How do we know he hasn't been doing that?" I asked.

Ensley shrugged. "If he has, they've remained disciplined. I haven't sensed any use of magic, or none apart from when you were conducting the trials."

"And they used that as cover to steal the artifacts from the drow," I said, shaking my head.

"If Brightborn takes the bait," Brag'mok said, "this is the best opportunity we will have."

I shook my head. "Something about this just isn't sitting right with me."

"We could still wait for Aerin to return," Layla said. "I don't like Brag'mok's idea either, but it wouldn't be real. It's just a ceremony, right? Nothing says you'd have to consummate it."

I raised my eyebrow. "You're seriously considering that idea after all the jealousy before?"

"I know you love me, Caspar. This would just be a formality. It isn't like a wedding is a magic spell that forces you to fall in or out of love with someone."

I shook my head. "Not magical, but it *is* meaningful. Which is why divorce is so painful. What God has joined together, let man not separate."

Layla cocked her head. "So now it's religion that's the issue?"

"Yes and no," I said. "It's that. My beliefs about marriage, sure. But it's also my experience. Look, it's not an option. I don't care what her prophecy says."

"It isn't just her version of the prophecy," Layla said. "I mean, our prophecy spoke of love. Hers, it seems, speaks of marriage. Isn't it possible that both are right? That your heart would belong to me according to the elven prophecy, but you would marry her like the drow version of the prophecy suggests?"

I folded my arms. "I can't believe you of all people are pushing this idea."

"I'm not," Layla said. "I'm just saying if you aren't sure luring my father through the gate early is going to work, there are other options."

"Layla," I said. "Say we went through with it. You'd have to go back to New Albion. You'd have to pretend you were remorseful through whatever penance or punishment your elders think is necessary."

"Most likely a series of lashings," Layla explained helpfully.

I cocked my head. "Yeah, that isn't happening. I'm not going to marry someone else just to send the woman I love to go get beaten to prove a false loyalty to her jerk of a father."

Layla smiled. "Well, when you put it like that… "

"And he might kill you," I said.

"I don't think so. I mean, he's still my father."

"Who has lied to you about his real intentions your entire life, Layla."

Layla nodded. "I suppose that's true, but he still has a prophecy. The elves still believe in it. If I go back, it allows him to set me up with another suitor and parade the guy as if he's the chosen one. If that happens, he might even be able to convince the elders to bypass the penance I'd normally have to suffer."

I snorted. "So now we both have to marry people we don't love, just to deceive your father?"

"Just an idea. Last resort sort of thing."

"Not happening, Layla," I said. "And if I'm honest, it hurts that you'd even consider it."

"To save your planet, Caspar? To save both our worlds? To see the prophecy fulfilled? I'd still love you, and we'd still find our way back to each other eventually."

I sighed. "Maybe. How do we know how everything would shake out? So much of all we've been planning ends at the same place. It depends on how your father decides to respond to what we do."

"He has a point," Brag'mok said. "In our experience fighting your father, the one thing we always knew would happen in battle was that he'd do something unpredictable."

"It's a game of chess," I said. "Right now, there's only one move we can make."

"And we need to be prepared to make the right move after he responds," Layla said. "Even if he doesn't do what we're anticipating. Even if the move we have to make isn't one we like."

CHAPTER THIRTY-FOUR

There were tanks, several Humvees, and camouflaged trucks that probably had technical names I didn't know. And yes, tanks. Did I mention they'd sent tanks?

"Holy crap," I said. "Those are tanks!"

Darrishaw smiled. "I told you we'd be prepared."

Layla smiled back. "Let's hope that's enough."

"These are tanks, Layla. It's like the Chuck Norris of the military."

"You mean, outdated and less effective than the reputation warrants?"

I gasped. "Sacrilege to say such things about Chuck Norris. You'd better hope he doesn't find you."

Layla rolled her eyes. "What would happen if he did?"

I stared at her blankly and ran my thumb across my throat, the universal sign that indicates throat-slashing.

Layla chuckled. "If he's so deadly, what are we doing here? Why not just open a portal to New Albion and send Chuck Norris after the legion?"

"We tried," Darrishaw interjected. "Mister Norris said he had a prior commitment."

"Something more important than saving the world?" I asked.

"It's Chuck Norris," Darrishaw said. "Whatever he's doing, you can be sure it's huge."

I giggled. At least I now knew Darrishaw was human. I'd thought he was a cyborg until now, given his stoic demeanor.

"We've been coordinating our plan with yours," Darrishaw said. "Brag'mok and Layla will stay with us and provide us intelligence about what's happening on the ground while you try to open the gate like you suggested."

I nodded. "Sounds good."

"We took the liberty of providing a standard-issue wetsuit. We figured you'd appreciate it since the plan calls for you to get a little wet."

"Thanks for that. Certainly better than trying to start a war in my skivvies."

Darrishaw replied, "Of course. Also, this suit will allow us to monitor your vitals, and you'll also be issued standard comms."

"Comms for underwater?" I asked. "That's pretty cool."

"You won't be able to speak, but there's a basic set of controls wired into the device. One click does nothing. That's just to avoid accidental messages. Two clicks means enemy incoming. Three means you're clear and we should open fire on the location."

"Is there a signal if he's in trouble and needs help?" Layla asked.

"Press and hold the button on your comms for three seconds. But we'll also be monitoring your vitals."

I shook my head. "When I'm in the ley lines, I don't need to breathe. I can't say if my vitals will read normally or not."

"Good to know," Darrishaw said. "We'll monitor for abnormalities, and if the medical team identifies anything that signals a crisis, we'll act."

"And someone will be in my ear the whole time?" I asked.

Darrishaw nodded. "You should be aware of our intentions.

You'll be given instructions to click twice to confirm or approve any order before we issue it."

"And if I disapprove?" I asked.

"Click three times."

"A lot to remember," I said.

"Don't worry. We'll be in your ear. They will periodically ask you to respond in certain ways to confirm you are still viable. They may ask you to click twice, three times, whatever. If you make an error, they'll ask you to do it again. Two errors in a row will be taken as an SOS, and we'll move to exfil."

"Exfil?" I asked.

"Exfiltration. It means removing a soldier, or in this case, the civilian subject from a hostile position."

"So if I need exfil, I can either request it by pressing and holding the button, or if I screw up any of the signals, you all will assume I need help and come for me anyway?"

Darrishaw nodded.

"Thing is," I said, "I doubt the soldiers can even enter the ley lines without magic. Second, even if they managed to get there, I'm not sure they'd survive it."

Darrishaw nodded. "Then let's hope we won't need to do it, but if push comes to shove, given your unique abilities, your survival is the priority."

"Over the lives of the other soldiers?" I asked.

"We've been told to ensure your survival at all costs," Darrishaw said. "So if saving you would put my men in danger, how about you do me a favor and don't screw this up?"

"Yes, sir!" I said, feigning enthusiasm. I didn't intend to mess this up. It wasn't the first time I'd dealt with the ley lines, and I was more powerful now than I'd ever been. I could feel the magic as we drew near to the source. I could not only sense just the magic in the ley lines, but also how it resonated with each of the five elemental spirits. As we got closer to the source of the magic in the earth, it was like the energies within me swelled.

The cool sensation of water. The burn in my chest from fire. The heaviness and grittiness of earth. The purity of air filling my lungs. And the thrill, the freedom, of aether.

By these powers combined, I am Captain Planet!

Okay, sorry. I couldn't resist. Watched too many episodes of that show growing up.

Captain Planet was better than the code name they'd given me on comms: Magic Seal.

Made me sound like an off-brand press-and-seal sandwich bag.

I should have been flattered. I figured the term "Seal" was reserved for those who'd completed their BUD/S training. I only knew that much since one of the members at Holy Cross had a grandson who was a Seal. We'd prayed for him regularly, even when he was in BUD/S. She was proud. We all were, for her.

I shook my head, thinking about it. I wasn't part of those people's lives anymore, but it wasn't the job I'd miss. It was the people. I could keep in touch with most of them through e-mail, social media, or Philip, but what would they think of me? Most of them weren't thrilled about all the recent changes. My excommunication would probably be viewed as vindication that they were right to be concerned, or so they'd believe.

I probably wouldn't reach out to anyone from the church. That chapter of my life was over. It didn't mean I wouldn't miss the people, and it certainly didn't mean that I wasn't still fighting for their salvation.

But now, I was doing it differently. I was diving into the ley lines, hoping to lure a deadly elven legion to Earth for them. For the people I'd always wanted to give hope to. For the people I cared about. For the world, as broken and as cruel as it could be, that I loved. For love. For Layla, because this was her home now too.

They passed me around to several military folks who, in their fatigues, helped me into my wet suit, hooked up my comms, and ran me through a series of tests to make sure I understood how the signal system worked.

I was impressed by their competency. This was undoubtedly a unique situation. I couldn't imagine that they'd trained for anything like this, but they were operating like they'd done this mission a thousand times.

They couldn't have been as calm on the inside as they appeared.

I could see it in their eyes, a mixture of curiosity, determination, and fear. I was doing this to save them too.

I just hoped I could.

I shook Brag'mok's hand. Fucker didn't know his own strength. His hand enveloped mine, and he squeezed harder than I'd have liked.

I winced, swallowing the pain.

Then I glanced at Ensley, who'd made an appearance on Brag'mok's shoulder. "No pranks, right? You didn't fill this suit with Gorilla Glue or anything?"

Ensley giggled. "Damn! I wish I'd have thought of that! But no, no pranks this time. May the Furies be with you, my friend!"

I made a mental note. If we survived this, I'd have to ask him about the Furies. I suspected they had something to do with fairy magic. If push came to shove, I could use it, hopefully before any of the soldiers risked their lives in a futile exfil attempt.

When I looked at Layla, I don't know why, but tears started to well up in my eyes. She was tearing up too.

"I love you, Layla,"

"I love you too, Caspar."

I kissed her as if it was going to be our last time because when it came to things like this, there was always the chance it might be.

CHAPTER THIRTY-FIVE

I dove into the river. By dove, I mean belly-flopped. I'd tried to learn how to dive as a child. Took swimming lessons. Earned my swimming merit badge in the Boy Scouts. But when it came to diving, I sucked. I always hesitated a split second too long, kicking my legs out behind me and tucking my head. The result?

Belly-flops every time.

Thankfully, my swimming ability wasn't in question, nor was it relevant.

The moment I hit the water, I felt the elemental power of water and its coolness well up inside of me. I didn't need to swim. I created a current around my body. The rivers would obey me. I could have stopped their currents if I'd wanted to. I almost did, but I figured it would probably flood the city upstream. Instead, I created a current of my own that carried me deep into the water.

I knew where the gate had formed: right at the confluence. I could feel where it changed, where the current grew stronger as the force of the Meramec was added to that of the Mississippi.

But it wasn't the rivers' currents I needed to harness; it was the Earth magic, the magic of the elements coursing through the ley lines just beneath the muddy riverbeds.

So much power flowing through my body was overwhelming. I didn't feel human anymore. I wasn't just a man, charging through the water like a torpedo.

"Base to Magic Seal. Click twice to confirm status."

I clicked the button twice. So far, so good.

I didn't feel like myself. With so much power around me, consuming me, the woman's voice in my comm was barely audible by contrast.

I was the magic. The ley lines were part of me. How had Ensley described manipulating magic? It was like I had new arms and legs extending in four directions.

All I had to do was flex like Jag, admiring himself in front of the gym mirror.

I didn't know how much it would take to blow open the gate.

I pulled in magic from all four directions and concentrated on the confluence where the gateway usually formed. Streams of magic colored blue, red, green, white, and gold coalesced on my frame.

There was a pop in my ear, then static. So much for the military comm. It was waterproof but not magic-proof. I could only hope they wouldn't overreact and attempt an exfil. So far, everything was going exactly as planned, other than the comms shorting out. I'd hate for that little hang-up to spoil the whole mission.

When the magic forces collided at the confluence, a luminescent gold circle formed and expanded.

It was working; I'd blown up the gate.

Step two, try to draw the magic back out of it. Give the elven king the notion that we'd done it by accident while we were trying to destroy the gate.

I inhaled, drawing all the magic I could back through the gate.

It poured on me like a deluge. Like I'd uncorked a dam and all the water it was holding back came flooding through.

Too much.

I tried to slow it down. I tried to focus. I needed balance; that was what Aerin had taught me. But no matter how much I tried, more and more magic poured through the gate.

It consumed my body. Why it wasn't ripping me apart or exploding me into a million molecules I wasn't sure, but I couldn't contain anymore. I couldn't force it back into the ley lines.

I tried, but it was as if I'd overwhelmed the source.

The gold gate expanded into a massive column of magic, then poured out of the water and into the sky.

It carried me with it.

Other bodies all around me. I felt them. I could sense them, some of them attempting to strike me.

Elves!

Like a blur, hundreds of them flowing through the magic, each taking their best shot.

But they couldn't break through the magic that formed around me.

The king had taken the bait. He'd sent his legions through.

But this magic was more than I'd channeled into the gate. It was like I'd pulled more through the gate—the magic I'd previously used to recharge New Albion, all of it exploding into a mushroom cloud above the confluence. A magical bomb with all the elemental energies exploding all around us.

I had to focus. I had to get out!

Aether! I could use aether and air.

I harnessed their power and flew like a missile out of the cloud of energies. All I saw below was devastation. The tanks overturned. The whole convoy of military vehicles overturned, some of them on fire, pillars of black smoke pouring out of them.

I harnessed the power of water. Giant bulbs drawn easily from the rivers doused the fires.

Where was Layla? Brag'mok?

A green orb formed in front of me as I soared through the sky.

"Ensley!" I shouted. "Where are they?"

"Just over the ridge. They need your help!"

I nodded and followed Ensley. I couldn't port there since I didn't have a good visual.

Darrishaw was lying in a pool of blood. A dagger like the Blade of Echoes was sticking out of his chest.

Brag'mok was fending off two assassins in black with the broadsword in his hand.

I tossed a stream of fire at each of them, sending them tumbling back.

Brag'mok took advantage and thrust his sword into the gut of one, then withdrew it and did the same to the second.

A third assassin charged him from behind.

I reached for the power of fire again, but an arrow took him out from behind. I followed its trajectory.

"Layla!" I shouted.

She probably didn't hear me, but I dove after her.

She didn't see the assassin behind her, and he was only twenty feet away. I had fire ready to go, and I released it.

The purple magic around him was angelic power. It was Fred. He threw a dagger as I blasted him with fire, but a shell of magic formed around him. He thwarted my blast and disappeared in a violet haze.

I hit the ground, barely landing on my feet. I turned. Layla lay with her bow held tightly in her grip and a dagger in her back.

I ran to her, pulled the dirk out of her back, and pressed my hand into her wound.

"Layla!" I screamed. I had to focus. I'd healed people before. I'd healed a stroke. I'd cured a girl of spina bifida. Surely I could handle this wound! I visualized her wound closing as I channeled the power of aether into her body.

Layla gasped for air. She was alive.

"Caspar!" Ensley shouted. "Behind you!"

I turned. A hundred yards away on one of the bluffs stood King Brightborn. An elf beside him carried a massive flag on a pole—his battle standard, I presumed.

And hundreds if not thousands of legionnaires stood beside and behind him in single-file lines.

Several of them, the most magically adept of them, I assumed, extended their hands to the sky, and they drew on the magic that was pouring out of the gate.

Then, as if they'd had a fairy portal of their own, a circle of magic passed over them, and the entire legion disappeared.

CHAPTER THIRTY-SIX

I pulled a fairy portal over us, and we appeared in my apartment. It was either there or go back to the cult building. I wasn't eager to deal with anyone, not until I knew what had just happened.

We couldn't stay there long, and the cult building wouldn't be safe either. The assassins, at least a few of them, were gone, but Fred was still out there. And who knew where Brightborn and the legion had gone. Chances were good he had more assassins he'd send after us.

I laid Layla on the couch. Agnus jumped up next to her.

"What happened?"

"A dagger to her back," I said, ripping off the back of her shirt.

The wound had healed, but there was a spiderweb of purple spreading out from where the blade had struck her.

I tried to heal her, but it wasn't something I couldn't sense or counteract.

"It burns," Layla said, rubbing the spot where the blade had cut her.

"Purple magic, I think. Fred's blade must've been laced with it."

"It happened fast," Layla said. "As you started to form the gate,

Fred and the assassins started taking down soldiers one by one before we even knew what was happening."

"So many lives," Brag'mok said as he stood in my living room, shock on his face. "Too many lives."

"What happened, Brag'mok?"

"The assassins drew fire from the magic that poured out of the gate and destroyed the military before we could even react. Fred took out Darrishaw."

"Then I showed back up? The legion appeared. By then, it looked like the military force was all dead."

"So many more lives." Brag'mok kept shaking his head.

"What do you mean?" I asked. "Did that magic explosion harm the city?"

"Saint Louis is untouched," Brag'mok said. "I'm talking about New Albion. All the magic you drew through that gate. King Brightborn knew what was happening, even if his legions didn't. He didn't even *try* to stop it!"

"What was happening?" I asked.

"If all the magic was drawn from New Albion—" Layla said, her face white as a ghost's.

"They'd all be dead," Brag'mok said, finishing her thought. "If not immediately, they won't survive for long. Millions of lives! New Albion is as good as gone!"

I sighed. "The prophecy said more lives in a single day than in the history of all of the worlds' wars combined."

Brag'mok nodded. "I fear it is done. The prophecy has been fulfilled unless Brightborn brought the rest of the elves to Earth somewhere else."

I shook my head. "How could he possibly do that?"

"Fairies," Layla said. "If he's somehow convinced the fairies on New Albion to do it."

"But the fairies there," I said, looking at Brag'mok. "They saved you, right? Why would they now align with Brightborn?"

Brag'mok frowned. "The fairies are not aligned with one side or the other. They are and remain on the side of magic. Where they sense an abuse of magic, an injustice committed by such power, they intervene. It is why the fairies, themselves, have so frequently seemed to switch sides. Whoever has most recently misused magic in a way the fae do not endorse becomes the enemy."

I clenched my fist and slammed it on the coffee table. "Goddammit!"

"If no one has survived," Layla said, "that means the only elves that remain are with my father."

"And if they did survive," Brag'mok said, "chances are they're on Earth somewhere, just waiting for Brightborn to seize control of this world."

I screamed, then fell to my knees in tears. "I couldn't control it. I tried, but the magic just kept coming."

"This is not your fault," Brag'mok said. "You could not control it because Brightborn's sorcerers were pulling their magic through with them. They did this."

I shook my head. "But if I hadn't opened the fucking gate…"

"Caspar," Layla said, grabbing my hand. "You didn't do this."

I squeezed her hand back.

"I know, but how the hell am I supposed to unite anyone except the elves if all the giants and most of the elves who lived on your planet are dead?"

"The prophecy can only pertain to the living," Brag'mok said. "There are elves here on your world. There are drow, and perhaps the rest of elven kind is here somewhere. Not to mention, how many factions divide humanity?"

Layla sighed and winced in pain. "There's only one way to unite the elves on Earth," Layla said. "We cannot assume any of my people survived. We must unite with the drow."

"I'm not going to marry Aerin!" I shouted.

"It might be the only way," Layla said. "And we will need their help to defeat my father."

"I don't love Aerin!" I replied. "I love you, Layla!"

"No offense, Caspar," Agnus piped up, "but what's love got to do with it?"

I stared at Agnus.

"Sorry," he said. "I need to work on my timing."

"I'm not even going to consider it," I said. "We have to figure out how to heal you. This infection, I could swear it's spreading. It looks worse, and it's only been a couple of minutes."

"Caspar," Layla said. "If I die, you need to marry her."

"You're not going to die!" I screamed. "God as my witness, I won't let you die, Layla."

Layla pressed her lips together, then smiled and touched my face. "I love you, Caspar."

"I fucking love you too, goddammit!"

Layla chuckled. "And I believe in you. If you can't save me, promise me you will do what you have to do."

I shook my head. "We're not having this conversation."

"Caspar!"

"Ensley!" I shouted. "Aerin is the only one who knows anything about angelic magic. If anyone knows how to heal Layla, it's her. Can you find her?"

"I can try," Ensley said. "But she isn't using magic, and there's so much magic swirling around right now. It's too much."

I didn't have my phone on me. I'd left it with my change of clothes before they put me in this wetsuit. I couldn't text him, but I did have a computer in my apartment. If I was lucky, Jag would have his phone set up to alert him if he got an e-mail. If anyone knew if Aerin was back, he would.

I quickly fired up my computer.

"You've got to be shitting me!" I said.

"What is it?" Layla asked.

"Windows is doing a fucking update."

"I take it that's not a good thing?" Brag'mok asked.

"No!" Layla and I growled in concert.

I watched as it slowly crawled from one percent to two percent.

"We don't have time for this."

It moved a little faster, jumping five percentage points at a time.

It hit one hundred percent.

"Thank God!" I exclaimed.

Then it started back at one percent.

"Goddamn son of a bitch!" I screamed.

"Calm down, Caspar," Layla said. "Just take us to the church. The Elf Gate church. Jag is probably there or at the gym. You've ported to both places before."

I nodded. "Fine. Just trying to avoid, you know, porting into a trap."

"We aren't any safer here than we would be there," Layla pointed out.

I shook my head. "I know. Whatever. Let's go."

We'd try the Elf Gate church first. Jag probably wouldn't be there. It wasn't like he lived there or anything. But at this time, porting to the gym in the group exercise room would probably drop us into the middle of a Zumba class or some shit, and maybe right into someone's body. Not the best idea.

I drew on fairy magic, visualized the cult building, the same place I'd ported before, and formed the gate.

Agnus jumped through.

"Well, I guess he's coming along," I said.

"He is your familiar, after all," Layla said. smiling while rubbing her shoulder. "And it isn't safe to leave him behind. Not after the last time."

I nodded. She was referring to the time Hector had kidnapped, or catnapped, him. Knowing Agnus, that was what he was thinking about too. My apartment wasn't safe, but was any place right now?

Layla, Brag'mok, and I jumped through the portal. Ensley followed me.

I looked around the room. I didn't expect so many people to be at the cult building at this hour. I mean, the trials were over and the cult was divided and in disarray, but these weren't cultists.

I saw twenty people, maybe more, in colorful, ornate clothing. Several of them had blades sheathed at their sides. All of them had dark purple-gray skin and pointy ears. They were drow.

"I'm glad you're here, Naayak," Aerin said. I turned around, and she was standing right behind where the portal had been when it disappeared.

I shook my head. "Glad we didn't port into you. We could have ended up inside you."

Aerin cocked her head and smirked.

"Not like that, Aerin!"

Aerin giggled. "You said it, not me. That wasn't even what I was thinking. I was expecting you, Caspar, after all that has happened."

CHAPTER THIRTY-SEVEN

"The elven legion is here, Aerin," I said.

"I know, Caspar."

"And Layla has been wounded. I can't heal it."

"Let me take a look," Aerin said. "This way."

Layla, Brag'mok, Agnus, and I followed her to the back room with the couches.

"Fred hit me with one of his stupid daggers," Layla said, pulling down the top of her shirt and exposing her wound.

The magic had expanded and was now spider-webbing halfway down her back.

"It's his magic, isn't it?" I asked.

Aerin nodded. "It is."

"Can you do something about it?" I asked.

"I'm afraid I cannot," Aerin said. "But you might be able to."

"How?" I asked. "I tried healing her, but I can't do anything about that magic."

"You will need the artifacts Fred stole," Aerin said. "It's the only way to stop the magic from spreading."

Layla took a deep breath. "He wasn't trying to kill me. Fred knew we'd have to come to him to heal me."

Aerin nodded. "That is likely, though I doubt he was the mastermind behind this."

Layla shook her head. "My father?"

"We need to go to him," I said. "Wherever he is."

"No, Caspar," Layla said. "*I* have to go to him."

"But if I get the artifacts from him," I said, "I can heal you!"

"I agree with Layla," Brag'mok said. "It is risky. Fred will be protected by the legion. If you show up in the middle of them all, they'll kill you, Caspar."

I bit my lip. "I don't think they will."

"Why wouldn't they kill you?" Brag'mok asked.

"The assassins could have killed me already. Why the hell was one of them, presumably Fred, following me on the streets? Look, if these assassins are as good as Layla says they are, there's no reason I should be alive if they wanted me dead all this time."

Layla spoke up. "My father won't allow it. Because if they kill you—"

"If one of us dies, both of us die. We're soul-bound, Layla."

"Does the elven king even know about that?" Brag'mok asked.

"Of course he does," Layla said. "It's the reason he didn't kill Caspar when he had the chance."

"It's why my brother had to stab himself with the Blade of Echoes. To sever the bond between the chosen one and the blade before he sacrificed himself."

"When I healed Caspar, when I used the magic the Blade of Echoes had introduced to his body to heal him and he survived, I was uniting the magic of my soul and spirit to do it. It's why we're soul-fused. My father knew it, which was one reason why he was so pissed about it all. I bound myself like that to a human."

"So, if this angelic power in you now kills you, Caspar will die, too," Aerin said.

"Oddly enough," Layla said, "our connection is one reason why we're both still alive."

"If only there was a way to sever our bond," I said. "Bear with me. I'm just thinking out loud."

"You'd be dead before the night was out," Layla offered.

I shrugged. "Maybe I would have been. Before. When I didn't have this power, but Ensley can't locate the elves right now. There's just too much magic in the air. He can't sense where they are, so we'd have no way to find them and locate Fred to attempt to get the artifacts from him."

Layla shook her head. "It's too risky, Caspar."

"But if they think our bond is severed, there's a chance they'll show themselves. They'll come after me. It's our best chance to locate them."

"Still," Layla said, "there's no way I know of to do that. To sever a bond like that?"

Brag'mok grunted. "When B'iff stabbed himself, the bond between Caspar and the Blade of Echoes was severed, correct? That's why Caspar didn't die when the blade was destroyed."

I nodded. "I think that's correct."

"It is," Layla added.

"What if there was a way to bond Caspar to someone else? To replace the bond you two share..."

Aerin cleared her throat. "There is. But you're not going to like it."

I sighed. "Let me guess."

"When drow marry, we seal our union with a common bond to an object enchanted by aether. The connection binds us together. For the drow, to marry is literally until death parts us, for when one spouse dies, so does the other."

"So, the only way to do this is for us to get married? Why am I even asking that? Of course it is. For fuck's sake."

"It does not mean love, Caspar," Layla said.

"It is true," Aerin said. "I do not love you, Naayak. I know your heart belongs to her. But often, marriages are made not out of love but for politics, to forge alliances, to save kingdoms. Or in this case, the world."

"It still doesn't make sense," I said. "If they are hoping that Layla will return to them, there has to be a way to find them. Brightborn doesn't want her to die."

"He doesn't want me to die," Layla said. "But if it comes down to it, he knows we are desperate."

"If we sever our connection," I said, "we're doing exactly what he wants us to do. We're giving him a chance to kill me but save Layla. We'd be playing right into his hands."

"Perhaps," Layla said. "But it's either that or this magic consumes me, and both of us die."

CHAPTER THIRTY-EIGHT

The Elf Gate Cult...

Correction, the Order of the Elven Gate. Since I was working with these folks, it was probably time I started referring to them by the name they'd given themselves.

Of course, was it even the same Order now that Fred and others had divided their loyalties? I expected that, now that the elven legion was on Earth and they weren't ever going back, other members of the Order would likely follow Fred's lead. Sure, I'd done some impressive tricks taking down those elementals, but I was one man. Brightborn had a whole legion at his command. An army of badass, magic-wielding elves.

I might have persuaded them for a minute, given them a second's pause to consider the idea that I might be able to defeat them.

But let's face it. I couldn't square off with a whole legion. Even with all my newly acquired power, I was still one man.

Anyway, the Order was already set up for live streaming. For a second, I considered porting us to Holy Cross, my old church. Maybe I could convince Philip to do the service. I was kidding myself. If he was seen marrying me to Aerin, he'd meet the same fate with church authorities that I had.

Why did I even care? It wasn't like this was a real marriage, just a formality. A way to give the impression that Layla had reason to reconsider her loyalties and an excuse to untangle our fused souls.

But I didn't like that idea. I had to admit, there was something oddly romantic about the drow tradition of fusing souls when married. I mean, I wasn't sure how many drow there were—probably not many more than Aerin had brought with her. But I was reasonably certain their rate of mariticide was likely a lot lower than among human couples.

But the idea of tying one's life to one's spouse took that whole "flesh of my flesh and bone of my bone" thing that Adam said in Genesis to a new level. The drow took that shit seriously.

That was how it was with Layla and me, and I appreciated it. Our lives were bound together. I didn't resent it even a little. If she died, so would I, and vice versa.

Don't get me wrong. Aerin was hot. Next to Layla, she was the most beautiful creature I'd ever seen, and she was thoughtful, playfully flirty, and wise. What more could a man ask for? I mean, there's the whole female supremacy thing; that was an issue we'd have to work on. But other than, well, her entire worldview, she was a catch.

For some men, that would be tolerable or even thrilling.

But that wasn't the sort of thing you'd find in my browser history.

The doors to the church swung open.

My heart skipped a beat.

My first thought was the elven legion. If it was, maybe it was a blessing in disguise. Sure, we might get our asses handed to us, but I wouldn't have to marry Aerin.

My second thought was that it was the government. Maybe a

Seal team was pissed because I'd gotten the troops sent to back me up slaughtered.

I'd have to deal with that eventually. I wasn't sure how they'd respond, but I did know that they would be far less likely to back up one of our plans in the future. If they helped at all, I'd be doing things their way—which would probably get us destroyed.

But I didn't need to work with the government. They just complicated everything. I only hoped they'd still fight. Let them be a nuisance to Brightborn. A distraction, at least. As long as they didn't surrender.

But the figure that walked through the door was large and imposing. He walked with confidence, though his arms swung a good foot away from the rest of his body on either side.

"Jag!" I said, both excited to see him and relieved that it wasn't any of the other folks it might have been.

"Saw y'all show up on the security feed," Jag said.

"You have security cameras here?" I asked, looking all around but unable to spot a single one.

"The same cameras we used for streaming. I left the gym when I saw Aerin came back. And then you guys showed up."

Jag looked at Brag'mok and cocked his head. "How much you bench, bro?"

Brag'mok shrugged. "Probably two of you."

Jag grinned. "Mad respect, bro. Mad respect."

"Good to see you, Jag," I said. "Nice to see a friendly face."

"What did I miss?" Jag asked.

I gave Jag the short version of all that had happened, just the basics. Magic blew shit up. Elf legion was here. Layla was magically wounded. And now I had to marry Aerin.

"Marry her?" Jag asked, raising one eyebrow.

I nodded. "It's the only way we can think of."

"Care if I move in on your sloppy seconds?"

"Excuse me?" Layla stood there, her hands on her hips. "I'm not sloppy, and Caspar and I aren't breaking up, exactly."

"Dude," Jag said. "You're going to be a polygamist?"

I shook my head. "Not exactly."

"This marriage," Aerin said, "is a matter of necessity, not love. I have no intention of preventing Caspar and Layla…"

"An open marriage!" Jag exclaimed. "Dude. I knew you were a progressive minister, but that's…I don't know what it is. I envy you, bro."

I shook my head. "This isn't something we want, Jag. We have to do it to save Layla."

Jag nodded. "Over my head. But you have my support. Good thing you've been working that cardio. You're going to need it to keep up with these two sexy elves."

I snorted. "I don't think that's what this is about either."

"Dude, don't tell me you aren't going to consummate this?"

I shook my head. "I wasn't planning on it."

Jag scrunched his brow. He was confused. It just wasn't fathomable that I wouldn't take carnal advantage of the situation.

"Look, Jag," I said. "We just need to make sure this goes out on the live stream. Can you make that happen?"

"Totally," Jag said. "But I don't know we can send that to everyone. Children might be watching."

"What are you talking about, Jag?"

"The consummation, dude! What are you talking about?"

"Um, the wedding, Jag. Just the wedding."

"Oh," Jag said, looking genuinely disappointed that I was asking him to be a wedding videographer rather than the director of an adult film.

"Who is going to perform the ceremony?" Jag asked.

I shrugged. "I don't know, Aerin. This is a drow ceremony, right?"

Aerin nodded. "It is, but it would not be bad to include rituals common in human marriage. Our usual rite would not be immediately recognizable as a wedding. We want any who see it to have no doubt that we are getting married."

"Have a minister in mind?" Jag said.

I shook my head. "None of the pastors I know would do it. Not without getting themselves into trouble."

"Then you're in luck!" Jag exclaimed.

"How so?"

Jag stood up straight, tucked his tank-top into his sweatpants, and grinned. "You're looking at the Reverend Jagger."

"Reverend?" I asked. "When did you go to seminary?"

Jag snorted. "I didn't. I paid thirty-five bucks to the Church of Universal Life. I can do weddings, bro!"

I sighed. "This isn't going to be the wedding my mother always had in mind for me, but whatever. It's a second marriage. I can handle that. You're on, Jag."

CHAPTER THIRTY-NINE

This wedding was going to be a joke. Jag as the minister? The love of my life standing in the back of the room, watching it happen? And broadcasting to the world.

I didn't even have a best man.

"Hey!" Agnus blurted. "Where's the sandbox in this shithole? I have to go!"

I cocked my head. "Hey, Agnus. How would you feel about being my best man?"

Agnus cocked his head. "I have to poop, Caspar."

"Yeah, but would you stand up with me at this wedding?"

"Just don't call me a best man," Agnus said. "That's degrading."

I nodded. "I think there's a potted plant or two in the back room. The room with the couches."

"Brilliant!" Agnus exclaimed, taking off as fast as he could run.

Layla was sitting by herself on one of the chairs around the perimeter, the same place she'd sat for the trials. I walked over to her and sat down.

"This sucks," I said.

"It does," Layla agreed, staring into space.

"I'm sorry, Layla."

Layla said, "It has to happen. Just think, both prophecies were correct."

"What do you mean?" I asked.

"I will always love you, Caspar. That's what our prophecy stated—that we'd fall in love. And their prophecy, the one with the drow, was about marriage. I just assumed all this time that love and marriage would go together."

I nodded. "So did I. But you said it, this is just a ceremony. A ritual. It doesn't mean anything."

"But it does, Caspar," Layla said. "Your lives will be bound together when this is done. How can I compete with that?"

I shook my head. "There is no competition, Layla. When my heart stops beating, Aerin's will too. But a lot of people throughout the world die at the same time, and they have no relationship at all. I promise you, Layla, until my heart's last beat, every one will be for you."

A tear fell down Layla's cheek. "I just didn't realize how hard this was going to be. When we were talking about it, it made sense. In my head, I know this is the right thing to do. But in my heart, I fucking hate it."

I nodded. "So do I."

Layla rubbed her eyes.

I leaned over to kiss her.

She turned her face away. "Don't, Caspar. Don't make this any harder than it has to be."

I nodded and stood up. "I love you, Layla."

Layla nodded. "Me too."

Agnus sauntered back into the room.

"Everything come out okay?" I asked.

"It was an artificial Ficus, Casp," Agnus said, shaking his head. "And the soil wasn't real, either. I'm traumatized."

"Sorry, buddy," I said, swallowing a chuckle.

"Whatever," Agnus said. "Bachelor party?"

I shook my head. "Sorry, no time for that."

Agnus growled. "What good is it being your best cat if I can't even get you a few strippers?"

"How would you even go about that?" I asked.

"I was going to get you a Sphynx."

I shrugged. "Isn't that a breed of cat?"

"Hairless. Nude all the time. She wouldn't even need to strip."

I grinned. "I'll just take a rain check on that. After this is over."

Agnus huffed. "Whatever. It was more for me than you anyway."

I nodded. "All you have to do is stand next to me."

"You sure you want that?" Agnus asked. "When people watch and they see you and me, I don't want to overshadow you with my ravishing good looks."

"I get it," I said, reaching down and scratching him behind the ears. "But I think it will be fine. Not to mention, think of all the ladies who will see you there. This might pan out in your favor."

"Please," Agnus said. "As if I don't have enough honeys as it is."

"Honeys?" I asked. "Like who? You never leave the apartment."

"You don't know what I do there when you're gone," Agnus said.

I grinned. "A lot of lounging on the couch."

"If you want to call it that. Lounging…on the couch, on your pillow, on the kitchen counter. Yeah, me and my honeys, we lounge on everything."

"In your fantasies, maybe."

"Keep telling yourself that, Casp. But the next time you pull those soft sheets over your head, just know I've lounged all over them."

I shook my head. I wanted to laugh about it, but I just wasn't in the mood. Agnus was great for a lot of things, but sensing the emotion of the moment wasn't one of them.

Aerin stepped toward the front of the room. Jag was in the middle. One of the other drow approached with a plate, presumably containing whatever enchanted object would be used to bind us together.

Reluctantly, I walked over to what I assumed was supposed to be my position beside Aerin.

"Dearly beloved," Jag said.

I had to bite my tongue. Beloved? Like that was relevant. But we had to put on a show, and Jag was just reading from a sheet. Something, I presumed, that Aerin or some of her fellow drow had put together for him.

"We are gathered here to witness the union of Princess Aerin of the drow and Naayak, also known as Caspar Cruciger, the chosen one of the ancient prophecy of Taliesin."

I looked at Aerin. She was gazing at me in anticipation. She'd been looking forward to this moment since before we met. I'd resisted it the whole time. I was still resisting it, but it was inevitable.

That was what Aerin had said; I didn't have a choice.

I was marrying for love, only it was my love for Layla and my need to save her, not my love for my bride.

"These rings were cast from a single piece of enchanted silver," Jag said as one of the drow knelt in front of us, presenting a plate with two nearly identical rings resting on it.

"By placing these rings on one another's fingers, your lives will forever be bound together as husband and wife. Your lives will be as one. Together you shall live, and together you shall die. Place this ring on one another's fingers and repeat these words: with this ring, I bind my life to you, so long as we both shall live."

Aerin grabbed one of the rings from the plate.

"Your hand," she said.

I nodded and extended my hand to her.

Aerin said the words, "I bind my life to you, so long as we both shall live."

She placed the ring on my finger. I felt a tingle, the magic in the ring melding with the power of aether, the spirit, within me.

"Your turn, Casp," Jag whispered.

I nodded and grabbed the second ring.

Aerin extended her hand.

"I bind my life to you, so long as we both shall live."

My hand was trembling as I put the ring on her finger.

"I now pronounce you Mr. and Mrs. Aerin Nightshade."

I cocked my head. Of course, I'd take her name. Matriarchal drow rules. Blah. I hadn't even known that was her last name—our last name now—until Jag said it.

Naayak Nightshade.

That was what Aerin would call me from now on. I had to admit, it had a ring to it. No pun intended, given the exchange of rings that just happened.

The drow applauded.

"You may kiss your husband," Jag said.

The next thing I knew, Aerin had grabbed me and pressed her lips to mine.

I didn't kiss back, but it didn't matter. It was done. I turned, looking for Layla. She was gone. She couldn't watch this, and I couldn't blame her. I felt sick to my stomach.

Jag pulled his phone out of his pocket and tapped a few times on the screen.

"And the broadcast is over. It's done," Jag said.

"Good," Aerin said. "Now kneel before me, husband. Kiss my feet and pledge your undying loyalty to me."

I cocked my head. "I…"

Aerin started laughing. "I'm fucking with you, Naayak."

"Caspar," I said. "That's still my name."

"It is your duty to satisfy my every desire."

I grunted.

"I realize this is an adjustment for you," Aerin said. "But as we are now bound, you will find in time that you cannot resist me."

"We'll see about that," I said. "For now, let's focus on saving Layla."

Aerin nodded. "She has surely not gone far. It is only a matter of time before Brightborn comes for us. He knows where to find us. Until then, come with me. We must complete this union."

"Aerin," I said, "I'm not ready."

"I said, come with me, Caspar. You will not deny me."

Aerin grabbed my hand, and she was right. When she touched me, my body gave in to her.

I had felt it when she kissed me, but now a flood of desire washed over me.

I didn't want to, but she was right. Whatever this enchantment was, however it had been forged, it possessed me. *She* possessed me.

I didn't feel like a husband. I felt like a slave or a servant.

I knew what it was like to be possessed by desire. By craving. Alcohol first, now this magic that bound me to Aerin.

My stomach churned. Yes, I still loved Layla, but I craved Aerin.

Step one. Admit that I was powerless over the situation. That everything had become unmanageable. Steps two and three, hand it to my higher power. Aerin wasn't going to like it, but this magic, whatever it was, didn't own me.

She led me into the back room. It was dark. She turned on the lights.

Layla stood there. She was smiling slyly.

"What?"

Layla held up her hand. She wore a ring just like mine. Just like Aerin's.

"What is this?" I asked. "Is your ring…"

"All three rings are genuine," Aerin said. "This was the compromise that we agreed to."

"Compromise?" I asked.

"We are all three bound together, Caspar," Layla said.

"Then our souls are still…"

"All of our souls are now bound," Aerin explained.

"My father saw what we intended for him to see," Layla said. "Our plan is unaltered."

Aerin grabbed Layla's hand. "You may kiss your husband."

Layla grabbed me and kissed me deeply. I kissed her back.

"I will not come between you," Aerin said, interrupting our kiss.

I grunted. I was just getting into it. Aerin's words reminded me we had an audience.

"I felt something when you touched me," Layla said.

I snorted. "Yeah, me too."

"Carnal desire," Aerin said. "A side effect, I suppose, of our binding. It will fade over time."

"Aerin," I said, "I don't understand. I thought you had a prophecy."

"Our prophecy only dictated that we must be married. According to drow tradition, we *are* married, all three of us. The ceremony is secondary to the sharing of rings. Our prophecy says nothing about love, and it in no way excludes the possibility of a polyamorous marriage."

I raised my eyebrows. "Aerin, I don't think we can."

Aerin raised her hand. "The sacrifice is mine. I have bound myself to two who cannot be truly mine. As I said, I will not interfere with your love."

"But we have to keep up the illusion, Caspar," Layla said. "For now, we need to give the impression for my father's sake that you and Aerin and only you two are married."

"But Layla," I said. "Before the wedding, you broke down in tears."

"This wasn't the wedding I wanted, Caspar. And we're also married, even if it's a formality, to a third wheel."

Aerin raised her eyebrow. "A third wheel?"

Layla shrugged. "Sorry, I didn't mean…"

Aerin chuckled. "I suppose the metaphor is fitting."

"A third wheel provides balance," I added. "And given our current predicament, it might be what we need. At least for now."

"It is not only for the sake of the elven king that we must keep up this illusion," Aerin said. "It is also for the sake of the drow. They need to believe the prophecy has been fulfilled, and in truth, it has. But if they believe for a moment that our marriage is a sham, that we manipulated the prophecy to make you only appear to be the one who fulfilled it, Caspar…"

I nodded. "I get it, Aerin. We can act like a couple in public."

Aerin put her hands on each of our shoulders again. The wave of carnal desire was still there, but we had an understanding. I didn't like it. Polygamy wasn't anything I'd ever envisioned for my life. But it was a ceremony. A tradition. A magical ring that bound our lives together. That was it. When it came to love, it was as it had been before. It was me. It was Layla.

Aerin was right. She had made a sacrifice. I couldn't imagine what it must feel like to bind herself to two who wouldn't love her. As unconventional as this arrangement was, as frustrated as I was about how all this was arranged without me knowing, part of me felt for Aerin. What she had given up was a chance at real love. It was a sacrifice I had to honor.

CHAPTER FORTY

My head was spinning with conflicting emotions: the lust for both elves, my love for Layla, disgust with myself over the thoughts I was having about Aerin that I didn't want, and anger and frustration that this had to be what it was and that I wasn't consulted before we went through with it. I understood why. I was grateful they'd figured out a way to fulfill both prophecies, to keep my soul bound to Layla's, but also troubled. I have my values. Polygamy is not among them.

But I only loved Layla. This arrangement—this compromise, if you could call it that—part of me loved it. Two prophecies, seemingly in conflict, now fulfilled and the contradiction resolved. But I also hated it. I mean, I was just recently a minister in a conservative denomination, hiding that my elf girlfriend lived with me. Now I was a polygamist and officially excommunicated, and not even for that.

I'm not sure if the bond I had with Layla before was severed and replaced or just supplemented. Either way, I was glad that Layla was part of this. In a strange way, it was better to be married to both of them than to only be married to Aerin. At least this way, I could be with the one I loved.

BANG!

It came from the main room, from the entrance of the building...

"They are here," Aerin said. "Remember, Layla, they must believe your bond with Caspar has been severed."

Layla nodded. Then she kissed me on the cheek and left.

I started to follow her. Aerin grabbed my arm.

Wow. Would I feel that sense of desire, no matter how inappropriate the moment, every time she so much as touched me?

"We cannot appear together," Aerin said, "until she leaves with them."

"Do you think they are going to leave without fighting, Aerin? I have enough blood on my hands. I can't let anyone else die."

Aerin protested, "They are not here to fight, Naayak. They are here for their princess. With the legion's numbers reduced, Layla said her father would not order them to fight unless they were forced to, or unless they were in a situation where they had a distinct advantage."

I sighed. "But what if Fred is here?"

"He won't be," Aerin said. "Brightborn would not be so foolish. If fighting ensues, my subjects are more than capable, and if we hear conflict, we can intervene at that point."

I took a deep breath. "This sucks. I hate that she's going with them."

"No harm will come to her," Aerin assured me.

"How will we find her?" I asked.

Aerin glanced at the corner of the room.

"My clothes? What I was wearing before at the rivers?"

"And your phones," Aerin said. "I saw to it that they were retrieved. Thankfully, they hadn't been burned."

"Our phones," I said. "That's brilliant, Aerin. Truly."

I unlocked my phone and opened my location app. "Layla has her phone on, too."

Aerin nodded. "Technology. One advantage of having lived on

Earth. The elves won't even suspect that we can track her location."

I almost hugged Aerin, I was so thrilled she'd figured out this complication. She'd known we'd need to track Layla. But then I pulled back. Touching her and hugging her wasn't appropriate. Not that I didn't trust myself; I wouldn't give in to that temptation, but I didn't want to subject myself to the desire.

"I know this conflicts with your values, Caspar. This arrangement, I mean."

I nodded. "I'm a mess of emotions right now."

"I should have confided the plan to you in advance," Aerin said. "But Layla insisted you would not agree."

"She did agree to it?" I asked.

"Monogamy is not as common among elves or drow," Aerin said. "This compromise was not as foreign to her expectations as it might be for you. Such marriages are acceptable in elf societies. There's a story of another drow, one of my ancestors from ancient times, who had three wives and four husbands."

"Sounds like a harem." I laughed.

"Not as much as you'd think," Aerin said. "All the marriages were political. There was no intimacy. It was a formality to bind clans together."

"Clans?" I asked. "Must've been a long time ago."

Aerin nodded. "It was by such marriages that the drow became a single clan under my mother's rule and mine. But you are right; these marriages were necessary to unify us, to keep our identities protected as human society grew and we were forced into hiding."

"So, does this make me a prince?" I asked.

Aerin laughed. "Our males do not receive royal titles."

I shrugged. "Not the case for the New Albion elves."

"And they don't even know you and Layla are also married or that both of you are bound to me."

I shook my head. "One thing you said. If Layla knew I wouldn't agree to this, why would *she* agree?"

"It was part of the reason she was so distraught and why she could not watch the ceremony. Not because it violated her conscience, but because she knew it would wound yours."

I nodded. "But it did fulfill both prophecies."

"Indeed, it did."

"How long do we have to wait before we can follow them?" I asked.

"Not long," Aerin said. "Let us prepare ourselves for battle."

CHAPTER FORTY-ONE

Aerin and I watched as Layla moved to join her father. According to Jag, at least twenty elves had shown up at the cult building. Aerin and I didn't dare reveal ourselves. We didn't want the situation to escalate. We knew they were there for one reason: to find Layla. Once she appeared, the elves left with her.

Brag'mok sat on the floor, clenching his fists.

"Elves!"

I walked over and rested my hand on his shoulder. Even with him sitting, his shoulder was at the height of my own. "I know you want your revenge."

"Genocide," Brag'mok said, his shoulders shaking. "They wiped out my people. Then, quite possibly, millions of their own, so they could take their magic with them. All for the sake of a war."

I shook my head. "I can't even wrap my mind around that. So many lives lost."

Brag'mok shook his head. "The depravity of Brightborn is exceeded only by his blind ambition."

"I'm sorry."

"Not your fault, Caspar," the giant said.

"I'm just saying, you lost a lot. More than most. And it all started with me."

He nodded. "That was foretold long before you were born, Caspar, and none of it is your responsibility. At every turn, you've chosen peace and life. It is Brightborn who has manipulated everything toward war and death."

"I know, Brag'mok. We'll do whatever we can to stop him, I promise."

"You will have to go without me," Brag'mok said.

"Excuse me?" I asked.

"When you go to rescue Layla and secure the artifacts, I cannot accompany you."

"Brag'mok," I said. "You're a greater warrior than all of us combined. We might need you."

"That's the thing," Brag'mok said. "The rage inside me is too great. When those elves showed up, it took every bit of strength I had left to refrain from unleashing it all, and if I see Brightborn face to face…"

I nodded. "I get it. But if things don't go as planned…"

"I will let him know," Ensley said, suddenly appearing on Brag'mok's shoulder.

The giant grunted. "I will come if I must."

I said, "If things don't go as we planned, Brag'mok, you will be the last hope of our resistance. You'll be the only one left who can provide information to the government—the only one who has ever faced the elven legion in war. You'll be needed. If things are not going well, you must promise me you will not come to our rescue."

Brag'mok stood up and nodded.

"And you'll have to take care of Agnus for me."

"The cat?" Brag'mok asked.

I nodded. "He thinks he's self-sufficient, but he needs a lot of help."

"A big ask," Brag'mok said. "I mean, take care of a cat? You mustn't fail, Caspar, for the sake of the world. And my sanity!"

I chucked. "So that's a yes? You'll take Agnus?"

"Just don't fail," Brag'mok said, eyeing Agnus as he strutted across the room. He looked like he expected everyone to lay down palm branches and sing his praises as he walked.

"I'm not planning on it," I said, smiling.

Aerin walked over and took me by the arm. Again, I felt that sensation. Lord, I hoped I wouldn't be overwhelmed by lust every time we made skin-to-skin contact forever. Aerin had said it would fade eventually, or maybe I'd just get used to it. If I pitched a tent every time she touched me, it would be more than a little embarrassing.

Aerin pulled me to the side where no one else could hear us speak. "Come, husband. It is time to come to our wife's aid."

Our wife? I shook my head. Those words didn't sit well, but I knew what she meant. "You watching her location on my phone, Aerin?"

She nodded. "A strange place where they've settled. Based on the map, is this a park in the middle of the city?"

I nodded, assuming she meant Forest Park, but that was not where they had taken Layla.

I snorted. "Pruitt-Igoe."

"Who is that?" Aerin asked.

"It's a long story," I said. "But not a lot of people go into those woods without a death wish."

Pruitt-Igoe was a failed public housing initiative from the fifties and sixties. Giant high rises that, at the time, politicians had argued would solve the homeless and low-income problems in the city.

The government had funded the project. Nearly all of the initial applicants were African Americans, but accepting a home in Pruitt-Igoe came with several restrictions. Single mothers were given priority over married couples. Sounded reasonable, right? Until you realized that so many people were so desperate at the time for a place to live, for a chance at a better life, that it would divide families. Then, once the facilities were built and the apartments were filled, the government didn't fund its maintenance. Folks were off the streets. Out of sight, out of mind. That meant fewer government resources. The place fell into disrepair. Resentment against the system built, crime rates soared, and barely a decade after the place was built, it was demolished.

And no one had dared build anything on the property since.

Sure, there had been a few attempts, developers who took an interest in the area. However, every effort had failed, leaving it an urban jungle, overgrown with trees and foliage, in what had become one of the most dangerous and impoverished areas of St. Louis.

From time to time, gangs moved into the area. Bodies were often found there. Rarely did the police do much about it. They treated it like the armpit of the city. If they caught you there, they'd assume you were up to no good. It probably wouldn't end well for you, no matter what your intentions were.

And now, Brightborn and the elven legion had set up camp at Pruitt-Igoe.

Another outsider with aspirations to make things what they thought was better, but I doubted Brightborn intended to do anything with the land. He was using it as cover, a place where few would look.

I'd been to the perimeter of Pruitt-Igoe, but I'd never gone into it.

It was a land stained with blood. While the authorities and the government treated it as a cursed place, for many of the locals, it was a sacred site, a constant and ever-present memorial.

I couldn't begin to understand the pain and history that place represented to members of the surrounding community, but I could listen.

And in one respect, I agreed with the sentiment that the government wasn't going to solve this problem. Not the President, not General Breeland, not the senators.

"Are you ready, Naayak?" Aerin asked.

I nodded. "As ready as I'll ever be."

CHAPTER FORTY-TWO

I don't believe in ghosts. I used to watch *Ghost Hunters* and other paranormal investigation shows. Like a lot of people, I was sucked into them. The show never provided any conclusive proof of the existence of ghosts, but they did provide enough documentary evidence of unexplained phenomena that I was at the very least, curiously open to the possibility. The one thing I did know was that thousands of people had experiences they were convinced were the result of hauntings.

Walking into the Pruitt-Igoe woods with my new powers now coursing through me, I couldn't deny that something there was bringing the element of aether to the forefront of my consciousness.

I don't know if ghosts were the reason, but these were blood-stained lands. There was negative energy here that I couldn't ignore. Anger. Rage. Betrayal. Were these my emotions stirring in my mind, or the emotions of those who'd once called this place home?

Probably both.

Aerin gripped the hilt of her sword. The fire that enchanted her blade produced a gold-red glow that illuminated our steps.

Where were the elves? Where was Layla? We knew she was there. Most likely, Fred and Brightborn were too.

But the rest of the legion? Given the size of the area and the number of legionnaires I'd seen, a significant number of them were elsewhere.

Surely they knew we were there. How couldn't they?

One thing we knew for certain. As predicted, they hadn't executed Layla. If they had, we'd be dead, too.

I glanced at my phone. Layla wasn't far. At least, her phone wasn't. There was always the chance they'd dumped her phone in these woods and set us up.

The elves wouldn't know what to do with the technology, but Fred did.

A violet glow formed about twenty feet ahead of us.

Aerin and I exchanged glances and nodded.

When Fred appeared, we were ready.

"Welcome," he said. "We've been expecting you."

I cocked my head. "Expecting us? You aren't here to kill us?"

Fred grinned. "Oh, I want to, but His and Her Highness would prefer to see you delivered alive."

I cocked my head. "Alive? But why?"

"It is not my place to question our king's will, pretender."

"Pretender?" I asked.

"False messiah," Fred said. "I presume the king would prefer you to admit your fraud than make a martyr of you."

"He is no pretender, Fred," Aerin said. "You were there. You saw how he subdued the elements."

"A fine show. A convincing display of power for those gullible enough to believe that a human could fulfill an elven prophecy."

"I married Aerin," I said. "Surely he must know that defies their prophecy. Why does he need me to admit it?"

"Again," Fred said, "it's not my place to question my Lord's will. You would do well to follow my example."

I snorted. "I'm half-inclined to take you out here and now after what you did to Layla."

"What do you care?" Fred asked. "You married the drow!"

I shook my head. "Doesn't mean I want to see her harmed or killed."

"Those artifacts, entrusted to the drow for centuries, were not yours to take," Aerin growled.

Fred smiled and held up his hands. He had rings glowing with purple magic on each of his hands. "I agree. These artifacts are meant for the chosen one. I simply borrowed them that the king might bestow them upon the true savior."

"You didn't have the right!" I shouted.

"And you did, pretender?" Fred asked. "It seems these powers agree with me, too. Would you like another demonstration?"

I shook my head. "Not necessary."

Fred nodded. "Then you'd best come with me. And lest you get any foolish ideas, know that the king has assassins posted throughout these woods. One false move, and you'll regret it."

I shook my head. "You believe the king will rule this world justly? Look at what he did to his homeworld, Fred."

Fred stopped in his tracks and turned around. "You did that, Caspar. You forced his hand, and you nearly damned his daughter with your lies."

"I'm not the one who put a blade in her back," I retorted.

"You speak of justice," Fred continued, ignoring my remark. "Look at these woods. This place, what happened here? This is the desolation that follows human notions of justice. We've had our chance to rule the Earth, Caspar. The age of the elves is upon us, and it shall be our salvation."

I just shook my head. There was no sense arguing with him. He was right. Injustices perpetrated at the hands of humans had been a plague on the world. I'd always preached a new kingdom, a kingdom represented by the resurrected Christ meant to restore true justice to the world. I did lament injustice, but

Brightborn wasn't the answer. All he'd ever known was war. All he'd ever dreamed about was power. I wasn't going to convince Fred, though. Not about my faith, and just as surely not that the elven king wasn't the answer.

I simply nodded. With Aerin at my side, we followed Fred through the forest into a small clearing.

Two thrones hewn from gold were situated in the middle of the clearing. I didn't have a clue how he'd acquired them. Probably brought them from New Albion. He was seated on one, Layla on the other.

I could see the pain on her face. The purple magic had spread throughout her body, covering her face in what looked like glowing varicose veins.

I wanted to run up to her and take her hand. I wanted to hold her in my arms. It took every ounce of strength I had to hold myself back. She was spending whatever energy she had left trying to stay upright and alert.

"Caspar Cruciger," King Brightborn said. "This is the third time we've met. Tell me, what were your intentions when you followed us to this forest?"

I shook my head. "You can't have this world, Brightborn. I intend to stop you."

The king chuckled as he stood from his throne. "And Princess Nightshade. I expected better from you, considering our history."

"What history is he talking about, Aerin?" I asked.

"Why don't you tell your husband the truth, Nightshade?"

"We don't have a history, Brightborn," she said. "One chance encounter, and that was a mistake."

"A chance encounter?" Brightborn asked. "One that lasted an entire night?"

"What is he saying, Aerin?" I asked.

Aerin sighed. "He came to us nearly two years ago. He insisted he'd come to forge an alliance, one meant to ensure the arrival of the chosen one."

"An alliance?" I asked.

Aerin grimaced. "I agreed to marry him, but we had only one night together. We were never wed. He refused the ring at what was supposed to be our wedding, then left. This is the first time I've seen him since."

"You were foolish, Nightshade, to think I'd bind my life to yours."

"The custom is meant to prevent a betrayal between spouses," Aerin said. "And in forging alliances, the custom is wise. You would not accept the ring because you intended to betray us from the start."

"What I intended," Brightborn said, "was to glean information from you about the artifacts the drow guarded. And after one night of passion, you sure were willing to talk, weren't you?"

Aerin looked angry. "It was a grave error in judgment, Brightborn. If I had it to do it over again, I wouldn't have told you a thing. Nor would I have indulged your sick perversions for a single night."

"Perversions?" I asked.

"Don't ask," Aerin said. "The king is a freak."

"You have the artifacts, Brightborn. Why haven't you healed Layla?" I asked.

"Don't think I haven't tried," Brightborn said before raising his scepter. "Bind the imposter!"

I clenched my fists and gathered the power of fire. It welled up like an inferno in my chest.

But the elves who emerged from the darkness didn't come to me.

They grabbed Fred!

"Your Highness!" Fred screamed. "Please, don't do this!"

"Foolish human," Brightborn said. "You've served your purpose."

"I beg you, my king! I've done all you've asked! Please!"

The elves tied something like vines around Fred's wrists and forced him to his knees in front of the two thrones.

"But even with these powers, human, you were too weak to heal my daughter of the wound you inflicted."

"But you told me to do it! To charge the blade with my power. To strike your daughter with it, but not kill her. I did as you asked!"

"My daughter was stricken by the Blade of Echoes," Brightborn said. "And all the legion witnessed it."

"That was not the Blade of Echoes!" I shouted. "The true blade was destroyed!"

"So you say," Brightborn said. "But who other than you saw it happen? The blade that struck Layla appeared to be identical to the Blade of Echoes. It was vested with magic, was it not?"

"It is a forgery!" I shouted.

"Lies!" King Brightborn screamed back. "You are full of nothing but lies, human!"

I shook my head. "You and I both know the truth."

"What is truth?" King Brightborn asked. "If it is not witnessed, can it be truth?"

I grunted and shook my head. "Unbelievable."

"Now, Caspar, or should I call you Naayak Nightshade, you must seize the artifacts from this human's hands. You will use this power to heal my daughter so all will see that she has survived a strike by the Blade of Echoes. That they will know the truth—that Layla Brightborn is the chosen one foretold by the elven prophecy."

CHAPTER FORTY-THREE

"It will never work, Brightborn," I said. "The prophecy also dictates that the chosen one should love an elven princess."

Brightborn snorted. "It appears that our version of the prophecy was a copy. The drow possessed the originals all this time. And in their telling of the prophecy, it was said that the chosen one must marry an elven princess."

"She can't marry herself. This is preposterous."

"Is it?" the king asked. "That ring on my daughter's finger. It resembles one that you, Aerin, once intended for my hand. It appears my daughter has already married an elven princess. And to think, it was meant to be a drow all along. What better way to fulfill her role as the chosen one and unite the elves as a start than by marrying into a race of elves that has been separate from us for centuries?"

I raised my hand and showed the king my ring. "She married me, too, Brightborn."

"An unfortunate turn of events," the king said. "Which is one of two reasons I haven't killed you yet, human. I still require you to retrieve these artifacts from this pitiful human's hands."

"And help you further your delusion?" I shouted.

"You will have to kill this man," the king said, "to retrieve the rings from him. And you'll have to use all the elements to do it."

I shook my head. "I'm not a murderer!"

King Brightborn huffed. "Says the man who killed Hector."

"I had no choice!" I told him.

"And you have no choice in the matter again," the king said. "I could have you struck down here, where you stand."

"You wouldn't!" I retorted. "It would kill Layla!"

"I admit," the king said calmly, "it would be most unfortunate. But I still have my legion, and your world is still ripe for the taking. It would be a loss, but such are the costs of war."

"Your men couldn't strike me down even with their best effort," I said.

"Maybe, maybe not. But if you fight, the infection that spreads through my daughter's body will soon claim her life, and you'll die with her."

"Caspar," Aerin said. "You must do as he asks."

I protested, "But I…"

"Listen to your wife!" the king said. "Isn't it dictated by drow custom that husbands should submit to their wives?"

I stepped toward Fred. He looked at me with fear in his eyes. "I'm sorry, Caspar. I was wrong. Forgive me."

"Do it!" the king shouted.

"I forgive you," I told Fred. Sure, his regret was just that Brightborn had turned on him. I could have held a grudge, but I wouldn't. I couldn't. I'd spent my whole adult life preaching forgiveness, even for those who might betray me. Forgive them, for they know not what they do. If Jesus could forgive the soldiers who were crucifying Him while they were doing it, I could forgive Fred.

I turned to the king. "I can't do this."

"You must!" Aerin interjected.

I turned back to her. She looked at me with wide eyes. "Do you trust me, Caspar?"

"I don't know."

"Then trust me!" Layla said, her voice raspy. "You can do this."

I looked at Layla. The pain in her face was almost too much to bear. She nodded at me. I nodded back.

"I love you," I said.

"I love you too, and I believe in you."

"What are you waiting for!" the king screamed, standing from his throne.

"Wait!" Fred shouted, "At least allow me one last chance to speak."

The king grunted and sat. He stroked his chin for a moment. "Very well, let the dead man speak his last words."

"My words are for Caspar alone," Fred said.

"Say what you must," Brightborn said. "But once you have spoken, you will die."

I knelt beside Fred. He whispered in my ear, "It takes all five elements to free the rings from their host. That was how I stole them from their boxes. But I had no power at all, and I was able to wear them. You do not need to wear these. You shouldn't."

I nodded and stood up. I wasn't sure what he meant, but it was something.

"What did he say!" the king demanded.

"At least afford a dying man the dignity to allow his last words to be what he intended," I said.

"No matter. Let it be done!" the king commanded.

I drew all the power I could. The cool sensation of water, the warmth of fire. The weight of earth, the weightlessness of air, and the strength of aether.

With tears, I released it all into Fred's body.

He screamed in agony. The sound of his pain was his soul. It connected to the power of aether, to my spirit, as if my insides were being torn apart.

It wasn't just Fred's cries. The cries of others, those whose blood soaked these grounds, rang out too. They fell on me like a thousand pounds, as if they were shouting, "Would you shed still more blood on this ground?"

I released my magic.

Fred's body fell to the ground with a thud.

I turned and looked at Layla. She was unconscious.

"Now, human!" the king shouted.

I pulled the two rings, still coursing with violet energies, from Fred's fingers.

Layla wasn't dead. Not yet. But it wouldn't be long.

Why had Fred told me not to wear the rings myself? What did he know that I did not? And more, he was the last person I could trust. No one had betrayed us worse than Fred.

But he had begged forgiveness, and I had given it. All my life, all my time in ministry, it was a message of forgiveness that had moved me. Without forgiveness, without grace, I would not be sober. I had asked for forgiveness. I was granted redemption.

Fred deserved his chance at redemption, too. And if with his dying breath, he had truly changed…

It didn't make sense. I should have just put on the rings and tried to heal Layla, but was there any guarantee I could do it? Anyone, Fred said, could use these rings. Only one with all five elements could remove them from the wearer, and if I failed, if I couldn't heal her, there would be no way to undo it. If anyone knew what this magic could do for its wearer, it was Fred.

Despite my better instincts, I chose to believe him. I chose to embrace his chance for redemption because if I had never had that chance, I would be dead.

I approached Layla.

"Put them on!" the king demanded. "Heal my daughter!"

I fixed my eyes on Layla, ignoring the elf king's impatience. Then I grabbed her hands. These rings were too big for her fingers, so I slipped them on her thumbs.

The energy in the rings flooded into her body.

"What are you doing!" the king shouted in a rage, standing up.

I raised my hand, and wielding the element of air, threw him back down on his throne.

Layla's body glowed bright, the power overwhelming her frame. Then it faded.

Layla gasped for air, then fell off her throne into my arms and wrapped her arms around me. My eyes welled with tears.

"Layla!" I cried. "I thought I'd lost you!"

"You'll never lose me."

The king grunted, then stood up. "Behold! She who survived the Blade of Echoes! The chosen one, Layla Brightborn!"

I looked around. Hundreds of elven legionnaires had gathered around us. I can't believe I didn't anticipate that. The king wanted witnesses.

"Seize them!" the king commanded, indicating Aerin and me.

"Father!" Layla begged. "Our lives are still bound. You can't kill him!"

The king nodded. "It doesn't mean we cannot imprison both of your unworthy spouses."

Layla unsheathed her blade. I gathered my power. The legionnaires closed in around us.

Layla jumped off her throne and channeled purple angelic power from her fingertips, sending a row of elves flying into the trees.

Aerin swung her blade, severing an elf's head from his shoulders. No blood. The wound was cauterized.

I gathered the energies of the elements. With earth, the trees responded, their branches bending and swiping legionnaires aside. With air, I trapped dozens of them in a whirlwind.

But there were too many.

I turned. Where the hell had the king gone? Fled for his life, most likely. Fucking coward.

"We have to get out of here!" Aerin shouted. "There are just too many of them!"

"On my position!" I shouted.

Layla and Aerin stood next to me. I harnessed fairy magic and forged a portal over my head, then started to pull it down over us.

A dozen balls of green energy flew into it and dissipated it.

"What the…"

One of the fairies appeared. He looked similar to Ensley if a bit rougher around the edges. "You who used magic to take life cannot be permitted to wield our power."

"Oh, for fucks' sake!" I shouted. "Ensley!"

Ensley appeared at my side.

"Back off, Develin!" Ensley shouted.

"You know the law," the fairy Develin said. "One who abuses magic cannot…"

"Stupid dogma!" Ensley screamed. "He never wanted to kill!"

Aerin swung her blade, striking an elf's arm from his torso, then with another slice, she cut off one of his legs. The wound cauterized as the elf screamed, hopping on one leg.

Layla was still shooting blasts of angel magic at the elves.

But without fairy power, it was just a matter of time before they overwhelmed us.

"I command you," Ensley said. "By my right as the king of the fae!"

"You are no longer our king, Ensley," Develin said. "By acclaim, and by the blessing of the Furies, that right belongs to me. And you are the traitor! You saw it! This man just wielded all the elements to kill a rival!"

Ensley charged Develin, spearing him with his shoulder into a tree.

"Fly, Caspar," Layla said. "Take Aerin with you."

"Layla…"

"They won't harm me. They think I'm the chosen one."

"Layla, I…"

"Just do it, Caspar!"

I ran over to Aerin. "On my back!"

Aerin jumped on my back piggy-back style. I drew on aether and air, visualizing us soaring through the skies. We took off.

Maybe, removed from the fairies, I could cast another gate.

I drew on the power, formed another portal in front of us, and flew as fast as I could into it...

But it dissipated the moment we should have passed through it.

I tried to draw on the power again. Nothing.

"It's Ensley," Aerin said. "It was his power you were wielding. That means—"

"He's dead. The other fairies killed him."

"I'm sorry, Caspar," she said.

I screamed at the top of my lungs as we soared through the sky.

CHAPTER FORTY-FOUR

"He was my friend," I said, sinking into the couch at the Elf Gate church.

Aerin sat beside me and took my hand. "I know I'm not the one you wish was here to comfort you."

I shook my head. I expected the lust to overwhelm me with her touch, but there was nothing. This was just a friendly touch. Maybe I'd already adjusted to that particular side effect of our binding, or perhaps it was because I'd just used magic to kill a man. I was so distraught that I didn't have any room in my body for lust at the moment.

"No, I appreciate it, Aerin. "

"You were incredible tonight," Aerin said. "No matter what the elf king says, you are the chosen one."

I shook my head. "Why didn't you tell me before about what happened with him?"

Aerin sighed. "I feared you wouldn't trust me if you knew. I realized from the start that convincing you to participate in the trials, to trust me at all, was going to be difficult."

I shook my head. "You still should have told me the truth."

"You're right," she said. "I'm sorry. If I had an ounce of the faith that Layla has in you, I would have trusted you."

I nodded. "I get it, Aerin. I know why you didn't tell me the truth. But if we're going to be married now, all three of us, no more secrets, okay?"

"Agreed," Aerin said, resting her head on my shoulder. Part of me wanted to shrug her off, but she was trying to comfort me. And it was innocent enough.

Brag'mok came running into the room. He was holding Agnus in his hands. My cat was hissing and swiping at him with his claws. "Take this demon cat! I can't do this!"

I laughed. "Come here, Agnus."

Brag'mok tossed him to the floor as gently as he could. Agnus immediately calmed, then he walked over and head-butted my shin.

"You two going to tell us what happened?" Agnus asked. "Everyone wants to know."

I nodded. "I suppose we should."

"Where's Layla?" Brag'mok asked.

"She's safe," I said. "I think, but King Brightborn and his legions are still at large."

Brag'mok nodded. "If you need anything, my broadsword is at your disposal."

"Thank you, Brag'mok."

"Do you want to tell those who have gathered what happened out there?" Aerin asked. "Or would you rather I do it? I know it must be hard for you."

"How many people, how many of my friends, are going to die for me before this shit is over?" I asked. "First B'iff, now Ensley."

"You inspired them," Aerin said. "I didn't know B'iff, but Ensley believed in you. That's why he was willing to fight for you. Why he was willing to die for you."

I nodded. "I just wish people didn't *want* to die for me. Too much death."

"There is still a sealed prophecy," Aerin said. "Perhaps once all is revealed, these events will make better sense."

I shook my head. "Making sense of death doesn't make it easier. Death sucks. Always. Especially when someone dies before they should have."

Aerin nodded. "Well, I'm here for you."

I sighed. "No offense, Aerin, but…"

"I know. I'm not the one you wish was here."

I nodded and turned to go out and relive the painful events. I would explain them to whatever followers of the former cult remained loyal to me.

But a purple glow appeared in the doorway.

"Layla!" I said, hugging her the second she appeared. "I didn't think you'd be able to come here!"

Layla hugged me back. "I told you they wouldn't kill me, Caspar. Doesn't mean I was inclined to hang out with those elf pricks."

"Ensley," I said. "Were you there when…"

"The other fairies overwhelmed him. I'm sorry. I held him in my hands as he breathed his last."

I nodded. "I'm glad you're here, Layla. I don't know that I could do this without you."

"Are you ready?" Aerin asked.

I extended my hand. Aerin took it. "We three come from different worlds. This night, we all came together despite different worldviews. Different dogmas. I still don't know how I feel about this polygamous marriage. Perhaps our unity can be an example to the world. An image of hope that unity is possible and our differences do not need to divide us."

CHAPTER FORTY-FIVE

Our numbers had dwindled significantly. With the elven legion here, it seemed more were willing to cast their lot with the king than an ex-preacher who had a few flashy tricks up his sleeve.

I could only wonder and hope the government's resolve to resist the elves hadn't wavered. It would be a lot simpler if Brightborn didn't seize control of the nation's military.

We weren't safe. The king had made it clear in the Pruitt-Igoe woods that his daughter's life for fulfilling his supposed destiny to rule the Earth was an acceptable cost.

But he still needed her. They now believed she was the chosen one. She was with us, sure, but the king had given them the show to believe. Why wouldn't they listen to the chosen one's father and the one they'd always followed as king?

We didn't know what Brightborn's next move would be. Had he wiped out all his kind on New Albion, or had he moved them off the planet before siphoning all the magic off-world? So far, there had been no sign of millions of elves showing up anywhere on Earth. If they were here, they were well-hidden.

I hesitated to say that what we'd done qualified as a victory.

But Layla had been saved, and the drow were, more than

anyone else, committed to our cause. At least they had been convinced by my success in the trials.

As far as the rest of humanity? The arrival of an elf king was still being treated by most of them as a fringe conspiracy theory. Doomsday preachers had taken to the streets proclaiming the coming of the Great Tribulation, begging people to prepare for the rapture, which I found annoying. Not just because I didn't subscribe to the particular view of the end-times those doom-sayers were proclaiming, but the idea of trying to drive people to God out of fear had never sat well with me.

Aerin, Layla, Agnus, and I didn't stay in one place too long, and I had to be careful about how I used my magic. With Ensley gone and the fairies aligned again with the elves, they'd surely know it if I unleashed my elemental powers.

The apartment wasn't safe, and other people lived there too. If the elves found us, the last thing I wanted was more bloodshed on my account.

We made periodic unscheduled appearances to Saint Ensley's. That was the name that the former cultists decided, in honor of my former fairy friend's sacrifice, to name their building. No more "Order of the Elven Gate" or "Elf Gate Cult." There was no more gate, so the name was obsolete. Instead, the remaining former cultists decided to name their movement, the resistance that proclaimed a hope tied to the elven prophecy, after a pesky little fellow who was more powerful than he seemed and had lost his life trying to save the world.

Brag'mok moved in with Jag. I wasn't sure the floor joists in Jag's apartment would hold the both of them at once, but they spent most of their time at the gym anyway.

We did not quit working out. We used the gym once in a while, but we had to avoid any sort of predictable routine—anything the elves could pick up on.

I knew we could not hide from them forever. At some point, I would have to figure out a way to practice my magic without the fairies finding us. Brightborn had not so much as shown himself since that night at Pruitt-Igoe.

He was planning something, preparing his plans to take over the world. We just did not have the slightest clue what his step one might be. When he moved, we would move.

The other drow found various places to stay nearby. They all had phones, so we could reach them if needed. And we *would* need them...eventually.

Motel-hopping did not suit us well. We were trying to find a place off the grid, somewhere we could stay and make a home that would not be on the books in case the government was compromised. It was a work in progress, but with Jag's help, I had a few leads along the Meramec River.

Aerin, Layla, and I were in the midst of touring a small patch of land one of the members of St. Ensley's owned. He had inherited a ranch from an uncle who didn't have any children of his own, but he did not know the first thing about raising cattle. So, the place had sat vacant for the better part of a decade and become a junkyard. Abandoned appliances, cars, and old toilets with flowers growing out of them littered the land.

It was not an ideal place to live under most circumstances, but given our situation, it was perfect. Eugene, the man who owned the land, was willing to keep our presence there off the books. The small farmhouse and the old stable, left there from the days when the place had been a ranch, were in disrepair. I was not a handyman, but I had YouTube and plenty of determination.

No sooner did I call Eugene to tell him we'd be staying there than I received a text from Jag.

Could you make an appearance at St. Ensley's tonight?

Probably. Why?

Trust me.

I wished I still had fairy power. Porting there would have been a lot easier. The only downside to this land that we were likely to move onto was that it was an hour or so away from the city. But it had enough space that it could, with some work, house all of us, not just Aerin, Layla, Agnus, and me. The rest of the drow could headquarter there too.

We crammed into the Eclipse. Agnus was on Layla's lap in the front, Aerin in the back.

I could not believe my life. Married to two princesses? It wasn't only uncomfortable from the perspective of my moral compass, it was also a double headache.

They could not agree about who had to squeeze into the admittedly uncomfortable back seat of the Eclipse. It was Aerin's turn.

And if I'd ever had any doubt that it was cramped back there, she made sure both of us knew it. This nomadic lifestyle just didn't fit with the lavishness of a princess' life that these two she-elves were accustomed to.

I didn't blame Aerin for her bitchiness.

If it had been Layla's turn to ride in the back, she would have acted the same way.

And Agnus, who always rode with Layla, would complain more than both of them combined. Not like it mattered to him. He was small enough that he could fit anywhere in that car. But for him, it was a matter of principle. Deities did not ride in the back unless it was in a limo.

We pulled up to St. Ensley's. A massive crowd had gathered outside the doors.

We had to park two blocks away. What the hell?

I pressed my way through the crowd. People crowded around us, trying to touch me. I reached the door and knocked on it three times.

No answer. Jag didn't realize it was us.

I texted him. **We're here. What in the world?**

It was a Sunday. It wasn't like St. Ensley's was a real church. It was more like a strategic outpost.

Fred's name had been on the title to the place. Luckily, it had been left to Jag in Fred's will.

The door swung open, and Brag'mok grabbed me and pulled me inside. Aerin and Layla squeezed in behind me.

"I think someone touched me!" Agnus protested.

"What's going on?" I asked, ignoring Agnus.

"There's someone here who I think can explain," Jag said. "Follow me."

As I followed the giant into the room with the awful couches, I was taken aback by the man who stood there.

"Cecil?" I asked.

"Hello, Reverend!" Cecil exclaimed, somehow leaping up from the couch without a struggle and gripping my hand.

"What is going on here, Cecil?"

"I told you, Reverend!" Cecil exclaimed.

"Cecil, I'm not a reverend anymore."

"Says who?" Cecil asked. "That backwards denomination you used to belong to?"

I smiled. "Yeah. According to them."

"I told you, Reverend. If they ever gave you the boot, we'd still follow you."

I shook my head. "I don't know, Cecil. Don't get me wrong; I appreciate it."

Cecil looked at me intently. "Reverend. When we saw that video and what you could do, none of us was the least bit surprised. We've seen it. Did I tell you Grace is trying out for her new school's soccer team?"

I smiled. "You didn't, but that's amazing. Truly, it is. And a new school? I take it you got that house you were trying to buy?"

"I did, Reverend. Thanks to you! Thanks to the Lord!"

I smiled. "I don't want to let all these people down, but I can't use magic right now. It's too risky."

"We aren't here for healing," Cecil said. "We're here for hope. Will you turn down people who need a little faith to get them through these trying times?"

I shook my head. "I can't turn them down. But you realize I have two wives, right?"

Cecil said, "So did Jacob in the Bible."

I snorted. Jacob did have two wives. He had been tricked into it like I had been, in a roundabout way. I hadn't thought of that parallel until now. Jacob also had a wife he loved and another he didn't.

But Jacob's beloved wife was barren. The other wife wasn't. She gave him heirs. Of course, Jacob was boning them both because, well, he had two wives. I mean, he was a man. Yeah, Jacob loved Rachel, but for some reason, Leah kept popping out babies. I suppose it was his duty as a husband. He couldn't just sleep with one of them.

I suppose the patriarch didn't have the same moral qualms about only being able to sleep with the wife he loved as I did. Based on the number of kids he'd fathered, he made the most of his polygamist marriage—the sacrifices some men have to make.

I smiled at Cecil. "Thank you for this."

Cecil nodded. "My pleasure, Reverend!"

"Jag," I said, "don't lock the doors against anyone. If they want to hear what I have to say, let them come."

"Sure thing, Casp!"

I hadn't seen so many people crowded into a building so quickly since I went to see Green Day in the mid-nineties.

I wasn't going to give these people half the show they had that night, but hopefully I could give them something more meaningful.

I stood up in front of the congregation and cleared my throat. I'd have to raise my voice to be heard. No sound system. No microphones.

"Today, it feels like the world we know is in upheaval. Perhaps you've heard the rumors. An elven king has invaded our world, and he intends to subjugate humanity. If you've heard these rumors, I can tell you today that they are true."

Gasps and murmurs sounded through the small hall.

I raised my hand, and the people quickly lowered their voices.

"Perhaps you've seen the video and were inspired by what I could do. All of that was real, too. But you might be asking, what can one man and a couple elf princesses, along with a giant and a cat, do to fend off a powerful elven king?

"Allow me to tell you a story. Two thousand years ago, another force arose to subjugate the world. To rule mankind and make the world obey. That was the credo of the Roman Empire.

"They took over nations. They even dominated and occupied Jerusalem until the son of a carpenter started preaching a message of love. Love, grace, forgiveness, and hope. And he gathered together a ragtag group of common men—fishermen, even a tax collector. Those common men, and a good share of strong but likewise common women, through faith, changed the world. In time, they overtook mighty Rome. Not with a sword, but with their simple faith.

"Can just a few of us, and today there are more than a few gathered, make a difference? Can we save the world? Can we thwart a tyrant who would rule us all and force us into obedience? With faith, with love, and with hope, yes, we can. With the hand of God at our side, yes, we absolutely can."

The crowd erupted in cheers. It wasn't a long, complicated message. Not a lot of deep theology. Not much dogma. But it had a lot of hope.

I looked at the crowd.

Common men and women. Different races. By the way they were dressed, they came from different backgrounds.

There were only three who stood out.

Three men. In black suits. And sunglasses. All wearing earpieces.

I stepped down into the crowd. I shook hands. I gave people hugs. I saw tears in people's eyes. This was why I had gone into ministry. Who would have thought that an odd elven prophecy would birth an opportunity that the church had not only failed to give me but had practically forbidden me to present?

I approached the three men and extended my hand.

They didn't shake it.

"Caspar Cruciger?" one of the three men asked.

I nodded. "That's me."

"Could you come with us?"

"Where are we going?" I asked.

"Just outside. It won't take long, but the President would like a word."

AUTHOR NOTES - THEOPHILUS MONROE

JUNE 2, 2021

Aside from being one of my father's favorite rock bands from the sixties and seventies, the phrase "three dog night" apparently goes back to when people didn't have excellent heating in the wintertime. On frigid nights people would call their "dogs" into bed to help keep them warm. Hence, the phrase "three dog night" is meant to describe a particularly cold night, a time when you might need three dogs in bed to stay warm.

In *Three Dogma Night*, we see the confluence of different versions of the elven prophecy. The action starts to get turned up a notch—and you can expect that to continue through the rest of the series. The night is getting cold—the threat from the elven legion real. And somehow, with these three "dogmas," these three versions of the elven prophecy (the elven version, the drow version, and the orcish/giant version) colliding, our hero must find a way to make sense of it all. Without, of course, compromising who he is or his values.

Caspar's struggle is no longer chiefly with the "powers that be" in the church. Still, other powers are making their presence and influence known. He's spent years standing up for what he believes is right against ecclesiastical authorities. Will he be able to stand firm in the light of the government's demands? How in the world is he going to navigate this Jacob-Rachel-Leah/Caspar-Layla-Aerin triangle that has been thrust upon him?

Stepping away from the story for a bit, my hope, in this story, was to present a dilemma for our hero that wasn't so simple as choosing between black or white. In the church, the authorities saw every dogma/doctrine as a matter of good or evil, right or wrong, true or false. More often than not, though, we are presented with situations in life where we have no clear or ideal path forward. What do we do when we're at a crossroads with one road leading into the frying pan and the other into the fire? Life gets messy sometimes. We sometimes find ourselves bound others in ways that are less than desirable or ideal. When life doesn't go according to "plan," where can we find goodness, virtue, or even ourselves? Can we find love when life doesn't give us the romantic ending we hoped for?

These questions aren't all answered for Caspar. At least, not yet. But then again, not all of these questions are answered in my life. I imagine, if you're reading this, you've found that some of the best things that ever happened to you in life came when things *didn't* go to plan. Some of the biggest blessings in my life came purely by accident. Sometimes, directly, as the result of bad things or difficult seasons. It wasn't always my dream to be a full-time author. I used to have different dreams. Some of those dreams, or hopes for my life, were broken. But I forged a new dream, a new vision for my future. The brokenness of the past allowed me to pick up the shambles of old dreams and forge something new—and I'd never go back, even if I could.

Thank you to everyone who has this story a read. Caspar's journey isn't over yet. Of course, neither is mine. Yours isn't either. And none of us know, no matter how much we've planned ahead, what the next chapter will bring. But as Shakespeare once put it (and as they often say in A.A.), "to thine own self be true." Everything else, I believe, will take care of itself. Even if we have to go through a "three dog night."

-Theo

AUTHOR NOTES - MICHAEL ANDERLE

JUNE 3, 2021

Thank you for not only reading this story but our author notes here in the back.

Can you believe it is almost the middle of the year? I started typing the date above, and I'm just kinda staring at it... *Twenty-seven days until the half-year mark?*

Shocking!

I appreciate my collaborator telling me where the 'three-dog night" the phrase came from. I had no idea myself. I figured the band just thought it was a cool name and used it.

Huh, I guess I might just learn something new every day.

Here in Las Vegas, I doubt I will encounter a three-dog night unless my wife and I travel up to the top of Mount Charleston and sleep up there for the night. Since I HATE being cold, I suspect I would agree to a three-dog night...and maybe a few extra.

(*Editor's note: I have four dogs, but only three sleep on the bed. I frequently have three-dog nights, especially in winter...whether I need them or not! They do help on those cold nights, though.*)

Or, you know, just adding a few blankets and a portable

heater seems like a great solution as well. Less bad breath and a whole lot less dog smell.

Now my mind has gone off on a tangent. Are there large doggy-shaped bed pillows for those who would like to be warm but also like the idea of dogs? I must go see.

<<Author heads off to go search with his Google-fu. Apparently, actually sitting in one place and finishing his author notes was the greater of two evils.>>

I'm back.

The short (really short because I was feeling guilty for not working on my author notes) answer is that you can get a few pillows designed to look like your pet in either square or cut-out shapes. But nothing like I was thinking. At least, my two-minute search didn't show me any.

I was thinking like a whole body… Wait a minute…

<<Author leaves again to go look up full body pillow.>>

HOLY #@%@!

There is a full-body pillow in the shape of a Labrador for $99.00!

If you are interested, search for "Labrador Retriever Plush Cuddle Animal Body Pillow - Chocolate Lab" and the one I found was on the Plow & Hearth website http://www.plowhearth.com.

Son of a gun!

I guess that if any of you like the concept of a dog in bed without the real dog (for whatever reasons), there is a full-body pillow available.

Once again, I learn something new.

I look forward to chatting with you in the next story!

Regards,

Michael Anderle

BOOKS BY MICHAEL ANDERLE

Sign up for the LMBPN email list to be notified of new releases and special deals!

https://lmbpn.com/email/

For a complete list of books by Michael Anderle, please visit:

www.lmbpn.com/ma-books/

CONNECT WITH THE AUTHORS

Connect with Theophilus Monroe

Website: www.theophilusmonroe.com

Social Media
https://www.facebook.com/pages/category/Author/
Theophilus-Monroe-Urban-Fantasy-Author-101469961530864/

Connect with Michael Anderle

Website: http://lmbpn.com

Email List: http://lmbpn.com/email/

Social Media:

https://www.facebook.com/LMBPNPublishing

https://twitter.com/MichaelAnderle

https://www.instagram.com/lmbpn_publishing/

https://www.bookbub.com/authors/michael-anderle